INTRODUCTIO

A Love Remembered

A deadly tragedy forces FBI agent Jonas Love to abandon his career and move back to Oregon. But when his treacherous job follows him, he regrets placing the woman he loves in danger. Can he save her and their love? Feeling forgotten by God, Darcy Nichols plans to leave her hometown to start a new life. But when a man from her past returns, will she risk opening her heart to him?

A Love Kindled

Someone's stealing Carver Love's cattle, but he won't turn to Sheriff Sheridan Hall because he doesn't think she's "man" enough to handle the problem. The truth is, deep inside his heart churns for her. Sheridan has her hands full with Carver—the stubborn rancher is more trouble than rustlers because he never remembers his place. But when they embark on a search for the cattle thieves together, will love erupt?

A Love Risked

ATV store owner Lucas has no fear, that is, until he meets his beautiful new bookkeeper. But losing his heart to her is a risk he's willing to take. After inheriting her grandmother's home in the Oregon Outback, Sierra takes the plunge and moves in, hoping to escape the chaos of the city. But she discovers that the simple life is the last thing she'll find while working for Lucas Love.

A Love Recovered

Bail bond recovery agent Justin Love believes the fugitive he seeks will soon make his way to Oregon. Too bad it's against Oregon law to make an arrest. But Justin's got something else in mind. Darrow Kincaid has been dating Smit Cooper for months and imagines she'll have a good life with him if he ever proposes. That is, until a stranger checks in to her lodge and starts a fire in her heart.

OREGON OUTBACK

FOUR-IN-ONE COLLECTION

ELIZABETH GODDARD

BARBOUR
PUBLISHING

Print ISBN 978-1-61626-587-8

eBook Editions:
Adobe Digital Edition (.epub) 978-1-62029-008-8
Kindle and MobiPocket Edition (.prc) 978-1-62029-009-5

Cover design: Kirk DouPonce, DogEared Design

Published by Barbour Publishing, Inc., P.O. Box 719, Uhrichsville, Ohio 44683, www.barbourbooks.com

Our mission is to publish and distribute inspirational products offering exceptional value and biblical encouragement to the masses.

ecpa Member of the Evangelical Christian Publishers Association

Printed in the United States of America

Dedication

These four novellas are dedicated to heroes—
those who weather the storms, and despite the harsh landscape this life can become, they continue to protect the ones they love, and sometimes, even the ones they don't.

A LOVE REMEMBERED

Chapter 1

Newton's Law of Gravity: What goes up must come down.

She took five running steps and leaped from Tague's Butte.

The force that countered gravity? Lift.

Wind rushed under the nylon fabric of the hang glider and carried Darcy Nichols forward. She was an eagle, soaring through the sky thousands of feet above the ground. Riding the wind, she savored the freedom of flight.

No matter how many times she'd launched from the six-thousand-foot knob across from Albert's Rim—the largest fault lift in the US—the view always left her breathless.

Exhilarated.

Leaning her hips to the right, she turned the hang glider toward the northeast into the straight line for her flight, maintaining a constant speed.

As she pushed her arms straight, forcing the control bar forward, the wing above her stalled. Then she caught the lift band, the thermal that would carry her higher.

Rising high into the wide open air space she craved, Darcy could see miles of the Oregon backcountry. She collided with molecules as she moved through the air, creating friction, or drag—another invisible force in the equation.

How high she could fly, how far she could go, and how long she could stay in the air depended on balancing the three forces of gravity, lift, and drag. Maybe she could make it forty or fifty miles. Someone had made it over eighty miles a few years ago.

It all came down to balancing invisible forces. They carried her through the air, allowing her to fly. But invisible forces were at work in her life, too, never ceasing. They ushered her through the days, weeks, months. . .through a lifetime.

A balancing act that left her exhausted.

Eventually, she'd need to radio Emily, her best friend, when she knew where she'd land. A few of Darcy's friends had been heading to Lakeview and agreed to drop her off at the jump-off point on the way.

With perfect conditions for hang gliders and extraordinary views, the region had earned the title, The Hang Gliding Capital of the West.

Darcy let the wind carry her away from her thoughts. She absorbed the view and took pictures as she swept over Albert's Lake, the water reflecting the blue sky filled with cumulus clouds. From directly above, the lake was indescribable—but she'd catch the image with her camera.

Her photographs ended up in her gift shop that targeted tourists traveling along Oregon's scenic byways. In the distance, she could make out Fort Rock, and on the horizon, the Christmas Valley sand dunes. A few miles east of Christmas Valley was Carnegie, the small town where she'd grown up. The views were spectacular, but the population was lean in Oregon's high desert, or the Oregon Outback as some called it.

The arid loneliness contradicted the beauty at times, making the land seem forgotten. Darcy shared that with the land—her father had died just over a week ago.

On Thursday, June 26th, he'd left her behind and alone.

She'd been preparing for his death these last nine months since he'd received the poor prognosis. Though he'd only been gone a week, after remaining by his side for months, Darcy needed today. She needed to feel lifted above it all.

In the sky, she could soar above the earth, and all the problems of the world appeared small. It wasn't all about her.

"Oh Daddy." There was so much she'd wanted to say to him, but it was pointless saying it now. All she'd ever wanted was what every child wanted—a father's approval. Why had it been so hard for him to give?

And now, that chapter of her life was gone forever.

A gust caught the delta wing, threatening to take her off course. In the sling, she leaned her body to the left.

North by northwest. Emily wouldn't be happy if she had to drive too far to pick Darcy up. An experienced pilot, she built altitude so that on her final glide she could go as far as possible, making it somewhere in the vicinity of Carnegie.

But even at thousands of feet above the ground, images accosted her mind. Her daddy's funeral in the pouring-down rain. And then. . .

The familiar silhouette leaning next to the centuries-old juniper tree.

A hood protected him from the rain, hiding his face. Darcy's pulse had raced. Was it Jonas?

No. Jonas Love had left town years ago thanks to her father's, Pastor Jeremy Nichols, counseling.

Jonas was the man she would have married, if it hadn't been for her father. In the end, Jonas was the one who'd hurt her the most. The best thing she could do now was start a new life elsewhere.

With only ten or fifteen minutes remaining in her flight, she fumbled with her radio and hailed Emily.

"What do you want?" Emily's voice barked over the radio.

Darcy's friend knew the drill. They'd done this for years. "I'm about ten minutes out. You could probably see me to the south."

"Come again?"

"Really?"

Emily laughed. "I'm on it. And, there's something else."

The wind whipped in Darcy's ears, nearly drowning Emily out. "What?"

"I'll tell you later."

Darcy shut off her radio. "I hate it when you do that."

An eagle again, Darcy lost herself in flight, savoring those last few minutes. Finally, she soared over the small two-lane highway that Emily would take to meet her. McFarlane's ranch was across the way, a small swath of earth where she was permitted to land. Too soon, her time in the sky was over, like the ending of a well-loved book.

Grass and earth came at her fast. She pushed the bar forward and stretched her arms, tipping the nose up and stalling the glider until it began to slow. . .slower. . . Darcy stuck her feet out and landed upright, running through the sagebrush and bunchgrass until she stopped. The wing dropped behind her.

Grounded, the exhilaration of flight slowly dissipated. She unharnessed from the contraption. When she looked up, Emily was jogging across the property. Breathing hard, she slowed as she approached, her dark blond hair bouncing in a ponytail.

"You didn't have to run," Darcy said.

"Didn't I?" Emily leaned over her thighs.

"On second thought, you probably need the exercise," Darcy teased.

"Are you prepared to walk home?" Emily raised her eyebrows.

"No, not really."

"Didn't think so." Emily drew in a long breath. "Let me help you with that."

"No. I have to fold it just right. It'll last longer. You know that."

"Yes, but I always have to ask, don't I?"

"Maybe. You can tell me whatever it was you were going to tell me later."

"Now?" Emily sounded cautious.

Darcy glanced up from packing the glider. "What is it?"

With an unreadable expression, Emily pinned Darcy with her sage-green eyes. "Jonas Love is back in town."

Invisible forces.

Evaluation. Debriefing. Decompression.

The bureau's behavioral science unit had evaluated Special

Agent Jonas Love all right. And . . .he'd endured the debriefing results.

Agent Jonas Love, you're relieved of duty. A megaphone blasted the words in his head again.

The Office of Professional Responsibility was conducting an internal investigation to see if Jonas was at fault. He'd turned in his creds and weapon.

And now, as Jonas sped over the sand dunes, gripping the handlebars of the quad. . .he decompressed.

A leave of absence. A minivacation. Whatever. The bureau was proactive when it came to covering their rears. To be fair, they wanted to protect their agents, too.

But if he was going to succeed at his current assignment—to decompress—he'd have to get a memory wipe. Was that too much to ask?

Sand dunes met the horizon in all directions. The guy at his brother's ATV shop had assured him that Lucas was out there somewhere, taking a break from work, doing what he loved. Jonas had grabbed one of the rentals—the latest and greatest in high performance all-terrain vehicles.

A big rise, maybe thirty feet or more, loomed ahead. He juiced it, power shifting for the big push over the top.

At the crest, he launched into the air. Flying, he stood on the quad, his legs gripping the sides. Then he thrust his arms up, pulling a no-hander. He'd forgotten the exhilaration, the thrill.

Gravity yanked hard. The quad pulled away from him. The machine beneath him plummeting, he gripped the handlebars.

Sand rushed at him.

His muscles taut, expectant, he watched the ground loom larger. On impact, the four-wheeler bounced, jarring his body. Plumes of desert sand burst up, encircling him. The machine jerked forward almost leaving him in the dust.

Almost.

The whir of the engine underneath buzzed in his head. Barreling downhill, he picked up speed and nearly lost control. He slid to a stop. Heat penetrated his helmet. He pulled it off and wiped sweat from his brow, feeling the grime of wet, grainy dirt.

Another daredevil rushed over the hills. Jonas watched the guy take a big risk—side hilling on a steep dune. He was booking it too fast for Jonas's taste. The quad teetered.

It's going to roll.

Jonas sent up a quick prayer. This guy reminded him of Lucas, always pushing the envelope. ATVs could injure or crush, but Lucas never cared. He wanted to live on the edge.

Ride on the edge.

At that moment, the quad tipped. The guy jumped off on the other side and made it to safety. He pumped his arm and gave a triumphant shout.

Jonas set his helmet on the quad's seat and started toward the crazy man, waiting for him to pull off his helmet. Then Jonas would know with certainty that it was. . .

"Lucas!"

While Lucas stared, Jonas trudged across the deep sand, resistant to his every step. By the time he reached Lucas, he was beyond winded.

Jonas bent over his knees, catching his breath. "You couldn't meet me halfway?"

A huge smile plastered his brother's face—the one that always got the girls. "Jonas!" He grabbed him like a bear.

Jonas returned the hug, thankful to see his brother again. He admitted that he'd stayed away for too long.

Lucas released him. "Dude. I can't believe it's you. What're you doing here?"

"You're not glad to see me?"

"Sure. You could have called or something. Then I would have cleaned the place up for you." He grinned.

"Yeah, right." Jonas moved to the quad. "So, you're into quad tipping now, is that it?"

"Hardly." He positioned himself to roll the ATV again. "Okay. On three."

Jonas came to his side and put his hands under the vehicle. "One, two, three. . ."

They pushed together. The quad rolled over again, and the sharp incline kept it rolling. At the base of the dune it stopped upright. Lucas had been lucky to escape.

He sucked in a breath. "Another one bites the dust."

"You think it's ruined?" asked Jonas.

"Maybe. I don't know. But I need to make sure it's completely safe for the next rider. It's a rental." Lucas grabbed his helmet and straddled the vehicle he'd just expressed uncertainty over. "How long are you here for?"

"I'm not sure." Jonas pulled on his helmet and fastened

it, then opened the throttle wide, spraying a rooster's plume behind him.

For the moment, he felt alive and savored it. He knew only too well how quickly a life could be snuffed out. He was still reeling that a member of his team had been killed during an FBI raid he'd led, along with an innocent victim.

His evaluation and debriefing had been hard enough, but he was beginning to believe he'd chosen the wrong place to regroup.

He'd never gotten over Darcy.

The whir of another quad zoomed past. His brother waved, then turned performer with his personally directed freestyle-riding act.

He hoped by now that his younger brother had grown up, taking life more seriously. On the other hand, maybe Lucas was living every minute to the fullest. Before Jonas could decide which was true, he pulled into the parking lot of Oregon Adventures, Lucas's ATV business.

He followed his brother to the side of the building to return both quads. Lucas explained to the mechanic what had happened with the ATV he'd ridden.

The man shook his head. "Another one?"

Lucas ignored the mechanic and focused on Jonas. "Seriously, you never told me how long you're here for. I mean, do you have time to get some lunch? Or are you staying longer?"

Jonas's stomach rumbled. "Lunch is good for starters."

Lucas led him to his apartment at the back of the building.

When he spotted Jonas's motorcycle—a royal blue Suzuki

Hayabusa—he released a low whistle. "I'd be tempted to max it out. Two hundred fifty miles an hour, right?"

"Something like that." Jonas grinned.

"And you still have your license?"

"What makes you think I've driven over the speed limit? That would be breaking the law."

"Why have such a beautiful thing if you can't experience it to the fullest? When can I take her for a ride?"

"When you convince me you won't kill yourself."

In the kitchen, Lucas made tuna fish sandwiches. He spoke around his mouthful. "So why are you here? Some case you're investigating?"

Jonas's appetite fizzled at the words. "Taking some time off. Thought I'd hang out here, if that's all right."

Lucas stopped chewing, his left cheek stuffed. He took a swig of a soda then swallowed. "What? You didn't get fired, did you?"

Jonas leveled a frown at Lucas. "Like I said, I'm taking a break."

He looked at his plate. Instead of a sandwich he saw an agent's body—the death, his fault. Maybe he'd never been cut out for that type of work. Maybe he would become a private investigator instead, though there wasn't much call for that in a small town like this. Rumors and gossip took care of things, bringing them into the open.

"What about Darcy? You're going to see her, right? Her dad died last week. Did you know that?" Lucas wiped his mouth.

"Yeah. I went to the funeral."

Lucas's eyes grew wide. "You did? Then you saw her already. And where have you been all this time? The ranch?"

"Carver says hello."

Lucas frowned. He never got along with Carver, their older brother. "And Darcy?"

"I didn't talk to her." Jonas finished his soda and crumpled the can.

Enough time had passed that they both should have moved on. Yet he'd done nothing but watch her at the funeral. On the grimmest of days, he'd wanted to console her. Instead he stood back, keeping his distance out of respect. Her father had kept them apart, and she'd abided by that. Jonas couldn't just walk back into her life the day her father was buried.

Jonas had been a senior in high school when her father had come to see him. He'd gotten into the wrong crowd. Darcy's father had given him the sort of talk only a father would give a troubled teenager. Jonas's own father had died in a ranching accident two years before, leaving behind four sons. His mother, eight years before that.

Jonas had taken her father's words to heart and made something better of himself. For her. But he doubted she even knew about it. At least he'd seen Pastor Nichols in the hospital before he died, during a moment when Darcy hadn't been there. Jonas owed him everything and told her father how he'd changed his life, keeping the recent events to himself.

Pastor Nichols's regret-filled eyes had brightened a little.

His next words to Jonas could change his life again. Darcy's father made Jonas promise to watch over his daughter. The only problem—Jonas wasn't sure if he was up to the task.

Nor was he sure that Darcy would be happy to see him.

Chapter 2

Her first day back at High Desert Art since the funeral—another Monday had come and gone. Julie, her summer help, had manned the place during Darcy's absence. Returning so soon had been more taxing than she'd expected.

She locked the door of the shop, then picked up a burrito at Taco Bell, despite the abundance of food well-meaning people had brought to the house.

A huge burden had been laid at her feet upon her father's death. She surveyed the contents of a home filled with thirty-five years' worth of things collected by her parents—it all now belonged to her, at least after probate. Her father had opted to own his own home, choosing a housing fund rather than a parsonage, in case something happened to him. Even a small estate probate could take several months, but she doubted it would take long considering her father's debts were paid, and she was an only child.

How would she ever go through everything? That task alone could take her years. She slumped into her father's leather chair to eat her burrito. Her thoughts turned again to the news

Emily had shared with her on Saturday. The man standing next to the old juniper during her father's funeral had been Jonas, after all. She'd wanted to believe her imagination had conspired to work against her.

Too much was coming down on her at once.

Escape seemed impossible.

But she had to try. She put the sign on her gift shop door today, telling the world it was for sale.

The doorbell rang. Darcy jumped up and surveyed her appearance in the mirror. Not good. She wore the raggedy but comfortable gray sweats she'd changed into when she got home. Her hair fell in limp strands around her face, tanned from her hang gliding excursion on Saturday. Also not good. She needed to be pale and mournful or the gossips would say she hadn't grieved her father's death.

The visitor was probably another little old lady wanting to give Darcy her condolences. When would people finally leave her to grieve alone?

Darcy knew all the casseroles on her kitchen counter and stuffed in the fridge were meant to reassure her, but she also knew that many a woman had wanted to garner the widowed pastor's attention. Darcy wasn't the only one feeling the loss.

A thought rushed by in a gust. Was it Jonas? Darcy's palms grew slick. Hating her feral thoughts, she shook her head. If he'd wanted to see her, he would have spoken to her at the funeral. He'd had a week since then to contact her. No, Jonas had left her behind without looking back, then and now.

Forgotten.

She yanked the door open. "Emily. What a relief."

Darcy pulled her friend inside then quickly shut the door.

"See, this is exactly what I was afraid of." Emily looked Darcy up and down. "You went hang gliding. Your first time in months. That's good, but aside from that, you've buried yourself in this dark and depressing dungeon of a home."

"You forgot. I went back to work today, too." Leaving her friend to stand in the foyer alone, Darcy returned to her father's chair and wrapped her legs underneath. "I have to grieve, and to think. It takes time."

Emily scrunched up her nose. "What is that smell?"

Without waiting for an answer, she sauntered into the kitchen. From where Darcy sat, she could see Emily lifting foil on various casserole dishes. "Someone expected you to eat all this?"

Her best friend had given her the space she'd needed. Maybe Darcy should have allowed her to stay at the house like Emily had wanted.

"Help yourself."

"You could have shared some of it before it went bad."

"There's some in the fridge that's still good, if you want."

"Later." Emily came back into the living room and plopped on the beautiful sofa. She ran her hand over the fabric. "I don't think I ever sat on this."

"That's why it's still in perfect condition. Mom never let anyone but guests sit there, otherwise it was covered with plastic. Dad continued the ritual. I ripped off the plastic because of everyone stopping by, but never put it back."

Emily stood. "Let's get out of here."

"I'm not exactly dressed."

"I'll wait. I'm taking you out for some fun."

"I can't have fun so soon after Dad's funeral."

"It's all over town you went hang gliding. You don't need to hide anymore."

Darcy frowned, knowing that other news was probably all over town as well. Why hadn't Emily asked her about the store?

Darcy stood. "Give me ten minutes."

"You get two because after that you'll show me up."

In the same bedroom where she'd spent her entire life, Darcy changed into jeans and a floral cotton shirt. Minutes later, Emily was driving Darcy around in the Camaro that she'd gotten for graduation ten years ago. At the last light in town, she punched it, speeding north along the highway.

"Where are we going?" Darcy asked.

"Out of town."

Darcy nodded, allowing Emily the reins, and stared at the scenery racing by. Maybe she and Emily could leave town together for real and go to nursing school somewhere. Unable to sleep at night the last few weeks before her father's death, Darcy had stayed up late and researched nursing schools and other occupations.

She'd opened her small store in town to please her father. He wanted her near, and she needed something of her own.

The car slowed and sputtered a few times.

"Uh-oh," Emily said. "I don't believe this."

"What's the matter?"

Emily pulled onto the shoulder, where the car died. "I

ran out of gas."

"You what? How could you do that?"

"Relax." Emily blew out a breath. "I'm sorry. I guess I was so anxious to get you out of that house, I forgot to look at the gauge. But the ATV shop is up the road. We can get gas there."

Emily climbed from the car. Darcy did the same, and glared at Emily over the top. "You did this on purpose."

"Why would I do that? It means I have to walk."

Emily was a real piece of work. She knew exactly what she was doing. "You and I both know the ATV shop belongs to Lucas Love. This is your little prank to get me to his shop."

If Jonas was still in town, he was probably staying with his brother. Darcy stared into the distance at the sand dunes. To the west was Fort Rock—a volcanic tuff ring resembling a fort. "I don't want to see him."

Why stir up the past?

"I'm sorry about running out of gas. But that doesn't change that we need to walk to Lucas's shop to get some more."

"You go. I'm walking back to town."

"What are you afraid of?"

"Jonas and I were over years ago." Darcy pushed past her friend, wishing she'd worn running shoes.

ꕥ

Jonas borrowed Lucas's four-wheel drive and peeled out of the Oregon Adventure parking lot. While Emily was inside the shop flirting with Lucas, Jonas intended to give Darcy a ride. Lucas could help Emily with the gas for her Camaro.

This was the sign he'd been looking for. He needed some way to break the years of silence between them. He floored the pedal, intending to reach her before she made it back to town. The truck's glass-packs announced his arrival long before he drew near, but he doubted she was expecting him. He slowed up next to the slim figure walking on the road.

Ash-blond hair pulled tight in a ponytail, it bounced as Darcy walked with purpose. She didn't look at the truck. Did she know it was him, or was she expecting Lucas?

Driving next to her, he hung his arm out the window. What did he say to her after all these years? "Can I give you a lift somewhere?"

Brilliant.

She ignored him. So. . .it was going to be like this. Jonas wasn't prepared to be ignored. Oddly enough her reaction gave him hope that she still cared. Otherwise, she would have smiled and made small talk because his presence wouldn't have done a thing to her—good or bad.

Jonas gassed the truck and pulled off the road, directly in front of Darcy. He hopped out before she could walk around, and stood right in front of her, crossing his arms. She stopped and drew her posture up to meet his gaze.

Pain and hurt lingered in her eyes. Had she really hung on to those emotions after almost a decade? No. She had to be grieving for her father. Jonas was nothing more than a jerk from her past.

"Darcy." He nodded.

"Jonas." She glanced away.

"You look good." And she did except for the dark circles under her misty hazel eyes. Brought on from her loss, he was sure. She was too skinny. Again, her father had been ill for months before she finally lost him—the man who had driven them apart. His long illness and subsequent death had to weigh on her.

Her face had a good healthy sheen to it. Jonas hated that he hadn't given her more time and space.

"I heard you ran out of gas. Can I give you a ride somewhere?"

"No, thank you. A walk is good. I need the fresh air."

Jonas pursed his lips, wanting to say so much more to this woman he'd once asked to marry him, but he couldn't force her into the truck. Now it was his turn to gaze into the distance.

Why couldn't he just say everything that was on his mind? Get everything out in the open? How did he tell her that he'd changed? Why he'd left in the first place?

The things her father had told him before he'd died?

Then again, he had no right to push himself into her life like this, especially mere days after her father's funeral.

Frowning, he nodded. "I'll leave you to it then."

Feeling like an idiot, he climbed up into the truck, and drove back to Lucas's shop so he could give Darcy's scheming friend a ride to her car with a couple gallons of gas.

By ten that evening, he'd worked himself into a mood while he and Lucas sat in the small bachelor-pad living room, watching the evening news.

They were like two lonely, old men.

So far, Lucas hadn't said a word to him about the chance he'd blown. But in the dim light he could see his brother working his jaw. It was only a matter of time.

The news went to commercial break. "Dude, why don't you just call her?"

"What's the point? She doesn't care about me. It's been too long. I thought she'd be married by now. Besides, she wouldn't talk to me today."

"Her best friend said she still likes you, maybe even loves you. Just call, you know, like an old friend. You can work your way up from there." Lucas grinned. "Maybe."

"What makes you think I'm interested in her anymore?"

Lucas contorted his face. "Come on. She's the *one*, bro, don't let her get away. You got nothing standing in your way this time with her old man gone. Practice what you're going to say in the mirror if you have to."

"Don't talk about him like that. It's disrespectful." Jonas hadn't shared with Lucas what her father had told him in the hospital before he died. No one knew that Jonas had visited the man. At last, he had the permission he'd sought years before. The only person standing in his way now was Darcy.

"Sorry," Lucas said, surprising Jonas.

"Besides, you expect me to take advice from you? You go through women like you go through four-wheelers."

Standing to stretch, Lucas tossed his soda can in the trash. "That's because I haven't found the one."

He left the room, leaving Jonas to ponder his brother's words. Maybe he was right. Jonas called the Nichols's house, hoping the number was still good. She didn't answer the home phone. That could be for any number of reasons. How did he get his hands on her cell number? He should have gotten her number from Emily.

Before he could call Emily, his phone rang. Jonas frowned at the number. Tom Jennings was one of his coworkers at the bureau. Dreading the reason that Tom would call, Jonas answered.

"Tom. What's up?"

"Watch your back. Gambini is threatening you from behind bars."

"He has no reason to come after me." Jonas pressed his head against the chair back, wishing his words were true.

"Keep telling yourself that." Tom sighed. "Look, I just thought you should know. We've got a surveillance team watching his cronies, just in case."

Great. So much for decompressing.

"Everything going okay there?" Tom asked.

"As well as I expected. I appreciate the heads-up. Keep me apprised of any new developments."

"Will do."

When the call ended, Jonas thought about Robert Gambini, the crime boss he'd helped put away. The man couldn't do much from behind bars, and his associates were being watched. Jonas should relax. Forget about it for now. He was here to recoup. He tried to shove the thoughts aside, but it was difficult.

After the events that led up to his time off, Jonas had allowed himself to dream, if only a little, about a life with Darcy, living in Carnegie, the small town where they'd grown up. Here in the Oregon Outback where two of his brothers still lived.

But everything looked different now. He couldn't recapture the past, what he'd lost. Nothing ever stayed the same. Darcy didn't want to see him. Nor would he ever be free from the threat of criminals he'd helped to incarcerate.

Even if Jonas resigned, leaving the FBI, it was unlikely that would make any difference to a man like Gambini. If he found Jonas, then another innocent victim could die.

This time, Jonas could endanger someone he loved.

Chapter 3

Tourists mingled in the aisles, perused Darcy's photographs and sketches, and examined cheap junk from China—gifts to take home to friends and family. The late afternoon sun beamed through the glass front, warming the store and creating rainbows from the hanging prisms that sold for $19.99.

The busy day should have helped her forget yesterday as she assisted customers and answered questions, but her mind was far from today, insisting on living in yesterday.

What are you afraid of?

Emily had cut to the heart of the matter, asking a question Darcy couldn't answer. Darcy's friend had simply exercised her muscle as a friend in her efforts to bring Jonas and Darcy face-to-face. As Emily's friend, Darcy would forgive her.

Eventually.

Then Jonas himself had appeared on the lonely highway to rescue her, riding in his brother's big noisy truck like some kind of hero.

Darcy's heart had beaten desperately against her chest, demanding to be let out. But she'd held on with all her strength, and in the end, kept her heart imprisoned. She'd not been able to look at him for long. The way his dark eyes searched her soul, she imagined him looking for remnants of the love they once shared. Her fantasy had almost set her heart free.

But that was all it was—a fantasy.

Trim and muscular, he looked even better than he had at eighteen. She didn't appreciate his attempt to jockey himself back into her life. Had she done the right thing in giving him up back then? Her father had thought so.

What was she afraid of?

Loving him again. Losing him again. There. She admitted it. Releasing her pent-up breath, she grabbed the counter, steadying herself.

Her father's death. Jonas's reappearance. It was too much, too fast. The walls were closing in around her.

"Are you all right?" A woman stood at the counter, facing Darcy.

Smiling, Darcy focused her thoughts on the bright sun pouring into her spacious shop.

The woman's teenage daughter placed their merchandise on the counter. Darcy rang up three small plastic dinosaurs and a dolphin wind chime, boxed and bagged the items, and thanked the woman and her daughter for their visit.

Next in line was an elderly woman, Mrs. Olson, one of her father's parishioners. She placed one of Darcy's framed sketches on the counter.

The ancient gnarled juniper. . .her father's funeral. . .Jonas, leaning against it.

Her breath caught. All she could do was force a smile and pretend the sketch wasn't suffocating her.

"I've always thought your sketches were lovely. My great-granddaughter wants to be an artist. She lives in Idaho. I'm taking this to her for her birthday."

Darcy made the appropriate small talk, and then Mrs. Olson reached across the counter and pressed her hand, aged with liver spots, over Darcy's. Her wrinkled smile was kind. "I don't care what anybody else says, I think it's good that you're back at work and keeping busy so soon after your father's funeral."

Resisting the urge to ask what people were saying, Darcy thanked her. Several impatient customers standing behind Mrs. Olson peered at Darcy, frowning.

"Was there something else?" Darcy asked.

Mrs. Olson leaned in. "Maybe now God has given you another chance with that handsome Love brother."

She winked, then removed herself from the line, carrying the packaged sketch with her—and all the air in the room.

Darcy's gaze sifted through the customers and gifts until she spotted her help, making eye contact. "Julie."

Her assistant sidled in behind the counter. "What's wrong?"

"I need a minute."

"No problem." Julie smiled and turned her attention to a young couple.

Darcy excused herself and, once she was alone in the employees' back room, she sucked a deep breath into her deflated lungs.

After so much time, people moved on with their lives, didn't they? But even dear Mrs. Olson, one Darcy counted as a true saint of the Lord, thought Darcy and Jonas were meant to be together.

Once Darcy gained her composure, she forced herself back into the busy shop. Near closing time, Darcy found herself alone with Julie. The crowd had made the day pass quickly, but she was exhausted. She still needed to close out the register.

Julie approached her, still looking energized. "Everything all right?"

"Sure, why do you ask?"

A knowing grin edged Julie's lips. "You've been distracted today. I'm here to listen, if you want to talk. I'm not looking for gossip, don't worry."

Darcy laughed. Maybe it would be good to unload her burdens. Whether she said anything or not, people talked. They made up stories if they needed to. "What is it you want to know?"

Hands behind her back, Julie's gaze traveled through the curios, gifts, and art, to peer through the glass storefront. "I know you and Jonas were an item once. What happened?"

Darcy sighed. "I thought everyone knew that story by now."

"I know a story, but I want to hear the truth from you."

Darcy admired Julie for asking for the truth instead of listening to the tales. How could she deny her? "All right. But I warn you, it's not terribly interesting."

"The whole town seems to be holding its breath. Like yours was the romance of the century."

Then the whole town is going to pass out. "Or maybe just

the decade. I'm not that old." Darcy hoped she could give the *Reader's Digest* version.

"Jonas and I liked each other early on. I was thirteen when I first had a crush on him. By the time I was seventeen and he was eighteen, I was head over heels in love with the guy. And he returned it, I thought. But my father didn't like the Love family, especially the brothers, who he thought were wild hooligans."

"That never helps when a girl's daddy doesn't approve." Frowning, Julie stared at the counter.

Was Julie going through something similar?

"Jonas proposed—well, not officially. He asked me to wait, and I think maybe I'm the one who messed everything up because I went to my father and asked for permission."

Darcy shook her head. "Jonas was right about waiting until the right time. I think my father had been too busy shepherding his flock and didn't realize how serious we'd grown. He wasn't prepared to hear that Jonas and I wanted to get married. My father forbade me to see him again."

"So what did you do?"

The doorbell rang, and a man pushed through the door. He appeared to change his mind and left before he'd even browsed.

Glancing at her watch, Darcy noted they only had fifteen more minutes until closing time. Thank goodness. "What did I do? I suffered behind the closed door in my room, praying my father would change his mind. Hoping that Jonas would wait for me. I dreamed about running away with him and propositioned him."

If only God had answered her prayers for direction then.

"Obviously, that didn't happen. But did you try to elope?"

"Jonas turned me down. I think he'd been sitting under my father's counsel. At least that's what I heard much later. In the end, Jonas left town."

Julie gasped. "Without even saying good-bye?"

"That hurt me the most." Darcy saw that clearly now, despite Mrs. Olson's suggestion that God had given them a second chance.

"But, you still love him, don't you?"

Finally, it was five o'clock. "Some people you never get over."

"That's too bad."

Darcy sighed, her last words ringing in her ears. Was that how she really felt about Jonas? "I think you're good to go, Julie. I'll close out the register and clean up."

Though Julie's eyes remained concerned, her smile brightened. "You sure?"

"I'm sure. Have you got a date tonight?"

"Yes. I appreciate you sharing your story with me. I'm sorry that you've had to endure the town gossip. That has to be tough."

After Julie left, Darcy opened a few boxes, a shipment she'd received earlier that week. She hadn't told Julie the rest of the story. Over time she'd fallen back into the routine of life. She'd forgiven her father, but felt like he owed her something. Last week's funeral brought her full circle. She'd given up the love of her life to do the right thing because she loved her father. Yet, he'd not given her the one thing she needed—his approval.

Though she was in the back, she heard the doorbell, the

telltale signal she had another customer. With her distracted thoughts, she'd forgotten to lock the front door after Julie left. Darcy made her way through the back room and into the main shop. "I'm sorry, but we're—"

The subject of her thoughts today, and her conversation with Julie, stood in the center of the store amid the art and junk. Lean, rugged, and tougher than when she'd known him before, the expression on his gorgeous face was hard, except for the torment behind his eyes.

The walls closed in around her.

Escape was impossible.

ᴖ

"What are you doing here?"

Did she really have to ask?

Dark and accusing, her hazel eyes stared at him like he'd committed a crime. Her thick hair was pulled behind her head again, a few strands hanging free, framing her pretty face and accenting her healthy complexion.

She looked good. But he already knew that.

Memories of running his fingers through her lush mane clawed at him. A decade ago and he could still remember. He scraped his hand across his freshly shaven jaw.

He'd wanted her to be his wife, he should be able to talk to her. But he'd been young then. Too young.

"Well?" She stepped over to the cash register.

How did she scramble his brains in less than fifteen seconds? He couldn't think to answer. Nor was she going to make this easy on him.

All he wanted was to make progress.

She opened the register and started the process of closing it out, counting the cash, as though Jonas didn't mean a thing to her. Never had. They'd spent a decade apart—could he still read her?

Yes. With the realization, he grinned.

In her eyes he recognized what he'd been looking for.

I need you to know why I left. That I've changed. "I'm sorry for disturbing you. I just. . ."

Lucas had coached him to approach her as an old friend. Start at the bottom. But with their history, would that work? "I wanted to know how you're doing."

"I'm doing well. As you can see, I've got my own business here." She barely glanced his way.

"I was sorry to hear about your dad's passing. Thought we could talk." He was floundering.

Darcy slammed the register drawer and yelped, yanking her fingers back.

Jonas rushed around the counter. "Let me see that."

He took her hand in his and examined her red finger. He resisted the urge to kiss it. Like that would make it feel better.

Her soft skin sent his mind reeling back to years gone by, to what they had together. To what he'd lost in submitting to her father's counseling—but he'd gained so much as well. Her father had helped him make sense out of his life.

Did she know that? *Lord, please give me the chance to explain.*

Darcy eased her hand from him. "Why are you here? Really?"

I thought we could be friends. Too little, it wasn't the truth.

I still love you. Too much, it was too soon.

"I rehearsed a thousand times what I'd say to you once I saw you again." He'd taken Lucas's advice.

Ignoring her swollen finger and Jonas, she zipped the vinyl money bag stuffed with cash, then laid it on the counter. She looked up at him, her gaze expectant.

Much better.

"I don't think it helped." A cute little grin tugged at the corner of her mouth.

He loved that. To see her smile at him like she used to would be a good next goal. But was it reasonable? He pushed both hands through his hair.

"I think you're right. Let me start over." He cleared his throat. "I know it's been a long time, but there are a lot of things left unsaid between us."

Darcy thrust her hand up to stop him. "I prefer to leave the past where it belongs."

She shoved from the counter and went into the back room. Jonas followed and watched her grab her purse and keys, holding the money bag under her arm. Did she realize that was dangerous? Or was Carnegie still safe compared to the rest of the world?

"Can you do that, Darcy?" Jonas stepped closer. "Can you leave unfinished business between us?"

She didn't resist as he removed the keys and purse from her hands, the bag from under her arm, and placed all the items on the table.

He took both her hands in his, and though he was being presumptuous, he stepped into her personal space. Her nearness ignited the full force of his love for her. An explosive force, knocking him over, sending questions like shrapnel to pierce him.

Why hadn't he returned sooner? How could he explain anything to her when he didn't have the answers himself?

But she couldn't handle the full weight of his confessions right now. That much he knew.

"Why don't you join Lucas and me for a picnic after church Sunday? We'll go hiking. Do something fun. Anything you want. I'm not sure how long I'm going to be in town and. . ." He grinned, hoping to disarm her. "I wanted to see you. Can you blame me for that?"

Okay, shut up. Give the girl a chance to speak.

"I don't know. Let me think about it."

What was there to think about? Jonas swallowed his question. Her answer was something. "Okay."

He couldn't rush her. Building bridges took time. He'd made progress, and that was all he'd come here for.

Chapter 4

"Thought I'd find you here."

At Emily's voice, Darcy turned from where she sat. Emily made her way through the sliding glass door at the back of Darcy's house and crossed the grass in need of mowing, then sat next to her in a wicker lawn chair. "You didn't answer your phone."

Darcy pressed her head against the chair back and listened as the birds started up again, the cicadas, too. "Just needed some time alone, that's all."

"Oh great, now I've invaded your peace and quiet." A few seconds of silence. Did she expect Darcy to dispute her statement? Then, finally, "Listen. About the other day—"

"You're forgiven." Darcy kept her eyes closed, relaxing the tense muscles in her neck and shoulders. They'd been friends long enough, few words were necessary.

"So. . .any news?"

"Somebody called me tonight. They're interested in buying the store. I haven't even listed it yet. Just put up that sign."

"Wow." Emily's chair creaked. "That's fast. Who wants to buy it?"

"I don't know them personally. Just someone who happened in the store this week. We were really busy, by the way."

"Business is good. You sure you want to sell? I mean, then what would you do?"

"Everything is happening so fast my head is spinning. I thought I knew what I wanted when I put that sign up, but I never expected someone to take me up on the business before the idea even settled in my head." *Or my heart.*

"You haven't given yourself much time to grieve your father's death. Making big decisions probably isn't a good idea yet."

Darcy opened her eyes and gazed at her best friend. "Thank you for cleaning my kitchen, by the way."

She'd come home this evening to find the counters empty of the casseroles that had grown rancid.

"I left you a couple in the fridge, in case you didn't look. That Tater-Tot one looks good, and the lasagna. Maybe we could eat that after church Sunday, that is, if you're going."

A new pastor had taken her father's position months ago, after he'd stepped down to deal with his illness. And now, it was a little difficult to sit there, listening to a man who wasn't her father—the only preacher she'd ever had.

"Do you want to go on a picnic?" Darcy shut her eyes again.

"That could be fun. What did you have in mind?"

"Jonas invited me to go with him and Lucas." Even with her eyes closed, she could tell Emily sat up and stared at her.

"Are you kidding me? That's the best news I've heard all day."

"I haven't accepted yet. Still thinking." Too much, too fast.

"Why did he suddenly show up? And at my father's funeral no less."

"Well, a picnic is a start. Maybe you can get your answer. I think you need to give him a second chance. Everyone deserves that, don't they?"

"I had put him behind me." Darcy paused, finally recognizing the words for what they were. A lie. "Or so I thought. When I saw him on the road the day you decided to run out of gas, and then again, when he stopped by the store this week, I couldn't get over how handsome he was." Darcy smiled at her friend. "Better-looking than when we were kids, and that's what we were. Just kids. There was something different about him. He was confident, sure of himself."

"See? There you go. Add to that the fact that he contacted you shows he's still got a thing for you."

"Except that he mentioned he didn't know how long he'd be here. What is the point in stirring things up, if he's going to leave again?"

Emily stood and stretched. "You can't know what he meant by that. Just get the facts before you make a decision. One picnic doesn't mean you're in love and getting engaged or married."

Darcy wasn't sure what it meant, other than a fierce battle to protect her heart. "I feel like I'm opening a door and the past is going to rush in. I don't want that pain again."

The very last thing she needed to do with the hope of a future in front of her, was set herself up to get crushed again under the weight of the love she'd once had for him.

"Who says it has to be a door to the past? Maybe it's a

door to your future with Jonas, a man you once loved enough to marry. A man you might still—"

"Why is this so important to you, Emily?" Darcy swung her legs over the side of the chair and sat up. "I almost think you care more than I do."

"Because." Emily pressed her hand over her heart. "You're two people who were kept apart—sort of like Romeo and Juliet. Like Rose and Jack in *Titanic*. . ." She paused at Darcy's look. "What? Too dramatic?"

"You could say that." Darcy hung her head. Exhaustion from the busy week, from her loss the week before, slammed her all at once. "In the end, only death kept them apart."

The words unsettled her.

"What are you thinking?" Emily asked. She'd started pacing the backyard, kicking around a few sticks like a little kid.

"That I need my phone so I can let Jonas know that you're coming with us." If she didn't explore this, she'd always wonder.

Time with Jonas would do one of two things—open up the possibility that he would fill the hole he'd left in her heart, or leave her cut and bleeding again.

This thing she had for Jonas was like a deep, flood-ravaged gorge that carried her forward in the rushing water. Depending on where you stood, the river was either beneficial to the environment or it was destructive.

Beneficial or destructive.

Darcy wasn't sure where she stood.

☙

"Okay. Close your eyes now," Jonas said.

Darcy sat on the tailgate of Lucas's truck. Swinging her

legs, she squeezed her eyes shut.

Emily was busy folding the blanket they'd used to eat their picnic lunch. Jonas and Lucas had made Darcy's favorite—fried chicken. It had been a risk. The women appeared to enjoy having someone else cook for them for a change.

Sunday had turned out to be a beautiful day. Perfect for a picnic—the kind where a guy could romance a girl, even if he was rusty like Jonas.

The sun behind Darcy created a halo around her hair. Ten years had been good to her—she'd grown into a beautiful, sophisticated woman, from the girl he'd been in love with. Jonas could hardly believe his luck that she wasn't married, or in love with someone else.

Though he wasn't sure his efforts would have been deterred by news that she had a boyfriend, now he realized he definitely wanted back in the game. Truth was, he wasn't sure when he'd gotten out. It hadn't been a conscious effort on his part, just time flying by while he became an FBI agent, then while he threw himself into his work.

Jonas wanted to imagine that they hadn't lost any time. That they had been together, instead of apart. Or better. He wanted to fast-forward to when they were together again.

But progress took time. Today, he would continue building the bridge that connected him to Darcy.

"When can I open my eyes?" she asked.

"Not yet. I'll be right back." He tugged the gift he'd purchased from underneath the front seat then rushed back around the truck.

Darcy waited with her eyes closed. Holding the gift wrapped

in brown paper, Jonas felt silly. He wasn't any good at this.

He handed it to her. "Okay, you can look now." He was going about this all wrong.

"What's this?" She smiled as she took it from him.

"It's for you."

She stared at him, leaving the gift unopened. "Jonas. . ."

"Just open it already." He grinned, covering his panic.

As if weighing what accepting a gift from him would mean, she hesitated. But when she ripped the paper off, he couldn't help his broad smile.

Holding the box filled with art pencils and an expensive sketch pad, she glanced up and looked long and deep inside him, searching for something. "You shouldn't have," she whispered.

Had she found what she was looking for? He hoped so. "It was my pleasure. I know how much you love to sketch."

"Thank you. This means a lot to me." Her eyes glistened.

"It's not like you needed any art supplies, I know. I just—"

She touched his hand, stopping him. "You don't have to explain. I understand. It's a very thoughtful gift."

Jonas cherished the look of hope in her eyes. He desperately wanted to ask her the question that kept him awake every night.

Can we recapture what we once had? "I thought you might like to draw while we're here." He sounded like he was eighteen again.

"Um, I don't know." She gave a nervous laugh.

"I used to enjoy watching you sketch." He'd brought up their past. What an idiot.

"I guess I could." She nodded. "Sure."

Relief swept over him. If he could only keep the light banter going forever, well, not forever, but grow it from here. He had to give her time. But with everything in him he wanted to rush things.

"I didn't get you anything. I'm sorry." Color rose in her cheeks and she glanced away. Cute.

"You accepted my invitation. That's enough." *That means everything to me.*

With every second he spent with her, the love he once had burned more brightly. Lucas was right. Darcy was the *one,* and she always had been. But in going away to make something of himself for her, he'd lost her.

"What should I sketch?" She'd tugged the ponytail out of her hair and shook it free, then looked at him.

Gorgeous, thick cords of her luscious hair hung over her shoulders. Though it was tough, Jonas resisted lifting his hand to her hair. "Let's walk, then if something you see inspires you, we'll stop."

He started on the trail near where they'd picnicked, Darcy beside him. Emily and Lucas had gone ahead, leaving Jonas time alone to give her his present.

Spotting them in the distance, he trudged forward. Darcy kept up with him easily. He shared a little about his career in the FBI. At some point, he'd planned to explain how her father's words impacted him, sending him along a much narrower path than he was headed, despite his intentions toward Darcy. For that, he was grateful to the man. But now wasn't the time.

Lucas and Emily dropped out of sight.

Jonas stopped. Where had they gone?

"Guys, remember when we used to explore in here?" Lucas's voice echoed, sounding like he was in a cavern.

Jonas smiled. Of course, he hadn't explored the Crack-in-the-Ground since he was a kid living here. The result of volcanic activity in Oregon's past, the fissure was two miles long and seventy feet deep in places. A local tourist attraction, along with the four craters to the north.

Trusting Darcy to follow, he picked up his pace until he stood at the edge of the fissure. He saw now how Lucas had climbed down since they were beyond the main entry point. Part of the wall had caved. Sand, dirt, and rock filled in the rest, giving him easy access to the bottom.

He turned to assist Darcy in descending, but she hadn't kept up with him. She still stood a good fifty yards back. "Come on. Don't you want to explore?"

She shook her head. What was the matter with her?

"You guys go ahead," he called down to his brother and Emily, "but don't be too long."

Lucas didn't answer, but Jonas wouldn't worry.

He trotted back to Darcy. "What's wrong?"

She gave him a look like he should know. "You don't remember?" she asked.

Remember what? In her eyes he saw pain and raw fear. A familiar memory trickled into his thoughts—her trembling voice when she told him about falling into the fissure as a child. Being stuck in the dark, feeling like the walls were closing in on her. How terrified she'd been.

"I can't believe I forgot. I'm sorry." He blew out a breath and studied her. All his efforts to be the most thoughtful guy on the planet and he'd forgotten this. Had it cost him? Had it just erased the gift, the picnic with fried chicken, destroyed the bridge?

He frowned, feeling the regret of everything he'd lost. Wanting to take her in his arms. Bury his face in her swanlike neck and gorgeous hair.

"I shouldn't have expected you to remember," she said, offering a soft smile. "I just can't go down there. It makes me feel trapped."

"No, you prefer hanging from a nylon cloth, thousands of feet above the ground."

"And that scares you." She laughed and finger-combed her hair then made a ponytail again. One of those familiar habits he loved—she'd release her hair from a ponytail and a few minutes later, put it up. Then the process repeated all over.

"It does." He nodded, drawing closer. "Are we going to hike while we wait on them?"

"No. I found my inspiration." Darcy scrambled onto a boulder, grabbed a pencil from her pack, and positioned her sketch pad. She stared at him as she sketched.

"What. . .me?"

"You're an FBI agent who faces death almost every day in his job, and yet there's something that terrifies you. You're an enigma, Jonas Love."

Losing you again scares me more. . .

Chapter 5

Thursday morning, the sun rose an hour earlier than usual, or it seemed to Darcy. She wanted to sleep in and since this was her day off, she was at liberty to roll over and smash a pillow over her head. But her to-do list wouldn't let go.

Tonight, she was supposed to meet with a potential buyer for the store and, if she sold it, that was one more step to her freedom. She loved her father, mourned his absence, but her life had never been her own. At last she could exercise some control over it.

She could make a fresh start somewhere else.

Stretching her arms, she remained in bed and stared at the ceiling. What would it feel like to sleep in a different room, to call a different place home, to have an apartment or a new house all her own?

When she rolled to her side to glance at the clock, the sketch of Jonas she'd drawn while on their picnic Sunday caught her attention. She slid it across the nightstand and held it up.

You are a gorgeous man, but. . .

"But what are you doing back in my life?" What were his

intentions? This had to be leading nowhere. Just like before.

After the picnic, he'd called several times during the week, even stopping by the store to see her. Jonas had invited her to spend today with him, but she'd refused because of everything she needed to get done.

Just being with him did crazy things to her heart. She was supposed to be protecting her most precious possession, wasn't she? She couldn't afford to offer it to him with so many uncertainties in her future. Emily's talk of their love story was something best left to a romance novel. Darcy had already played a main character opposite Jonas in a love story that ended badly.

She wouldn't make that mistake again.

Jonas had been kind to her, thoughtful at every turn, but Darcy sensed that he was acting out of guilt, attempting to make up for what happened between them. That wasn't something she wanted to build a relationship on. With her heart on the line, too much was at risk, especially since she didn't know what he wanted from her.

Was it friendship?

Forgiveness?

Love?

He clearly loved his job with the FBI. She recalled his anguish as he told her about how someone on his team was killed, and that he was in Oregon to regroup. That told Darcy she wasn't part of his plans for the future. Then why was she torturing herself with thoughts of him, or even giving him the time of day? Why couldn't she shove the remnants of her love for him from her heart?

Ignoring the clashing thoughts, she closed her eyes and tried to remember how it felt to be in his arms. To kiss Jonas, the man she loved. The man she would have married.

If not for her father. She released a pent-up groan, threw the covers off, and got out of bed. Allowing her thoughts to go there wasn't helping anything.

The here and now was all there was. All she had left. That. . .and a future of her own making.

Dressed in her comfy sweats, Darcy stood in the living room and stared at the mountain of knickknacks, collectibles, and paperwork to organize and put in an estate sale once probate was complete. She expected that news to come through any day now and had already contacted a woman who lived in Ridgeview and specialized in estate sales.

Darcy exhaled.

The aroma of coffee, set to brew the night before, wafted into the living room. She poured a big mug of the dark brew, adding fat-free milk. After drinking half the cup, she opened the front door and made her way down the driveway to retrieve the rolled-up newspaper. A quick read through the morning paper, and she could start her day off right.

A red minivan pulled next to the curb in front of the house, startling her. A woman hopped out of the driver's side and rushed around to the passenger side, tossing Darcy a little wave. What in the world?

Once the passenger door was hanging open, Mrs. Olson stepped from the car and smiled. "There you are."

Darcy didn't know what to make of the woman stopping

by, but moved closer to the van so the elderly woman wouldn't have to walk to her. "Hello Mrs. Olson. What can I do for you?"

"Please forgive me for coming uninvited." She looked at the younger woman standing next to her—a woman Darcy had never met. "This is my granddaughter, Candice. She drove over yesterday from Idaho to pick me up. I'm going to visit my great-granddaughter for her birthday. Remember, I told you about that."

Candice offered Darcy an apologetic grin. "I'm really sorry about this. She insisted that we stop here before heading out. We were going to leave the gift on your doorstep with a note."

Mrs. Olson pressed her hand over Darcy's like she'd done at the store. "That sketch of the juniper—I just can't keep that. It belongs to you. I could tell it was special to you. The thought has niggled me ever since."

"Oh Mrs. Olson. You didn't have to do that. The sketch was for sale. It belongs to you now."

Candice lifted a small gift bag from the van and handed it to Darcy. "Better just take it, hon."

"But if you'd like to return it, I need to give your money back."

"No. It's my gift to you. Read the note later."

Perplexed, Darcy watched Mrs. Olson climb back into the van then her granddaughter steered from the curb. She waved at the little old woman with the kindly eyes. How strange. She made her way back to the house with the gift bag and grabbed the note from inside, ripping it open. It explained what Mrs. Olson had told her in person, except for one thing.

The note suggested the sketch was missing something. Perhaps that was the real reason the woman had returned it—she didn't think it was complete. Desperately needing more coffee now, Darcy poured enough to fill the cup and took a long swallow.

She removed the sketch from the bag and studied the centuries-old juniper.

Mrs. Olson was right. Darcy did love this sketch. Like all her other photographs, paintings, and sketches, she loved them, but had to let them go. What could the woman think was missing in the sketch? Darcy crawled onto a tall chair that hugged the counter.

At her father's funeral, she'd seen Jonas leaning against the tree. At the time, she hadn't known it was him. He was the only thing missing in the picture, but Mrs. Olson couldn't have known that.

Had she also seen Jonas next to the juniper that day? She'd been at the funeral. Darcy huffed. Things were never that simple.

Mrs. Olson had suggested that God had given Darcy and Jonas a second chance. Maybe—maybe Mrs. Olson was much more perceptive than Darcy about her sketch. About her life.

Invisible forces. . .

ᴄƨ

The plate of eggs slipped from Jonas's grasp and crashed to the floor. He resisted swearing under his breath.

Lucas hovered over the stove, frying bacon. His turn to

cook. "Having a bad day so you had to throw a plate?"

"Sorry about that. I'll clean it up." Jonas wiped at the mess with a paper towel.

"I'll make more eggs."

"Never mind. I'll just have coffee."

"Too bad. You need your energy." The bacon started smoking.

"Pay attention to the bacon instead of me. You're going to burn it."

After the plate was collected and eggs wiped from the floor, Jonas slid into the chair and slurped coffee, his mind a tangle. The next thing he knew, Lucas set a plate of bacon and more eggs in front of him.

"Thanks. You didn't have to, you know."

Lucas slid into the chair opposite Jonas. "You've been a bear since yesterday. Well, more of a bear than usual. Was it that phone call last night?"

Jonas nodded.

"Care to share?"

Shaking his head, Jonas dug into the eggs and bacon, though he couldn't taste a thing. Tom had called again last night issuing him another warning. What Jonas couldn't figure was that if Gambini was serious about his threat, why would he bother warning Jonas?

Jonas had brought trouble with him, putting his brothers in danger.

Putting Darcy in danger.

Darcy wanted to keep the past behind her. He wished he

could do the same—that Gambini would just stay in the past. Jonas should leave now, head back to Chicago. But then he would never get another chance with Darcy.

Lucas finished his plate and got up to make more. Jonas couldn't believe it. "You're kidding, right?"

"I burn a lot of calories in this business." He cracked an egg against the side of the pan and dumped the contents, doing the same with three more. When they were ready, he sat at the table to shovel them in.

"I take it things aren't going so well with the love of your life," Lucas said between bites.

Finished with his eggs, Jonas tossed his plate in the sink. "I don't think she wants to be friends."

"No kidding. You need to speed things up. Guess you weren't born with a good sense of timing."

Jonas laughed. "So much for your advice."

"Have you told her how you feel? I mean, really feel?"

"No." Jonas was ready to pour it on the line, but he didn't want to rush her.

"Have you kissed her?"

"What is this? The Inquisition?"

"Just answer the question."

"No."

"That's all you need to get things on the right track. Just in case she's forgotten how things were between you."

Jonas had enough of his brother's love doctor counsel. This time, he wanted to do things right. His cell buzzed in his pocket. He tugged it out.

Darcy. . .

Before he schooled his expression, he looked at Lucas, who gave him a knowing grin. Jonas slipped outside, hoping to have a private conversation. "Hey there."

"I'm sorry if this is too early." Her tone was soft, sweet.

Jonas shut his eyes and leaned against the side of the house. He loved the sound of her voice. "No. I just finished breakfast. What's up?"

Idiot. Did there have to be a reason for her to call?

"Are you working today? I mean, helping Lucas."

"That depends." He smiled, expectation thudding in his chest. "What did you have in mind?"

"Well, you'd invited me to do something with you earlier. I'm sorry that I have so much on my plate today. Would you be interested in coming over? You could help."

"How soon would you like me there?"

"Anytime is fine."

"I'll be there in ten minutes."

"Whoa." She laughed. "I need to shower and get dressed. Give me an hour, okay?"

"See you then." He ended the call, a smile on his face. If the day went well, Jonas might believe he'd fully. . .*decompressed.*

The thought sent his mind racing back to the bureau. His job. His life in Chicago. After the internal investigation was complete, they'd call him back. He'd need to be cleared to return to work.

But he didn't want to think about that right now. He was running out of time to make things happen with Darcy.

He shoved through the door and into the kitchen. Lucas stood at the sink washing the breakfast dishes and sang a rocker screamo song about Jonas having a date. He sounded awful—but then that was the style.

He threw an orange at his brother. "It's not like that. She just wants my help."

Soapy hands on his hips, Lucas turned to face him. "Just one kiss. That's all it takes."

"If only the girls could see you now." Jonas laughed.

Frowning, Lucas wiped his hands. "Darcy wants the same thing as you. Your mission, agent man, should you choose to accept, is to kiss the girl. Make her remember what you had before. Make her want what you can have now."

"You should write a love advice column," Jonas replied with as much sarcasm as he could muster. He headed to the spare room to clean up before seeing Darcy. As much as he hated to admit it, Lucas was on to something.

He'd spent enough time evaluating their relationship; maybe it was time to take the next step. Maybe today would be the day he would tell her everything. Or better.

He *would* kiss her.

Chapter 6

All it had taken was Mrs. Olson's strange appearance this morning.

The doorbell rang. Darcy glanced at the clock. Jonas was ten minutes early.

She took one last glance in the mirror to reassure herself the new pair of jeans and lavender knit top she wore flattered her shape.

She was pathetic. Darcy needed to hear what Jonas wanted. Friendship or love? And if it was love he proposed, she wanted to hear his five-year plan.

Yeah, right. One step at a time.

She opened the door and smiled. Jonas cracked a playful, lovable grin. The shimmer in his dark eyes stirred her heart to flight—she was soaring again, only this time she was about to drop, falling straight to the ground.

"Sorry if I'm early."

She swung the door wide. "No problem. Come in. But when you hear what I've got you doing, you might wish you'd come late or not at all."

He stepped through the door, leaving her in the wake of

his musky cologne. Behind his back, she frowned, wondering if she'd made a mistake. Why did her heart and mind have to battle over this?

Jonas swung around to face her. "You've been busy."

He referred to the boxes everywhere, of course.

"Yeah, well, not busy enough. I've gone through boxes from the attic, looking through stacks of things. There's plenty I need to pack as well. Some things I'm going to store for a while. Other things I'm going to sell in the estate sale."

Jonas's smile slipped.

Darcy kept hers in place. "And this is where I need your help."

Pressing his hand over his mouth in a thoughtful pose, he surveyed the room scattered with cardboard and junk. "You're really going to sell all this stuff so soon after your dad's funeral?"

The look in his eyes bordered on a challenge. Darcy couldn't stand the accusation there. She made her way to the kitchen, aware that Jonas followed her with his gaze. He expected an answer.

What did he know about it? He'd been gone for so long. He had no right. She squeezed her eyes shut, stifling her retort. She didn't want to get into that.

"You want some coffee?" she asked.

"Sure." Jonas approached the kitchen counter. "I'm sorry. It's not my place."

Darcy poured the coffee, then raised her gaze to meet his. She offered a smile in truce. "If it's all the same to you, I'd rather not discuss my reasons for doing things the way I am."

She wasn't sure there was any sense to packing up the house other than the sooner she took care of what was a necessary task, the sooner she would be free.

To do what, she wasn't exactly sure.

After showing Jonas where she wanted him to start, he positioned himself on a footstool and began packing items she'd put in a pile. Today, Darcy planned to go through her mother's dishes—the Noritake china she'd been given when her mother had died. Of course, Darcy had continued the tradition, always using the china for Sunday dinners when they hadn't been invited to someone else's home after church. That hardly ever happened. Looking at it now, she finally realized what a state of confusion she was in.

She'd been wrong to think she could do this so soon, and sagged against the counter. Everyone had been right—it was too soon. But it had to be done. There was no good time.

"Darcy, did you see this?" Still sitting on the footstool, Jonas peered at her from the living room.

Glad for the distraction, she set the dish on the counter and went to him. "What is it?"

He held up a photograph. Prom night. Darcy's junior year. She and Jonas stood together. He wore his tux, she, her sky-blue prom dress. She laughed. "Oh, I forgot about this."

She attempted to pull it away, but he wouldn't let go. Smiling, she tugged harder. "Let me see."

He relinquished his hold. Darcy pretended she didn't see the regret in his eyes and studied the old photograph.

"You were a lot skinnier then. Better looking, too." She

laughed. That was so not true.

"Now it's my turn." Jonas stood. He took the photo from her and stared, his gaze thoughtful. "I remember that night. We were young, and our lives were full of hope and promise. That night, we still had a future together."

Jonas laid the photograph in the box, packing away the memories. He leveled his gaze at her and took her hands in his. The tenderness in his touch, his skin against hers, sent heat rushing through her.

Friendship? No...

Her breath caught in her throat. "What are you doing?"

"I'm done wasting time." Impatience edged his voice. He inhaled deeply. "From the minute I saw you at your father's funeral, I've wanted to be with you, tell you everything. But I didn't want to rush you."

"Jonas..." Her voice was raspy.

"And if I'm rushing you now, just say the word and I'll stop."

She'd wanted this, hadn't she? She wanted to know what Jonas was thinking by putting himself back into her life. But anguish whirled inside. This was all too fast.

He brought her hand to his lips, pressing them against her skin. Tingles swept over her. He took a step closer, his face near hers, his breath warming her cheeks.

It had been so long...

She'd dreamed of this moment. And yet, she was terrified.

The walls were closing around her. He would suffocate her if she let him.

"Kiss me," she whispered, closing her eyes.

ꞓ₿

The longing he'd seen in her eyes sent him over the edge. The moment had finally arrived. With her soft body against him, her arms pulling him closer, Jonas teetered on the brink of passion, the love he thought he'd buried gushing from all the hidden places in his heart.

He kissed her thoroughly, completely.

Remember what we had. . .

He breathed in the honey-vanilla scent of her. How many years had he longed for this? To wrap his arms around her? To kiss her once again.

Never again would he let her go.

He had to control the flood of emotions, or he'd overwhelm her. Though he feared releasing her—would she ever be in his arms again?

He eased back. "Darcy. . ."

She pressed her lips against his again. He gripped her arms and gently untangled her from him. "We have to stop."

Hurt flooded her eyes. "What's wrong?"

He gripped her wrists before she could step away. "Nothing. I. . .didn't want to get carried away."

Not until I've made you my wife.

Darcy freed herself from his grip. "What are you doing here, Jonas? What do you want from me?"

Her question was loaded with years of hurt and resentment. She'd waited for the right moment to stab him.

And this was it?

He'd rushed her—she needed more time after her father's death, whether she thought so or not. And he had rushed her.

"I wanted to give you time and space. Time to get used to me here. Space to grieve for your father. But the truth is. . .I want you back. I want what we had back then but lost."

There. He'd said it.

She pulled in a breath. "Why'd you leave in the first place without so much as a good-bye? Ten years and not a word. How can you expect us to pick up where we left off"—she snapped her fingers—"just like that?"

"Your father wouldn't let you see me, you know that." Jonas raised his voice to meet her tone, then regretted it. Softer now, "I got into trouble, after losing you, I just didn't care anymore. All I had for a father figure was Carver. He was too busy with the ranch."

Darcy sank into the sofa. "I'm listening."

That was all he wanted. But it was so complicated. He wasn't sure he could explain. "I got into trouble and landed in jail. I wasn't charged with anything. The sheriff just wanted to teach me and my friends a lesson. Your father visited me there and at the time, I thought he'd bailed me out. Maybe he did. From that moment forward, though, I had to agree to meet with him for counseling."

Darcy looked at her hands.

"I hated that at first. But the man knew how to talk to me. Over time, he made me realize I would never be good enough for you. Not until I turned my life around. Until I made something out of myself. I left town, got a degree. . .you know the rest."

"And the reason you never contacted me in all this time?" Darcy twisted her knife.

She had him there. Everything he could think of sounded like pathetic excuses. "Because by that time, it had been years, Darcy. Years. I thought you found someone else, or you'd forgotten about me."

"Nice try, but you hurt me. Really hurt me."

"I never stopped thinking about you." Jonas heard the desperation in his voice, hating that it had come to this. But he was willing to beg.

"You picked a crazy time to walk back into my life. This time, I'm the one who's leaving. Tonight, I'm meeting with someone who wants to buy my business."

She punched him with that. The room tilted a little and her drive to pack up the house made more sense. "You're. . .leaving?"

"Sure. Are you the only one in town who hasn't noticed the For Sale sign on the store? As soon as I get that squared away, I'm putting this house on the market."

"Why?" His voice cracked like he was thirteen again.

Why was she doing this to him? What a jerk he was to even ask. The love of his life was slipping away. There was nothing he could do about it.

She'd slipped away a long time ago. He'd let her. Making something of himself for her father, for her, had taken too much of a toll on them.

"It's my turn to make something of myself. Maybe we can get together in oh, say, another ten years."

Chapter 7

She wasn't sure how it happened. Or why.

She'd wanted the kiss. He'd given her that and much more. Told her everything she wanted to hear. How then, did she end up throwing it all back in his face? More like smearing it.

Despite the deep ache in her heart, after Jonas had left earlier, Darcy worked on digging through the junk she found in boxes in case she found something important or valuable. Other stuff, she packed away. Memories—some good and others not so much—taunted her much of the day.

That wasn't even counting her emotional battle with Jonas. She'd started the day wary of spending time with him, then Mrs. Olson's appearance had prompted her to invite him over. At least now she knew what he wanted. Never mind that she'd sent him away.

Resentment long buried had boiled to the surface, heated by her passion for him, by his kiss. For a decade, she'd held on to it with fervor. If only she'd known.

Treating him like that had been wrong, but it had felt good to hurt him back. She'd lashed out in anger; she saw that now.

Multiple aftershocks of deep regret shook her to the core. The only thing keeping her grounded was the fact he couldn't be too devastated—she hadn't gone anywhere yet.

He said he wanted her back. But that would take careful consideration. Time and space, like Jonas said. The kiss had been a huge indiscretion, but she wanted to know if his kiss would still make her knees weak.

Was that so wrong?

She rubbed her temples, remembering the passion. And Jonas had actually backed off. There was more between them now than before. If she decided to throw down the drawbridge to her heart, allowing Jonas to cross over, this time she couldn't blame the hurt she incurred on her father.

The blame would be Darcy's alone.

And finally, she had this chance to do what she wanted with her life. Her father's passing had lifted all expectations that she remain in town, run her little store, and type up his sermons. Freedom came with a price—she was alone and forgotten. The thought corded around her that if she entangled herself with Jonas she would no longer be free.

Enough of the mental wrangling.

Darcy headed for a quick shower. The day had left her drained. She needed to be sharp when she met with the potential buyer. After showering, she changed into business slacks and a nice, professional-looking, collared blouse. She could at least hear what the man had to say. He'd perused the store today, her day off, and wanted to hear more about the business over dinner.

If only she didn't have that same feeling in the pit of her stomach that she'd gotten when going through the Noritake earlier today. *It was too soon. . .*

She shouldn't make any life-changing decisions now. With so much of herself poured into the store—her hang gliding photographs, sketches, and paintings—she couldn't easily transfer the essence of what made High Desert Art special to someone else.

What am I doing? Dread battled with hope for a future.

But she was already dressed and ready to meet Alberto Marino, the interested party. Darcy stepped outside and discovered she had a flat. She could change it, but she would be late and have to change her clothes as well, and. . .she could think of a thousand more excuses. But did she need one when the truth was staring at her?

She leaned against the car, thinking. The flat was the reason she could use to cancel the dinner, and canceling the dinner made her happy. It wasn't the right time to sell her store.

She quickly dialed Mr. Marino.

"A phone call from you doesn't bode well for me," he said, his voice smooth like honey.

How perceptive. "I'm sorry. I've decided I don't want to sell the business. At least, not yet." The truth hadn't been so hard, had it? And she didn't even have to use her flat tire for an excuse.

"There is potential in the future? Then you should still dine with me. I want to hear what you can tell me about the tourist business and the town. I'm interested in moving to the area. And that way, should you decide to sell in the future, I'll know if I'm interested."

"I have a flat tire. Can we reschedule?"

"I'm leaving tomorrow. I'll come over to your house, change your tire, and then take you to dinner. How can you pass up on that?"

Darcy started pacing, feeling a little trapped. She had to get over this anxiety brought on by the smallest pressure—almost like a panic attack. Almost like she was a kid again, stuck deep inside a crack in the earth and lost forever.

"Okay."

She gave him her address. Half an hour later, she was sitting next to Marino in his car telling him about the small town where she'd grown up, about the scenic byway and the Oregon Outback. He seemed especially fascinated with her hang gliding, and that connected back to her photographs that she sold at High Desert Art.

At last, she realized he'd been driving for a while. "Where are we going?"

"I found a restaurant I liked in the next town over. I hope that's all right."

"Sure, but that's a long drive."

"Perfect. You and I have plenty to talk about." When he glanced her way, she wasn't sure she liked the look in his eyes.

"I've already told you a lot. What more do you want to know?" She made sure her tone was warm, despite her sudden unease.

"Actually, I'm interested to hear more about your boyfriend."

Alarm sprang through her. "That's an odd question. Especially since I don't have a boyfriend."

Marino laughed. "Ah, I'm sure that didn't sound right. I want to make sure your boyfriend won't be angry if he sees us together."

"If I had a boyfriend, I would have invited him along." She smiled, but she was getting odd vibes from the man. A stranger. She was in the car with a complete stranger. Yet business professionals did this every day. She was overreacting.

Still, the walls shifted closer, tighter. Suffocating. "I'm starting to feel sick. Why don't we just call it a night? I think you've heard enough to make a decision. Can you take me home now?"

Marino kept driving, making no attempt to respond or turn around. Hadn't he heard her?

Darcy leaned over and cupped her mouth. "There's a rest stop a mile up the road. I need to use it." She tried to sound like her only concern was the queasiness whirling in her stomach.

The place was located where she and Jonas had picnicked near the Crack-in-the-Ground. Thankfully, he pulled into the rest stop. Maybe she'd misunderstood him.

"Thanks." She stepped from the car, planning to call Jonas in the restroom if she could get a signal.

Marino followed her to the women's entrance. "I forgot my cell. Can I borrow yours? I need to make a call while you're using the facilities."

"Sure, why not?" She tugged her phone from her purse, handed it over, then fled into the restroom. Great. She couldn't call for help if she needed it now, and the rest stop was empty of travelers.

Whatever was going on, she wanted to go home, and Marino wasn't obliging. Why had he ignored her? She paced, her palms sweating.

☙

On his Suzuki Hayabusa, Jonas raced up the highway, touching speeds far above the limit—but not nearly the speed the motorcycle was capable of going. Still, in this remote region and time of day, there wasn't another vehicle for miles.

Jonas needed to blow off his frustration. He was a failure. If he weren't a failure, he wouldn't need to decompress. If he weren't a failure, he'd be with Darcy right now, getting his second chance.

He'd kissed her, hadn't he? She'd responded, hadn't she? Then what went wrong? He'd rushed her, that's what. Just like he'd rushed his team into the house during a raid. Though he'd followed the book, as it were, something in his gut told him to wait.

He hadn't listened.

The only gas station for seventy-five miles sat lonesome and waiting on the right side of the road a tenth of a mile up. Jonas stopped at the station, knowing it might be another seventy-five or more before he found another place to buy gas. Though Lucas tried to talk him into staying, he needed to get out of town.

He didn't consider where he was going, or when he'd be back. He just drove.

He handed his credit card to the attendant—amazed the station owner had brought the place into the twenty-first century—who filled the tank.

Despite the way Darcy had laid into him, he held on to hope. He'd told her he wanted back what they once had. She'd been angry, cutting him deep with her words. But her anger was born of hurt that she'd locked away for a long time. With all that she'd harbored against him, he wasn't surprised at her outburst. But he had been surprised at her kiss—it was like she'd released the passion of a thousand kisses, bottled up for a decade.

Darcy didn't know about his visit to her father while the man lay in the hospital, just before he died.

This time, he wouldn't fail.

Jonas would listen to that sense in his gut, that sense that told him it wasn't the right time to tell her. He couldn't tell her what her father said until all was settled between them, if it ever was.

Finished with filling the tank, he hung his head. "Lord, please, help me make this right."

His phone buzzed in his pocket. Jonas yanked it out, hoping Darcy was calling, though he knew she was dining with the potential buyer at that moment.

Darcy's ID. His pulse spiked. "Darcy?"

"No, not Darcy. If your girlfriend was here, she would call me Alberto Marino."

The buyer was answering her phone? Something wasn't right. "Where's Darcy then?"

"But if you were here, you would call me Carl Gambini,

Roberto Gambini's nephew."

Noooo! His heart stopped. . .

Then started.

The worst kind of dread shot through him. "You listen. Your fight is with me, not Darcy."

"You have something that belongs to me. If I don't get it back, I'm going to destroy your life, everyone you care about—just like you did to my uncle—and there's nothing you can do to stop me. I already searched through the stuff you left in Chicago, and I didn't find what I was looking for, but I found something almost as good. Pictures of a beautiful woman. The one woman you love. If you don't return my money, I'll hurt her. And when I'm finished with her, I'll hurt your brothers."

Though Jonas was trained to respond, he was in a state of utter shock. His mind scrambled to figure out what money Gambini was talking about. But Gambini wouldn't want to hear that he didn't know, and a denial wouldn't buy him any time or help Darcy.

"I'll bring you the money in exchange for Darcy."

"You'd better have the full half mill."

A half-million dollars? "Where do you want to meet?"

"I'll call you within the hour. If you want to see Darcy unharmed, you better not contact the authorities. You, of all people, should know what can happen."

Gambini ended the call. He'd sucker punched Jonas, who should have been on the lookout for trouble. But he honestly considered Gambini's rants from behind bars nothing more than idle threats. It was difficult for a stranger to show up in this town without the locals knowing about it.

And with that he realized. . .Darcy's buyer. Jonas threw his leg over the bike, straddling it. It was his fault. Again.

He wouldn't waste time berating himself. He had to save Darcy.

Help me make it right. . .

Jonas called Lucas. "I need you to drive the roads and look for anything out of the ordinary. Darcy has been kidnapped by the relative of someone I put away. I don't want him to hurt her, so you need to use stealth. Do. You. Understand?"

"Got it."

"I'm on my bike about an hour out and headed back. Keep calling me if you have to. Call the sheriff, too; let her in on the news, but again, don't draw any attention or it could mean Darcy's life."

"Don't worry, Jonas. We'll get her back."

Next Jonas called Tom. "Gambini's nephew has kidnapped a woman. Her name is Darcy Nichols. He wants to trade her for a half a million dollars that he thinks I took. Know anything about that?"

Jonas gave Tom the rest of the particulars and was assured help was on the way, though details were sorely lacking.

If only he'd stayed away from Oregon's high desert country, away from Carnegie and Darcy, then she'd be safe right now. But Gambini had discovered her photograph in Jonas's apartment.

She'd never been safe with Jonas holding on to her. She'd never be safe until he let her go.

Chapter 8

Outside the restroom, Darcy pressed her body against the wall, listening. She stood around the corner from Marino.

She'd slipped out the moment he made the call, and from her hiding place, she heard every word. His name wasn't even Marino. It was Gambini.

By the conversation, she knew he was talking to Jonas. Jonas had stolen money from him, and now he wanted to trade Darcy's life for the money. Her pulse thundered in her ears. Her breathing would give her away if she couldn't calm down.

She'd been frozen to the ground, listening, and now it might be too late to run. They were out in the middle of nowhere, surrounded by miles of arid, deserted land and, beyond that, ten thousand acres of sand dunes. Thank goodness she'd worn flats. Still, Darcy would never make it to Lucas's, but she could hide. An image of the perfect hiding place appeared in her mind.

Oh no, Lord, please no. . .

Gambini disappeared from sight. Darcy guessed he was going to check on her. This was her chance to escape. She propelled herself from the wall and into the Oregon wilderness.

"Are you finished yet?" His voice echoed through the small opening in the wall of the restroom. He had to think she was an idiot.

Running as fast as she could, she didn't look back.

Gambini shouted. He'd spotted her, but now she had the advantage. She had a head start, she could run, and she knew where to hide. At that moment, she would give anything to be hang gliding, the earth far beneath her.

But she did her best to fly with her feet.

If she could put enough distance between them, she could lose him, weaving through trees and sagebrush, then hide in the fissure. It was her only chance.

She kept up her pace for a quarter mile. Though she was in great shape, she couldn't catch her breath. With the sun quickly setting, Darcy held on to hope that she could use the night and her familiarity with the area to outlast Gambini.

Footfalls approached from behind, coming up on her fast.

She darted behind a copse of trees, crept around boulders, and veered up the path to the Crack-in-the Ground, to the place where Lucas and Emily had been able to climb down beyond the main entry point.

Memories lashed at her. She and a friend were exploring the crack while their parents picnicked nearby. They'd been warned to stay away. Darcy had scrambled over boulders and hidden in a deep hole—a place not readily visible to tourists. During her climb down, she'd somehow dislodged a rock that slid against her arm, wedging it against the rock wall. She called for help. Hours passed before she was discovered. Her friend was afraid to tell her parents where they had gone for fear of getting in trouble.

Darcy could use her knowledge of the place to hide now. What if something happened to her this time? What if she was never found? She swallowed the acid rising in her throat. She'd rather take her chances with a geological oddity, than with Gambini.

Darcy scrambled down into the thousand-year-old fissure. She stood at the bottom and gazed up the seventy-foot rock wall that lined either side.

As she pushed farther along, she descended deeper and the shadowed crevice grew dark. The twenty-degree drop in temperature wrapped her in a blanket of cold. Finding what she was looking for—a rocky outcrop hiding a deeper hole—Darcy shoved herself in a corner, pushing down the panic.

Always the panic. The anxiety.

Completely shrouded in darkness, she wouldn't go deeper. Couldn't go deeper into darkness. Into that small, tight space. Unless her life depended on it.

Listening, she steadied her breathing.

Minutes crept by before she slid to the ground. Had she lost her abductor?

She would wait for Jonas. He would find and save her, wouldn't he? She could trust him on that, forget that her childhood friend had left her behind to save her own skin.

Thoughts of Jonas turning into a rogue FBI agent involved with Gambini sent her heart racing, quickening her breath.

Jonas couldn't have stolen the money. She wouldn't believe it. Gambini was the liar. That had to be it.

Her life was at stake because of that money.

In the end, only death kept them apart...

Her words to Emily about tragic love stories accosted her. Darcy shuddered at the thought. *Lord, give us another chance.*

Did she believe that Jonas was innocent because she loved him? Because she needed him? No—it went deeper than that. She knew in her core that he couldn't be involved in something illegal, despite his troubled youth. He hadn't carried that with him into a law enforcement career.

He'd changed for the better.

"If only you could see him now, Daddy," she whispered. *Then maybe you'd approve of us this time...*

She still wanted her father's approval. In the cool darkness, Darcy imagined that her father had given his blessing for them to be together. He finally told Darcy how proud he was of her—fulfilling her hope, her dream.

Against the smooth, cold stone, she had a startling revelation. A tear escaped, warming her cheek.

His approval would not fill the emptiness.

The phone vibrated in his pocket. Jonas slowed to a stop on the side of the road, hating that he had to lose time.

"Lucas, what have you found?"

"There's an abandoned sedan at the rest stop a few miles north of Christmas Valley where we took the girls for the picnic."

"That could be anything."

"Illinois plates."

The odds jumped a few notches. Maybe Gambini had driven to avoid being tracked.

"Search the area. If you find anything, wait for me and the sheriff. Do not act on your own. I'm just fifteen minutes out."

Jonas urged the bike back on the road and accelerated, not caring that he had to pass cars already driving too fast. He hadn't been good enough for Darcy a decade ago. Her father had called him a troublemaker with no direction.

He'd taken the man's advice. But even Special Agent Jonas Love was trouble for Darcy.

None of it made any difference. His life had ramped out of control. If Darcy was going to survive, Jonas had to let go of the reins. He needed divine assistance—someone who did a better job of running things than Jonas did.

Lord, please protect her, save her. I'm giving her up completely to You, if that's what You want.

It was hard. . .giving her up. But it felt right.

Waiting. Listening. Darcy shivered in the black night. Pebbles and dirt skittered from the surface into the fissure.

She held her breath. Desperate for peace and safety, she silently sang the words to Psalm ninety-one. *"I will say to the Lord, You are my refuge, and my fortress, my God in whom I will trust. . ."*

Thud. Someone had dropped to the ground.

Gambini was coming. Footsteps crunched between the crevice walls. He would find her. She searched for a rock—something to use as a weapon—and stood, pressing herself against the cold wall, willing herself invisible.

She heard faint breathing, not her own. Fear wrapped around her throat, cutting off her breath. She remained quiet. Listening.

Inhale. . .exhale. . .inches from her.

Could he hear her heart pounding?

The walls again. . .closing in. Darcy was trapped. There was no escape. Her anxiety sucked all the oxygen out.

I'm in a vacuum. . .can't. . .breathe. . .

She imagined invisible forces propelling her through the air, through her life, and to this place. But no invisible force controlled her path now. Or stood in her way. Only a man intent on harming her.

His will over hers.

Her will, now, over the panic, the anxiety.

Let him feel the full force of *her* will.

She swung the rock, aiming for a head. A hand gripped her wrist. Squeezed. The rock dropped.

Another hand stifled her scream. She bit into flesh.

"Shh. It's me, Jonas." His voice was sharp, strained. She'd bitten hard.

Darcy's legs grew limp. She trembled, relieved.

Jonas kept his hand over her mouth and whispered in her ear. "He's still out there. We have to be quiet. Do you understand?"

Darcy nodded. When he removed his hand, he sucked

her to him like a violent whirlwind, gripping her, hugging her. His tense muscles shuddered—and she knew he was relieved to find her.

She held on to him as if holding on to life. She wanted to whimper, to sob. But this wasn't over yet. His hands caressed her, his arms held her tight, and in his embrace, she could hear his silent question—was she okay?

When he released her, he took her hand, leading her quietly along the fissure away from where Darcy thought was the best place to hide. What was he doing? Did he have a plan to get them to safety?

Moonbeams filtered into the crevice in places. Jonas carried a weapon strapped to his waist, and he tugged it free now, held it at the ready.

Small rocks trickling down the wall. Jonas stopped.

He turned to her, pressed his finger against his lips, then nudged her back into the darkness.

She was scared for him. At that minute, she never wanted anything more than to be free to love him. Jonas moved to leave, but she reached out for him. He pressed into the darkness with her and cupped her cheeks. Then he kissed her, infusing her with his love.

"I have to go," he whispered. "And finish this."

Then, he disappeared into the darkness. Darcy prayed hard for him. Would they get their chance together? She never should have decided to sell her store. Never should have thrown things in his face. If she hadn't, neither of them would be here now.

Jonas was risking his life for her.

Pop! Pop! Gunfire exploded. Darcy covered her ears and stifled her scream.

Another round of gunfire erupted.

Then. . .silence.

Jonas didn't return. Darcy feared the worst, but neither did she hear anyone else walking the fissure path. No pebbles falling or crunching underfoot.

She left the shadows where Jonas had tucked her, no longer caring about her own safety. She had to know. Using the stone hedge as a guide, she crept forward.

In the moonlight, she spotted Jonas's silhouette. He leaned against the wall several yards away. Heart rate spiking, she made her way to his side.

Was he injured? Where was Gambini? Fear and sorrow erupted in her heart—her most precious possession. She'd wanted to protect it. But now all she wanted was to give it away. Give it to Jonas.

"Jonas," she whispered. "What happened?"

He pressed his hand against his chest, near his shoulder, and in the light of the moon she could see blood oozing between his fingers.

"You're hurt." A sob caught in her throat.

He slid to the ground. Darcy dropped beside him and there, she cradled his head. "I love you. Don't leave me."

Bright, white pain seared his shoulder and chest. The edges of his vision grew dark, even in the shadows.

Jonas wanted to tell her he loved her. There had never been anyone else.

Would he get the chance?

He didn't have the breath to speak. Why had he wasted his chance when he had it? Loud thrumming vibrated inside the fissure. A chopper. Help had finally come.

Jonas mustered his strength, tugging Darcy close. "It's over. You're safe now."

The beam of a light shone on her face, revealing her tearstained cheeks. Darcy kept her eyes on him.

"Jonas, I love you. Do you hear me? Stay with me."

Someone shouted. Sounded like the local sheriff—what was her name again? Jonas replayed Darcy's words in his mind, in his heart, until her face, the rock walls, the flashlight, and voices, all faded away.

Chapter 9

She had to see Jonas.

Authorities questioned her about the abduction, keeping her away for too long. She hurried through the hallway of the local county hospital, grateful they hadn't sent him to someplace like Portland.

That meant his injury wasn't serious enough to warrant travel to a better hospital. Room 235, where he recovered, loomed three doors away. He'd taken two bullets but was in stable condition, they'd said.

Two bullets!

The fact that he was an FBI agent had taken time to sink in. Gambini, gunfire, and bullets had done the trick. She drew near the room and heard voices inside. Not wanting to interrupt, she paused and lifted her hand to knock, listening to the voices to see if she recognized them. Were his brothers inside?

A gruff voice, "Patrick Honor was involved with Adrian Gephardt and his Internet fraud scheme. Money swayed him, Jonas. He took it to keep you off Gephardt's trail, but he didn't follow through with his agreement."

"And that, in turn, infuriated Gambini," Jonas said. "Because

I linked the Internet fraud to his mob operations."

"Right," the gruff voice again. "Honor was now a target. On the next raid, though he tried to assist the target's escape with vital information before you arrived, he was killed. We searched Honor's belongings, and then the boxes you put into storage. That's where we found the half-million dollars."

Darcy pressed herself against the wall, not wanting to hear more. Dreading what would come next.

"Honor's fingerprints were all over the bills. In his panic, he became careless. When he couldn't keep you off Gambini's trail, then he knew he was in trouble and hid the money in what he thought would be the most unlikely place."

Darcy exhaled. A nurse sitting at her station frowned at her.

"That's what it meant then. When he was dying, he told me he was sorry. I thought he was sorry for getting hurt during the raid. For dying on me."

"All you need now is a psych evaluation, then you're cleared to return. It'll be good to have you back, Agent Love."

Jonas said something, but Darcy couldn't make it out. Was he going back to work? Her heart sank right to her ankles.

"We're done here. Once you're fully recovered, we'll be in contact."

The men from the FBI were leaving, and Darcy stood at the door eavesdropping. She dashed around the corner and gasped for air, trying to comprehend what it meant.

His plans didn't include her. Had never included her.

He'd come here to wait out an inquiry over his conduct during a raid. She'd told him she loved him and still, he was leaving. He'd been half-unconscious before Darcy had been willing to give up her heart. Maybe he hadn't heard.

Devastated, she couldn't bear to face him now. Not until she gained some measure of control over her emotions. She took the quickest escape route and bumped into a man leaving another patient's room.

The man gripped her shoulders. "Darcy, are you okay?"

Darcy stared into the eyes of the new pastor of her father's church. "Pastor Reeves. What are you doing here?"

He gestured to the room behind him. "I stopped by to visit Mr. Donaldson."

Reeling from the fact she was about to lose Jonas again, Darcy eyed the exit. So. Close. "I'm sorry to hear that. Will you excuse me?"

She pressed past the new pastor. He called after her, "Wait, Darcy. I have something I need to give you."

Darcy was at the door, the only thing standing between her and freedom. She felt the cool glass against her palm.

"It belonged to your father," he said, gently.

She hesitated, peering behind her. He closed the distance between them and shoved the door open for her, allowing her through first. Outside, he motioned to a bench. Darcy didn't feel like sitting, but refusing would mean she'd need to explain.

Pastor Reeves sat next to her. "Somehow I ended up with your father's old Bible. Then today, I discovered that I picked it up on my way out the door to the hospital. I didn't know why, but I do now. God wanted you to have this."

He handed it to Darcy. She ran her fingers across the

dried-out, old leather that bound the weight of a thousand pages together. A lump cinched her throat closed.

When she said nothing, Pastor Reeves continued. "I tried on several occasions to return it because I wanted to do it in person. I was never able to connect with you. You see, I discovered a private letter stuck inside. It's addressed to you."

She thumbed through the pages. A letter rested behind the front cover. Staring at the envelope, she hardly noticed when Pastor Reeves stood.

When finally she acknowledged him, he smiled down. "I'm glad you have what belongs to you. I'll leave you to your business."

As he walked away, she tore the envelope, mindful of the letter inside. When she unfolded the paper, her father's familiar scribble caressed the sheet.

"Oh Daddy," she whispered.

My dearest daughter,

I'm terribly sorry that I've kept you from Jonas. But you should know that he has made good on his promise to me. I would be proud to call him my son now. Should you require my approval to marry him this time, upon my passing, I wanted you to know that you have it. I hope you understand how much I have loved you.

With all my love.

The writing blurred. Tears dripped onto the page, smudging the ink.

Jonas stared out the hospital window and buttoned his shirt, compliments of Lucas.

No more would he blame himself for Honor's death. A brick of disappointment lodged in his gut. Darcy hadn't come to see him yet, and he'd been in the hospital three days. Should he give up?

Had she meant what she'd said to him? Did she love him?

Her actions spoke to the contrary, like a megaphone in his head. He could almost hear her saying, *'Agent Jonas Love, you're relieved of duty.'* The words that had sent him to Oregon in the first place.

He had to face the awful truth. Darcy would be safer without him. It was better if she felt nothing for him. He couldn't afford more jerks coming after him, hurting Darcy or others he loved.

The words he had to say would be harsh. Jonas needed all the practice he could get so he said them out loud. Lucas's advice on that seemed to work, but he wasn't going to look in the mirror while he did it. He had to draw the line there.

"Because I love you," he said under his breath. "Because I love you, I have to go back to the bureau. Back to my job and do my duty to keep thugs like Gambini from hurting people. I've turned control of my life over to God. It's in His hands now."

There was still the issue of the promise he'd made to Darcy's father. Jonas sighed, dreading the decisions he faced—opposing forces ripped at him, inside his head, inside his heart.

If he could just say it like that to her face. . .it was a start.

"Don't leave." The words drifted to him so softly, he almost didn't hear them.

Jonas angled his head. Had he imagined them? He swung around.

Darcy stood there, a sheen of moisture in her eyes.

She gave him a sort of smile-frown. "Don't leave."

He tossed all his well-meaning thoughts about leaving, his spiel about why, into the air. His arm open—one arm remained in a sling—Darcy ran to him. She pressed into him. He sank his face into her neck, breathing in the familiar honey-vanilla scent. Breathing in the essence of Darcy, the woman he loved.

How many times had he said he would never let her go? The last time he'd held her, he thought it might be his last. He'd left her to face Gambini.

"I thought you'd decided not to see me," he said against her hair.

Darcy pulled away. He brushed a blond strand from her cheek.

"I came to see you yesterday, but you had visitors." She took a step back. "I'm sorry, Jonas. I overheard them. And then today, I was in your room, and you were talking to yourself."

Jonas released a breath. "So you heard me say that I love you."

"And that's why you think you have to leave. But I'm asking you not to. Not this time."

"But my being here put your life in danger. How can I let that happen again?"

"I gave you up once before, because I wanted my father's

approval. I've wanted it ever since you left. Even after my father died. He never gave it. When I hid from Gambini, scared for my life, I prayed for God to hide and protect me. I never needed Him that much, and He didn't withhold. That emptiness that I thought my father's approval would fill is gone."

Darcy angled her head, her soft hair falling forward slightly. Jonas could read her tenuous smile. She was afraid that she couldn't convince him to stay.

"God sent you to help me. Hiding and waiting for you, I knew I had to forgive you and that, with or without my father's approval, I love you and want to be with you. But I have his approval, too." Smiling, she tugged a paper from her purse. "I have his consent. My father left me this letter, saying he would be proud to call you his son."

Jonas took a breath to speak—

"How did he know?" she asked.

If he told her, would she lash out again? So near the very thing he'd wanted for so long, knowing how fragile that was, and how easily he could lose it, Jonas feared she would bolt again. He stepped closer, taking one of her hands in his.

"Because. . .I went to see him while he was in the hospital before he died. It was then that he gave me permission to try to win your heart back. To marry you." Jonas searched her eyes for understanding. "I never forgot you, Darcy, never stopped loving you. He made me promise to take care of you if you'd agree to have me. But I couldn't find my way back into your life no matter how hard I tried."

Her smile warmed. "I'm sorry it took an extreme situation

for me to see things clearly. If you made a promise to my father, then you'd better keep it."

"Are you sure? The condition was that I win your heart back."

"I've never been surer of anything. You've always had my heart, Jonas. I just didn't want to admit it."

"Then I'm going to do this right." Jonas dropped to one knee, tugging the ring from his pocket. He'd been prepared to lay it on the line, one way or the other—whether he stayed here or he went back to the bureau—today, this was happening.

He held the ring up for Darcy to see. She gasped. "It's beautiful."

"It was your grandmother's. Your father gave it to me. Maybe he had it with him at the hospital, planning to give it to you, but then I showed up. I guess he was showing his confidence that we would end up together. Darcy Nichols, will you marry me?"

"I'm flying, Jonas." A tear streaked down her cheek. "Yes, oh yes."

He'd waited oh-so-long for this moment. Finally. . .

A LOVE KINDLED

Chapter 1

Sheriff Sheridan Hall stood one aisle over in the local ranch and farm supply, hating herself for eavesdropping. She pretended to compare the brands of insecticide for killing ants, which she'd stopped in to buy, and listened to Carver Love make a fool out of himself, or out of her.

She couldn't decide which.

"The way I see it, she could have gotten herself killed." Though his voice took on a hint of concern, he didn't deceive her for a second. He didn't think a woman could handle the job.

"But aren't you glad she was willing to put her life on the line for your brother when she faced-off with a Chicago mobster?" the other man asked.

Why was he interested in Carver's opinion? Everyone knew the rancher was arrogant and stubborn as the day was arid in the high desert country. Still, the town respected him.

"That's exactly what I'm talking about. We don't see many hardened criminals around here. My brother is a trained professional, a special agent. He can take care of himself."

The rancher had nerve letting everyone know his opinion of her—at least his opinion of her serving as sheriff of Rimrock County.

But then that wasn't against the law, or she'd have arrested him a long time ago.

She wanted to jump into the middle of that conversation and explain what really happened. There were two henchmen. Jonas Love was down after a battle with only one of them.

She'd paid her dues. Did a good job managing her deputies as they covered a large region. Because she was a woman, she'd worked three times as hard as any man to earn respect in her position.

The last thing she needed was an influential rancher undoing her work with a few well-placed words. From her perspective, his words were misplaced.

"But—"

"Don't get me wrong, she's—"

"Can I help you with something, Sheriff?" Tom Harvey, the owner of the supply store, stood in the aisle, with a grin that connected his ears.

Not only had he announced her presence to everyone on this side of the store—his voice deep and bold—he'd just cut off Carver's next words. Sheridan desperately wanted to hear them. It almost sounded as if he was going to pay her a compliment, but that was probably a stretch.

Aware the conversation on the other side of the aisle had stopped, Sheridan placed one of the boxes back on the shelf. "No thanks. I've got it figured out."

Tom's grin slipped. She knew the guy had a crush on her, something she refused to acknowledge. If he never asked her out then she wouldn't have to turn him down.

"I'll just be on my way." She nodded.

Tom took the box from her. "I'll ring you up."

"Thanks."

"Ladies first." He motioned for her to walk ahead of him.

While she didn't mind him being the gentleman, his actions magnified Carver's opinion that she wasn't fit to be sheriff. Bristling, she plastered a smile in place to hide her reaction and walked in front of Tom.

At the cash register, Tom rang up her purchase, and after she paid, he stuck the insecticide in a sack. Sheridan grabbed it, itching to be out of the store before she saw Carver.

"Sheriff." Tom kept her from a quick escape. "Sheridan," he said, turning personal. "There's something I've been meaning. . ."

She tugged her cell from her pocket. "Would you excuse me for a minute?"

Sheridan stepped away from the counter just as Carver plunked down a fifty-pound bag of dog food.

Now was her chance to make her getaway. Though she hated that she'd cut Tom off, she couldn't stand the thought of rejecting him. But she hadn't given him any indication she returned his interest.

In the parking lot, she hurried to her vehicle. After she opened the door to the Yukon marked RIMROCK COUNTY SHERIFF, she tossed the sack in, preparing to follow.

"Sheriff Hall," Carver's familiar voice called.

This time, her raised hackles might get the best of her. She should let the man know she wasn't intimidated by him. Without hesitation she slipped into the vehicle and closed the door, but opened the window. "What can I do for you, Carver?"

He strode toward her, carrying the bag over his shoulder. A few feet away, he let the bag drop to his feet. At just over five nine, the eldest of four brothers wasn't a tall man, but years working his father's ranch that now belonged to him had produced a sturdy cowboy, muscle-bound in all the right places. His worn and form-fitting jeans and T-shirt, taut against his physique, didn't leave much to the imagination. With his bronzed skin and dark hair, faded to wheat by the sun, the man had his share of good looks.

Despite her errant thoughts, she forced herself to stare at him, face him head-on. One bullheaded person to another.

Carver looked at her from behind dark sunglasses, so she couldn't read his eyes. After a few seconds, he tugged them off and squinted. "I'm sorry."

"'Bout what?" Sheridan slid her own sunglasses in place and started the ignition.

"What I said in there. You must have heard." Carver's piercing chestnut eyes held her in place.

If only she could shift into Reverse and press her foot hard against the accelerator. "That you don't think I'm man enough to be sheriff isn't news. After all, Rimrock County still has a few men who live in the Dark Ages."

His chin jutting out, strong and sure, he slid his sunshades back in place.

"You don't have to worry about hurting my feelings. There's no love lost between us," Sheridan said.

If she'd wanted to act like she'd been unaffected by his

words, she'd failed. To prevent herself from saying more, she nodded and backed out.

In the rearview mirror, she watched him stalk to his truck and lay the dog food in the truck bed.

At one time in her life, Sheridan had been enamored with the man.

When he smiled, the way his cheeks dimpled, creases forming around his chestnut eyes, she'd have thought her heart would stop, but that was years ago.

To be fair, she'd been young then. Impressionable. Some had wondered why Carver had yet to marry at thirty-five. But Sheridan knew. He was a stubborn mule of a man. His opinion was the only one that counted.

But at thirty-two and unmarried herself, she could hardly be his judge.

If only Carver showed her a little respect, she might fancy herself thinking about him as more than an egotistical rancher.

Which was exactly why she had to keep her distance.

☙

Carver maneuvered out of the parking lot. Turning right—the opposite direction from where the sheriff had headed—he steered toward the Circle L Ranch, just east of Ridgeview, near Carnegie.

He slowed up. The fifteen-mile drive out of town wouldn't give him enough time to bridle his annoyance with himself if he drove the speed limit.

Eventually someone would grouse. He didn't have to wait

long. A truck grill filled his rearview mirror. He chuckled, unwilling to bend to the pressure, wondering how long it would take the driver to pass him.

Sure enough, the obnoxious driver honked then swerved around Carver's dually—not an easy task—flinging hand signals as he did. Though he wanted to respond in kind, Carver stared straight ahead, acting like he didn't care—much like the sheriff had done to him in the parking lot.

The man wasn't from around here, or he would have avoided taking issue with Carver Love. He knew he thought too highly of himself. What kind of moron would speak so candidly in a public place where he could be overheard? An opinionated, mule-headed moron like himself, that's who.

Wouldn't be the first time his perspective had gotten him into trouble. But he was equally annoyed with Sheridan for her lack of backbone. The usually hard-hitting sheriff hadn't said a word to him. She should have challenged him on what he'd said. Either she didn't care, or she wanted to hide her animosity toward him.

No. That wasn't it either.

To use her words, *There's no love lost between us.* She hadn't gone out of her way to conceal her hostility.

Hanging one elbow out the window, Carver ran his hand over his face and sighed. He was a cattle rancher just like his daddy, and his granddaddy before that. He was sturdy and tough. Had to be. The high desert was harsh land. Carver had to be harsh in turn.

There was only one thing more difficult than managing

a cattle ranch in the arid country of south central Oregon. Tempering the soft spot he had for the fine-looking Sheriff Sheridan Hall.

With her antagonism toward him, he'd rather chew nails than have her find out how he felt. He certainly wasn't her only admirer.

Poor Tom. Didn't appear the guy would ever get his chance with the thorny sheriff.

Brown-and-white flashed in Carver's peripheral vision.

He slammed the brakes, jerking the wheel. A steer hit the grill then lumbered away like nothing happened. Carver's truck veered into the ditch, ramming an old fence post. He sat there, waiting until his pounding heart slowed. At least the steer had survived, though not unscathed.

If only Carver could say the same. Hank Hogan owned a spread nearby. Carver would let him know about the steer. Had to be his.

He swung the door open and climbed out to assess the damage. Dog food covered the road. Great. That was what he got for thinking about Sheriff Hall. He knew never to brake and swerve.

Carver marched around his truck where it joined with the post and frowned. The damage would take Bobby a week or more to fix and would cost Carver a pretty penny. He hated using his insurance for the little jobs.

If he hadn't been driving so slowly, things could have been much worse. A full-on impact could have killed the steer, and even Carver. He yanked his cell from the truck cab and called

Bobby. Carver stood in the road and shook his head at the mess he'd made as he explained the situation to Bobby, who was on his way with a wrecker.

And just up the road. . .

Oh no.

The siren blipped, lights flashed once. The sheriff steered her Yukon to the side of the road. She stepped out, looking official.

"You all right, Carver?" Animosity aside, Sheridan sounded like she cared this time.

"I'll live, and the steer that hit me will live, I think. But I've called a tow for the truck."

She crossed her arms and angled her head like she planned to challenge his story. "You say a steer hit you?"

He could have sworn she almost grinned. "Came right across the road straight at me."

Pulling her sunshades off, she frowned, stepping closer. Her emerald eyes sparkled in the sunlight. Her hat covered long, dark hair held back by a rubber band. While the dull brown Rimrock County sheriff's uniform was snug against her slim figure, it didn't do her justice. He'd seen her in a little black dress once, years ago. What he wouldn't give to see her like that again—a beautiful, tender, and pliable woman. Instead, her job had made her determined and unbending.

Just like him.

Carver admitted that some part of him admired her for her unwavering attitude. Maybe she was the only woman in the world who could handle him. He grinned at the thought.

She gave him a funny look. He was glad she had no clue what he'd been thinking.

"You're hurt." She lifted his hair then touched his forehead, but jerked her hand back. Her touch sent a stampede of heat charging all the way to his toes.

"You hit your head. I'll run you to the ER."

"If it's all the same to you, I'll pass."

"Don't worry. You're in good hands with me. I'm perfectly capable of driving you to the hospital." Hands on her hips, she scrutinized him. "If I can handle a mobster from Chicago, I can handle you."

Bobby's wrecker rumbled as he backed up to Carver's truck.

"Sheriff, I've already apologized. I don't have time for a visit to the ER. But I'd appreciate a ride to the ranch."

Bobby jumped out of the wrecker and attached the tow to Carver's truck. "Oh, I can drive you. We'll drop your truck off and be on our way. It's no problem. The sheriff probably has sheriffin' to do."

Thanks a lot, Bobby. "I appreciate your help." Carver inhaled and waited for her reply.

Sheridan studied Carver, contemplating her answer. He'd bet she was thinking about the hurtful words he'd said in Harvey's.

"I'll leave that up to Carver," she said.

He exhaled. "Bobby's right. You've got more important things to do than haul a rancher around."

Idiot. Was some crazy part of him hoping she'd argue his point?

"In that case, after I complete this accident report, I'll be on my way. Take care of yourselves." She climbed into the Yukon and, after a few minutes spent on her radio then writing in a notebook, she looked at Carver, nodded, then drove away.

Had she known he'd been watching from behind his shades?

Chapter 2

A week later, Carver hadn't been able to get his mind off his encounter with Sheridan. A few long days spent in the saddle had been a good idea.

Though the isolated land and the brilliant night skies had given him clarity, he wasn't any closer to solving his problem. Sitting in the saddle, he urged Kodiak through sagebrush and junipers along the rim to the secluded valley where they'd left four hundred head of his eight hundred cattle to graze. He hadn't caught sight of them yet. The Circle L Ranch covered seventy-five thousand acres of range, divided between his property and the Bureau of Land Management allotment—plenty of room.

He'd decided to join his trusted friend and cowhand, Ray Bolton, along with several others to bring the cattle in early this year. It was June, and the cows would have dropped their calves by now, but Carver usually waited until the fall roundup, after the calves were weaned, to bring them close for corralling and branding.

The work was all done on horseback. Nothing much had changed over the last century in terms of managing cattle because the wide open region was inaccessible by car or truck.

Carver nudged Kodiak to the edge of a rocky drop and looked out over the valley. A pebble clattered over the rim. Ray came alongside him on his own horse, ropes hanging over the saddle.

"Sent the boys farther down to locate the herd."

Carver nodded.

"Everything okay?" Ray asked.

"Why?" Great. He'd opened himself up for conversation.

"You're distracted. Don't tell me it's related to the ranch or your brothers."

"Okay. I won't." Beneath the brim of his hat, he could feel Ray's stare.

"You're never going to see eye to eye with her."

Kodiak sneezed and shuffled, growing impatient. Carver said nothing.

"On the other hand, you're not getting any younger."

This time, Carver tilted his head. As far as he was concerned, he was in his prime.

"And right now, after a couple days of riding, you're the definition of rank. A grungy cowboy. Neither of those attributes would appeal to the woman sheriff." Ray leaned forward in his saddle, clearly pleased with his advice. "I know about three ladies in town who ask about you every time they see me. I bet one of them would be happy to spend time with you. Why don't you fall for one of them?"

Carver eyed Ray. "Are you done now?"

Ray nodded. "I'm done."

What was taking the men so long?

Soon enough, he spotted the herd coming across a rise on the other side of the valley. One of the cowhands rode ahead of the group. Carver and Ray steered the horses along the path into the valley to meet him.

Riding hard, Conroy slowed when he reached Carver. He took off his hat and wiped his brow. "We're missing some."

A full ten seconds passed before Carver processed what he'd said. "Come again?"

"We only counted three hundred fifty head. We're missing cows and their calves."

Fifty cows that had calved? That was a hundred head of cattle.

"They're lost. Spread out and find them."

ଓ

Three days later, Carver stomped onto the wraparound porch of his ranch house, his body aching to the bone, and his heart and mind heavy with the loss of cattle.

After time spent in the saddle—he'd even called Lucas to help in the search, using ATVs—they'd come up empty-handed. Inside the mudroom, he tugged off his dirty boots. Behind him, the door opened and shut. He glanced up to see Ray.

"You call the sheriff yet?"

"I've hardly had a chance."

"You're not going to, are you?"

Carver stood to his full height and scratched his roughened jaw, measuring his response. "I'm responsible to take care of my own. A hundred head of cattle lost to rustlers? That makes me look like a failure in anybody's book."

"We've been friends too long. Friends are willing to speak the truth. You need to swallow your pride and tell her about the theft."

Rage and defeat thrashed in his gut. Calling the sheriff counted double against his pride—he'd all but proclaimed to the county that he didn't think she could do the job, and now he would ask her for help because he couldn't do *his*?

Maybe he was an egotistical chauvinist, after all. On second thought, there was no maybe about it.

He sighed, hating the realization, and yearning to scrape the dirt from his body. "Doesn't matter. What's done is done."

"She needs to know. We might not be the only victims here."

"This has to be someone we know, Ray. They know our habits. Where the cattle will be. They know how to drive them for days while living in the saddle. They know the region well. Tell me. What can Sheriff Hall do about it? She's only got a few deputies and a huge county."

Besides, with the way she felt about Carver, he knew his problems wouldn't exactly be a top priority for her. *No love lost between us. . .*

Ray exhaled then turned his back on Carver, throwing his hand up in an I-give-up wave. He stomped out the door.

Later that evening, after Carver had taken a long hot shower, he sat in his favorite recliner nursing his tired body and mental wounds.

He called the main number for the county sheriff's office,

expecting to get dispatch or the after-hours answering service. He'd leave a message.

"Sheriff Hall here."

Carver sat forward in the recliner. "Uh. . .Sheriff. I didn't expect to get you."

"Carver? Is that you?"

The fact she recognized his voice made him smile. "If I answer yes, are you going to hang up?"

ꕥ

Carver's dejected tone surprised Sheridan. She'd never heard him let his guard down like that. He was human after all.

"What's this about?" she asked.

Carver released a long, pathetic sigh.

What in the world? "What's happened?" *You're scaring me.* But then for an emergency he would have called 911. She'd just happened to answer the phone. Idiot.

"Nothing life or death. Some of my cattle are missing."

"I can send one of my deputies out right away." Rimrock County didn't have the funds for livestock police or investigative officers. They did have two brand inspectors, one of them part-time.

"It'll wait until morning. We made the discovery four days ago."

"Why didn't you call earlier?"

"I was searching the valley to make sure they weren't lost. But like you said, I can give the details to your deputy when he gets here." Carver hung up.

Sheridan stared at the phone. He called *her* and had the nerve to be short?

The man had a way of getting under her skin like a prickly-pear cactus. Why did he have to ruin the rest of her evening? Still, the fact that he'd stooped to call, had swallowed his pride, was as big as the Great Basin.

Dealing with this herself instead of sending one of her deputies might give her an opportunity to prove herself to Carver.

When Sheridan pulled around the circular drive at the Circle L Ranch house, her palms went slick. Ridiculous.

She climbed from the cab of the Yukon and straightened her slacks and shirt. Why hadn't she sent Ronny or at least brought him with her? Standing tall, Sheridan made her way around the vehicle, shoving aside her crazy insecurity.

Before she took the first step to the expansive wraparound porch, her gaze roamed over the large ranch house. Sheridan had moved to town ten years ago at twenty-two, so hadn't grown up with the Love brothers, but the way she understood it, they were troublemakers as boys, loving to live life on the edge. She'd never been to the Circle L Ranch, even during that time when she thought she and Carver had something between them—their brief romantic encounter.

She'd just moved to the area and spent an evening in his company during a county fund-raiser. He'd been kind and considerate then. A real charmer. A gentleman. He'd sparked something inside her. But it hadn't taken long for the real Carver to show himself. A month later, Sheridan tried to stomp out anything that had been kindled between them. Why a few embers had remained, she wasn't sure. The older he got, the more crotchety he became.

Still, people respected the family. Specifically, Carver Love.

With Carver holding the whole county's respect, she wasn't sure how she ever became sheriff. Now serving in that role she wanted—no, needed—a chance to prove herself to this man.

The front door swung open. Sheridan hadn't taken her first step onto the porch. Carver stepped outside. Instead of a snug T-shirt like he'd worn the other day, he was dressed in a crisp button-down, long-sleeve shirt along with a newer pair of Levi's. He cleaned up real nice.

"Having second thoughts?"

No. I always thought you looked good. Sheridan berated herself and refocused her thoughts.

She shook her head. "I've never seen the house before."

He closed the door behind him. Apparently, he'd decided she didn't need a tour. Had he started antagonizing her already?

"Thought you were sending a deputy?" He gestured to the outdoor furniture, wicker chairs, a table, and a couple of rockers.

On the porch, Sheridan walked by him, catching a whiff of his cologne, and sat in the rocker. That was a mistake. She couldn't help herself, she had to rock, and the chair had to creak.

"I decided this warranted my personal attention." She pulled a notepad from her pocket. "Tell me what happened."

Carver's eyes were tired. "I wanted to bring the herd in early this year. The cows would have dropped their calves by now, and we planned to brand them. When we got to the valley, we discovered a good many missing. Cows and their calves."

"And you've searched the whole region?"

Carver held up his hand. "I'm sure you mean well, but all the same, you're not that familiar with how things are done."

Sheridan bristled. She'd served in a law enforcement capacity here for the last eight years. As sheriff the last three. They'd not had any problems with rustlers until now. Measures were in place. Although not mandatory in Oregon, branding was the best defense. Transporting cattle to auction, for a change in ownership, or out of the state required paperwork. There was an aircraft up once a week somewhere in the county, watching the movement of cattle. The region was enormous. But she'd let Carver have his say.

"Out here, ranchers leave their cattle in the wide open range to graze for months on end. We expect to find a few missing, but that's due to natural causes. Wolves. Disease. A few might wander off, but not far from the rest. We always find them alive, or we find their carcasses. That said, we're missing a hundred head."

Ouch. Sheridan winced. "That's a devastating loss."

"We searched for them as long as we could, but finally brought the rest of the cattle, including those grazing on the southern border of the ranch, closer. I've been on the phone all morning, calling other ranchers to see if they've lost any."

"And?" Sheridan was agitated. If rustlers were out there, she needed to hear from the others as well.

"Some are riding out to check. Others won't know until the fall gathering. But nobody is admitting anything yet."

"What do you mean, *admitting* anything?"

"I mean, ranchers are a prideful bunch. If I'd had only a few cows stolen, I probably wouldn't have said anything to you."

Sheridan pushed to her feet, leaving the rocking chair to creak on its own. Maybe that was part of Carver's problem. He was a rancher. Prideful was an understatement. "Why on earth not?"

Carver rose, matching Sheridan's stance. "Because they were stolen from under my nose. You know how that makes me look?"

"They were miles away. How is that right under your nose?"

Carver paced the porch. She'd never seen him like this. He'd always maintained his composure.

"Tell me what you're thinking?"

"It has to be someone who knows how to live on a horse for days at a time, driving cattle. Knows the region. Someone we know right here."

She sucked in a breath. "How soon can you be ready to take me to the crime scene?"

Carver stared at her blank-faced, then broke out laughing. "Where my cattle graze isn't a place you can drive to."

Sheridan could easily translate. "Are you saying that because I'm a woman you can't take me to look at the evidence?"

"That's exactly what I'm saying."

Sheridan chewed on the colorful words she wanted to spew. "You are a piece of work, you know that?"

Oh, she did not just say that. If she was going to act the professional, she had to rein in her emotions.

Carver shoved his hands through his hair, oblivious to her comment. "I can show you where the cattle were on a map. They could have driven the cows for days until they reached a highway where they loaded them on a truck. By now, they could be on their way to Arkansas or selling them anywhere brands don't matter."

The man was frustrated, feeling helpless to do anything. Sheridan wanted to reach over and squeeze his shoulder. To reassure him. But what was she thinking? That last time she'd done that, touching his forehead where he'd earned a souvenir for landing in the ditch, a bolt of electricity had shot through her.

Instead, she moved to the porch railing and stared at the vast ranchland. The place was beautiful, peaceful, and secluded.

She turned and leaned against the whitewashed banister, attempting a softer tone. "I don't see you as the sort of man to give up." That was definitely something she admired about him.

"I never said I was giving up."

"I want to know what you're planning."

"They could have taken the cattle somewhere remote, grazing them until the calves are weaned. If that's the case, I'll find them." Carver seemed to transform right in front of her, his expression steel. "Either way, this isn't a job for you. You don't have enough manpower to help. I just thought you should know in case this turns out to be a bigger problem. More ranchers involved."

Sheridan dropped her arms to her side, getting the distinct

impression he'd dismissed her. She worried the man would find the rustlers, confronting them alone. "Don't take on these men without the law, do you understand?"

"I can't make promises. Now if you'll excuse me, I've already wasted enough time today." Carver nodded and stepped toward the door. "Good day to you, Sheriff."

Of all the. . .

Unwilling to stand there and let him close the door in her face, Sheridan stomped to her Yukon. The front door of the house clicked shut before she reached the driver's side.

Sheridan climbed in and drove a mile up the long, winding driveway before she allowed herself to release her pent-up anger. That man made her crazy.

If she could just figure out what, besides his good looks, drew her to him.

Chapter 3

Carver stepped into the hangar at the small county airport. He spotted Kevin Wells standing next to his Cessna Skyhawk, doing the preflight check.

Kevin glanced up. "Good to see you, Carver."

Two long strides later, Carver stood next to the plane. "Thanks for agreeing to this on such short notice."

"No problem. I hope you find what you're looking for."

"Well, if nothing else, this will tell me where they aren't. I don't want to waste any time on the ground, looking in the wrong area."

Kevin walked around to the back of the plane. "Go ahead and hop in. We're still waiting on one more person."

What? Maybe he should reschedule, but he couldn't afford to waste more time. Waiting for the sheriff to arrive first thing this morning had already put him behind. He'd done the right thing telling her about the cattle, but he didn't want her involved, getting hurt, especially because of him. This was no business for a woman. He'd seen the look of incredulity in her eyes, but that was nothing new where he was concerned.

"You know I don't like anyone infringing on my business.

I thought this was just you and me. Who else is coming?"

"I am." The familiar female voice crawled over his back and into his heart, causing it to miss a beat.

Carver closed his eyes. He hung his head, unsure what this new development would mean, then turned. "What are you doing here?"

She made her way from the hangar entrance over to him. "I'm going with you."

When he slid his gaze to her, she was grinning. "I told you I didn't want you involved," he said.

"Then you shouldn't have called me."

Blood pressure rising, Carver left his thoughts unsaid and climbed into the Cessna. He shouldn't have listened to Ray. But why didn't he want Sheridan's help? Taking her in the saddle on a long, hard ride was one thing, but having her along this time couldn't hurt.

When Kevin was seated next to Carver, and Sheridan strapped in behind him, Kevin taxied the four-seater plane from the hangar and, after he'd gained clearance, took them into the sky.

A light floral fragrance wafted around Carver. Sheridan. "You sure this is part of your job description, Sheriff?"

"This is a criminal investigation. Rustling is a felony. Why wouldn't it be part of my job?"

Kevin guffawed. "You two aren't going to be at this all day, are you? I was afraid it might be a mistake to have you together, but why don't you forget about your differences for now. Let's find your cattle."

Carver didn't much like being lectured. He didn't realize that he and Sheridan had drawn battle lines for everyone to see.

"I'm all for that," she said.

Great. She had to be the first to agree. Carver wasn't big on talking anyway, so he said nothing. Let them think what they would. Carver tugged his binoculars out and focused on the surrounding region.

He hadn't expected how difficult concentrating would be with Sheridan this close, her face looking out the window, searching with him. The plane banked right and headed toward the northeast.

"You tell me where I need to go, Carver," Kevin said.

"Let's look at the most remote areas with canyons and ravines. The cattle need water. Unless the rustlers, if they're still out there, are going to haul it in, they have to be near a water source."

"Good idea," Sheridan said. "At the risk of showing my ignorance, what exactly are we looking for? How can you tell if the cows we see are yours?"

"Mine will be white-faced, for starters. I'm hoping I'll have a sense of whether or not this is my stolen herd. If we get a reaction at all from men on horseback, that could tell us if they're the rustlers." Carver's spirits sagged. This seemed like an impossible task, but he couldn't give up. "On the other hand, if we spook them, they'll move again."

He recalled Sheridan's words that she didn't think he was the kind of man to give up. The way she'd said it almost sounded like a compliment. He liked that.

A half hour passed and they saw nothing suspicious.

"Over there, to your far left corner. I see something," Sheridan said.

Carver looked through the binoculars. "We don't want to alert them we're looking for them. Just want to act like we're out for a nice Sunday drive."

At least twenty white-faced cows and their calves grazed on a foothill. Kevin flew the plane close enough for a good look and continued on in the same direction.

Two men on horseback were heading into a gulch. They didn't look up at the plane. Carver's pulse throbbed against his collar.

"Did we find them?" Kevin asked.

"Maybe. I don't know. I'm afraid to fly around and take another look. We might scare them off."

"And then they'd be gone by the time you got there." Sheridan slid over into the opposite seat to look out the other side. "What do you think, Carver? It's your call."

"I don't have an answer for you yet. Let's cover as much area as we can to make sure those aren't the only cattle I need to check out."

"Sure thing," Kevin said. "This is a big region to cover, but what you've got on your side is that it's got a small population. Someone has to know something."

Kevin's words resonated with Sheridan. "I put my deputies to work on that after we talked this morning, Carver."

He didn't say anything, making her wonder if he approved. Not that it mattered.

Sheridan glanced at her watch. She'd known this could take all day, or at least until Kevin's fuel ran low.

"What about those men on horseback? Wouldn't we have seen them react to the plane if they were rustlers?" Kevin asked.

"I don't know. Maybe." Carver lowered his binoculars and squeezed the bridge of his nose.

The man had a reputation of being determined and hard-headed, but she'd never known him to be indecisive.

She leaned forward in her seat. "No. That's wrong. If they were regular guys out there, they would have glanced up at the plane. It's the only thing happening for miles around. It's a reflexive reaction. Curiosity. The fact they didn't glance up says they could be up to no good, didn't want us to see anything we could identify them with."

"Good point," Carver said.

Had Carver just agreed with her? This was going better than she expected. Still, it was a guess at best.

By lunch, Kevin had brought the plane back and taxied off the runway to park. Sheridan climbed out, her jacket flapping in the gusty wind. She waited for Carver to get out, too.

They thanked Kevin, then Carver made arrangements to pay the man for his time, trouble, and fuel.

"Uh, Carver, that won't be necessary," she said. "The sheriff's department has funds allotted from the BLM law enforcement contract for aircraft time. I'll make sure Kevin gets paid."

"This is why I didn't want you along. These are my cattle.

I'll deal with this in my own way." The creases etching Carver's eyes conveyed his stress.

"Carver, I don't want you going after these men alone." How could she get it through his head this could be dangerous?

"I know how to handle rustlers," he said.

"All the same, someone will be over to the ranch. We pay you a fee to board horses for mounted patrols. Someone will ride out with you."

With that, she walked to her own vehicle, doubting Carver liked her last words. She headed to the office. She needed to get a handle on this problem in case it grew, or worse, had been growing—as Carver put it—right under her nose.

Lord, please help me keep a handle on things. Carver wasn't making that easy.

Though Sheridan didn't enjoy spending time confined to a desk, there were always matters that needed her attention. On the drive back to town, she contacted Ronny about riding out with Carver. Ronny's little girl had a birthday tomorrow. He wasn't happy about Sheridan's request, but she didn't have the sort of experience Ronny did in the saddle. Carver had been right on that point, though she hated to admit it. They were two of a kind.

At the office, Sheridan nodded to Kelly and others of her meager staff. After grabbing coffee, Sheridan settled in at her desk to complete paperwork. Deputy reports, warrants, dispatch logs, and a few citizen complaints. But Carver was never far from her thoughts.

Hours later, she blew out a breath and straightened her

desk, relieved to have made a dent in the pile.

Kelly leaned in the door. "There's a disturbance outside McHenry's Round Up Cafe."

Sheridan slid around the desk and grabbed her hat, making sure her firearm was in place as she passed Kelly.

"Uh, Sheridan."

She glanced back.

"Ronny said it involves Carver." Kelly shrugged. "I just thought you should know."

What was that man up to now? She thought he'd already be riding to check on the cattle they'd located today, Ronny at his side. Sheridan pulled into the parking lot at McHenry's, unsure why Ronny needed her assistance. She hopped from the Yukon. Carver had his back to her. He reminded her of a wild mustang that had just been corralled, and Ronny, who dared to argue with him, looked like an inexperienced cowboy.

"What's the problem here?" Sheridan spoke with authority, inserting herself into the dispute.

When Carver turned, Sheridan schooled her surprise. He had a shiner.

Ronny stood straighter when he saw Sheridan. "Carver got into a fistfight with Joe Miller."

She couldn't believe this. "Carver, I thought you were going after the rustlers."

"And I thought you put your deputies to work, asking around town to see what they could find out."

Displeased with his tone, she skewered Carver with her gaze. "My deputies have been working on that all day, as they go about their daily activities."

"Well, they missed talking to Joe. He knows something. Even taunted me, but he wouldn't tell me who stole my cattle."

Sheridan looked at Ronny. "Where is Joe now?"

Ronny shrugged. "I questioned him then let him go. He's not talking if he knows anything."

"Sheriff, you're wasting my time by keeping me here. I'm supposed to meet up with Ray. He and what men we could spare have already headed out." Carver postured himself, challenging her.

"Ronny will go with you."

Carver's face turned red. "Ronny let Joe Miller go. I don't want Ronny coming along with me so he can mess up something else."

Then, to Sheridan's surprise, Carver stomped right by her toward his truck. Ronny looked from Carver to Sheridan like he wanted to see who would win this battle. Sheridan had no intention of losing face.

She stomped behind Carver. "Mr. Love. I need you to cease and desist. I haven't released you yet."

The man had the nerve to ignore her and opened his pickup door. Sheridan yanked the cuffs off her belt and slammed them against his left wrist. He glared up at her, eyes wide. "What the. . ."

Before he could react, she'd completed cuffing him.

He opened his mouth. "What are you charg—"

"Disturbing the peace. You are belligerent on so many levels, I can't even name them all, but there has to be a misdemeanor in there somewhere. If you want things to get worse, just keep talking."

Carver clamped his mouth closed, but his jaw tensed.

There. *Let's see who's man enough now.*

Chapter 4

"You need to remember your place." Sheriff Hall ushered him into a jail cell and removed the handcuffs.

He turned around as she slammed the door. He stared at her through the bars, her emerald eyes boring into him. Aware that he'd aggravated her, pushed her too far this time, Carver looked away. Maybe he shouldn't have pressed Joe for the truth so hard that Joe punched him. Maybe he shouldn't have defended himself, hitting back.

Sure he'd been disrespectful to the sheriff about her deputies, but he'd never held Ronny in high regard, and for the guy to just let Joe go?

Carver paced the cell, trying to decide how best to reason with Sheriff Hall. She'd left him to himself at the moment so even if he beat on the bars, she probably wouldn't hear him down in the basement. Nor would that set him free.

Exhausted from the events of the last few days, Carver sat on the cot. She'd not even allowed him his phone call.

But. . .he wouldn't call a lawyer, or quibble with her, because Carver loved Sheriff Sheridan Hall. Today was the most time he'd ever spent in her company. If he didn't have a ranch to run or rustlers to catch, he might prefer to stay in jail if that meant seeing her.

He'd been too stubborn to own up to his feelings, but deep down, he knew it was true. No other woman had ever captured his heart like her. Had ever fueled his mind, challenged him, like her. He'd tried to convince himself he didn't care. Admittedly, he'd been too outspoken about his opinion that he'd rather see someone else as sheriff. But that was because he hated to think of Sheriff Hall in the line of fire. Rimrock County hadn't experienced any serious crime until someone had followed his brother, Jonas, here.

That the sheriff—*Sheridan*—had faced a hardened criminal who could have killed her, well, that brought all the turmoil inside to the surface. His daddy believed there were certain jobs for women, and sheriff wasn't one of them. Call him old-fashioned, but Carver had struggled to disagree.

He eased down onto the cot and covered his face with his hat. Might as well grab some shut-eye because as soon as she let him out, and he didn't doubt she would, he'd have to make good time, searching for those rustlers.

Sheridan shoved through the door of the county offices into the evening heat, Ronny on her heels. She hadn't eaten all day and was starving, and she bet Carver was hungry, too.

"What are you doing? You didn't even read him his rights."

She whirled to face the deputy. "He's a child. I'm giving him a time-out."

A slow grin spread over Ronny's face. "I get it now. He doesn't like that you're sheriff, and you're showing him who's boss. The only reason you'd care to do that is because you like him."

"Don't underestimate me. I have every intention of booking Carver Love on charges if he won't see reason. Now, if you want to keep your job, you need to find Joe Miller. Find out what he knows. I can't believe you let him go."

Ronny frowned. "He doesn't know anything."

She lifted a brow. "He's not going to tell you with a crowd watching. Find him and get me something. Who are the rustlers? Where are they headed? Arrest him for brawling in public if you have to."

"Am I riding out with Carver when he goes or not?"

"No. I'm going." *You've done enough damage for one day.*

Ronny wouldn't argue further because he never wanted to go anyway. She watched him make his way to his vehicle, then she headed next door to order takeout. Barbecue sandwiches and two small bags of potato chips in hand, Sheridan headed back. What was she doing?

She'd bought Carver his favorite chopped beef sandwich. The fact that she knew his favorite disconcerted her. Somewhere she'd heard that he loved these sandwiches, and she'd stored that information, tucked it away in her memory. Why in the world would she do that? The man was just plain impossible to get along with.

Ronny was wrong. She didn't like him. Not one iota.

Taking the last step down into the basement where the cells

were—the place reminded her a little of a dungeon—Sheridan started having second thoughts about buying the barbecue. She might have to explain how she knew this was his favorite. Why she treated her prisoner to barbecue. If he pressed her, she'd have to charge him with something, or he could have her hide for mistreating him.

Unfortunately, her decision was on the emotional side. Still, she'd done it for his own good, to protect him. He was going after the rustlers in the wrong way and could end up getting hurt. A shiner was one thing, but he could get shot or worse, killed.

Sheridan needed to reason with him, and hopefully remedy the situation.

Carver was the only man in her jail, and the dungeon was quiet. She found him lying on the cot, hat covering his face. He'd been crestfallen when she'd closed the barred door in his face, and now he slept in his cell.

Something shifted in her heart.

She jingled the key in the lock. Carver sat up, catching his hat as it fell away. He positioned it back on his head. Sheridan crossed the distance and sat next to him on the cot. Carver scooted over to give her room, his eyes wide.

She held up one of the sacks. "I brought a peace offering."

A crease appeared in his forehead, and he opened the sack. He breathed in the aroma. "Barbecue? You brought me barbecue?"

"Did I get it wrong? I thought it was your favorite." Now she'd done it. Why had she told him that? What kind of sheriff did that?

Carver stared at her long and hard. Sheridan's throat twisted in knots. His gaze held admiration—was he glad she'd brought him the sandwich? Then why didn't he just say so?

In that moment, something passed between them. If Sheridan was a romantic, she would have thought Carver was about to kiss her. All over a sandwich. If she'd known barbecue would bend him to her thinking, she would have catered it to his home at least once a week.

But no. That wasn't it. Carver's look said he saw past the sheriff exterior to the woman inside.

"A peace offering?" Carver closed the sack and set it aside, disappointing Sheridan. "I appreciate your thoughtfulness, but before I eat, I need to know something."

Sheridan's stomach protested. "What's that?"

"Why have you locked me up when those rustlers are getting away?"

"Because I don't want to see you get hurt."

"You don't want to see me get hurt." The words were a statement, not a question. Carver looked away from her, thoughtful. "Have you ever before locked up anyone because you didn't want to see them get hurt?"

The man knew what questions to ask. "You'd be the first."

Half a grin cracked his face, and something akin to pleasure warmed his eyes. "Then I'll share a secret with you. That's the same reason I don't like you as sheriff. I don't want you to get hurt."

Carver's tone was warm, genuine. Caring. Reminding her of the past.

Their brief romantic encounter.

Heat poured through Sheridan's veins. "Now that we understand each other, do we have a truce? I'd rather not bristle every time I see you in town. I'd rather be friends."

Carver's half grin flattened. "Let's eat."

He ate, but his expression remained troubled.

When he finished off the sandwich and chips—Sheridan had only eaten half of hers—he wadded up the brown paper bag. "Now, are you going to let me out?"

Stuffing her unfinished meal in the sack, Sheridan stood to look down at Carver. "On one condition."

Carver rose, standing a head taller and meeting her gaze. Did she see a glimmer in his steely eyes? "I'm listening."

"You plan to meet your boys, right?"

His chin jutted out, his usual stance when he was about to challenge her, and he nodded.

"You need the law on your side, Carver. I'm going with you."

Chapter 5

Standing in his kitchen, the light over the stove chasing away the darkness, Carver slammed the rest of his water. He and Sheridan had teamed up to chase down the rustlers. He didn't like it one bit, but he didn't have a choice. She was the law in Rimrock County.

Carver smiled despite the long night ahead. As long as he lived, he'd never forget the day Sheriff Hall locked him in jail and bought him his favorite barbecue.

The sheriff had a heart. But he'd never doubted that.

He rubbed his hand over his jaw. And in that heart of hers, she held a soft spot for him. Just like he did for her. He prayed that whatever lay ahead of them over the next few days would bring them closer, but feared the opposite more likely.

In the end, Joe had spilled what he knew to Sheridan. He stumbled into a back alley late one night on his way to his car and overheard two men disagreeing about their plot to steal range cattle. Driving them east a good fifty miles, they'd graze them in the hills before loading them onto a semitrailer and heading out of state. Cutting through the Warner Valley on Hogback Road, they'd connect with Warner Highway and cross the border to Nevada. By the time the cattle were discovered missing, they would be long gone.

Idiots. They proved that too much drinking would loosen a man's tongue every time. What they didn't know was that Carver discovered his missing cattle because he'd changed his habits, bringing the cattle in earlier than usual. The men knew his habits.

They must know Carver. His blood stewed.

Even with this information, they could still miss the men. Lose his cattle. Sheridan had contacted the state police for help in watching the highways. Every cattle trailer would be inspected.

He and Sheridan would trailer the horses and drive to the region north of Warner Valley to search in the same vicinity where they'd spotted cattle from the air. He didn't doubt the men were skittish after they were spotted by a plane.

Carver's plans hinged on a call from Ray via his satellite phone and if they'd discovered anything. Ray and the boys would chase down the rustlers and hopefully run them straight into Carver and Sheriff Hall. In addition to the state police, she'd alerted her deputies and the sheriffs in neighboring counties.

This was their best chance, barring that it wasn't too late. Carver had about five hours to catch some shut-eye then Sheriff Hall would meet him at the ranch, and they'd make the drive. He grabbed a shower and just before he got into bed, he heard from Ray.

"We haven't found anything yet," Ray said. "We're settled in for the night and will get an early start in the morning."

"Sheriff Hall and I plan to be north of the Warner Valley by dawn."

"The sheriff? I thought you were dead set against bringing her."

Long story. "She's the law around here, Ray."

"I can't wait to hear what's got you singing a different tune."

Carver deserved Ray's surprise, so he'd let the barb slide. Ray had been his right-hand man for so long, the guy was like a brother to him. "Starting tomorrow I want frequent updates. Once we find a place to park the trailer, we'll head your way."

After ending the call, Carver fell back on the bed into an exhausted sleep filled with dreams of Sheriff Hall.

Sheridan. . .

A loud noise rattled his nerves, yanking him from a fitful dream in which she was in danger. He shot straight up.

Bang, bang, bang. Add to the knocking, the doorbell kept ringing. The bad dream hovering at the back of his mind, Carver glanced at the clock next to his bed. The one with the alarm set that was supposed to wake him up.

He'd overslept. Carver jumped out of bed and slipped into his jeans, then padded his way out of the bedroom, through the living room to the front door. He swung it open, knowing he looked like a worn-out cowboy barely this side of sleep.

Sheriff Hall's eyes grew wide and bright. "Oh, thank goodness. I thought you'd left without me. Either that or something bad happened to you."

The sheriff's eyes flickered over his chest, and a little smile tugged at the corner of her lips. Carver realized he was shirtless and, though he'd never considered himself modest after life with a bunch of cowhands, the veiled appreciation in her gaze sent heat rushing through him.

She combed her fingers through his hair. "You're a little scruffy-looking this morning. Like you just woke up."

Brushing by him, she stood in the foyer, the faint scent of her shampoo pleasing his senses. He ran a hand down his grubby face, feeling disheveled and groggy.

"I figured you'd have the coffee going and the trailer loaded by now."

"My fault. I overslept. Do me a favor and start the coffee. Give me a few minutes to get it all together. We can share the coffee in the truck."

Her smile did wonders to bring him fully awake. "I can't promise I'll wait to drink the coffee. But I'll be sure to make it strong."

Maybe the good Lord could redeem all the times he should have made her smile instead of scowl. How she could be so chipper after climbing out of bed in the middle of the night to help him, he didn't know. He almost wished they would have left last night, but both of them needed a few hours' rest.

Carver led her into the kitchen and flipped on the light, squinting against the onslaught of brightness. She found the coffeepot but before Carver took a step out of the kitchen, she tossed him a set of keys, which he caught.

"Remember, we're taking mine," she said.

"I remember, but why are you giving me the keys?"

"So you can get the trailer hitched." She filled the carafe with water.

Carver looked at her. "You're not planning to help?"

"You want coffee or not?"

How long did it take to fix a pot of coffee? Carver groused as he left the kitchen, but mostly at himself for getting up late. A guy couldn't exactly speed when he was riding with the sheriff.

Gripping the keys, Carver headed into the bedroom and shut the door, warmed by the fact that she'd entrusted him with them.

Sheridan stole a cup of coffee before the pot had finished brewing.

The sound of a door opening drew her gaze up, and in rushed Carver, looking like he'd spent a half hour smoothing out the rough places rather than eight minutes. She tipped the large mug against her lips to keep him from seeing the approval she was sure glimmered in her eyes.

His broad shoulders filled out the blue-and-white-striped western shirt just right. When he finished tucking the shirttail into his jeans in the back, he came toward her and squeezed her shoulders.

Sheridan tensed at his nearness. "What are you doing?"

With a teasing smile, he nudged her over a few steps.

He reached into the cabinet and grabbed two large thermal carafes. "Fill these with coffee. Then meet me outside, around back."

"Sure thing." Sheridan grabbed the mugs, her fingers brushing against the tanned skin of his hand. She kept her focus on the task, rather than looking at him. He might see the way he affected her, and she was still trying to figure things out.

Carver appeared to have changed his attitude toward her, becoming more accepting of her as sheriff. That went a long way in taming the animosity that always cropped up whenever she saw him. He was a good man. Maybe the time spent with him the last couple of days showed her they'd simply gotten off to a bad start ten years ago. She laughed inside at the absurd thought.

After securing both thermal mugs filled with hot coffee, she made her way out the front door and walked around the porch. He'd turned on the security lights. She spotted her Yukon, a horse trailer behind it. Carver and another man worked to secure the hitch.

Minutes later, they were urging two of the horses into the trailer. Sheridan opened the vehicle door to place the mugs in the holders, then slipped out of the cab and to the trailer in time to see the back end of the last horse.

Since she'd been sheriff, Sheridan hadn't had to utilize their mounted patrol, and depending on how long they were in the saddle, this could definitely test her skills, but she was confident she was up to the challenge.

Carver lifted a saddle and rushed by her, storing it in the neck of the trailer, followed by his cowhand. "We've got to make good time, Sheriff, so why don't you climb in. I'm almost done."

Sheridan pressed a hand on her hip. Just who was running this show anyway? She climbed in on the driver's side and started the ignition, waiting on Carver. The aroma of coffee drew her thoughts to the mug, and she lifted it to her lips.

Her door swung open. Carver filled the space, staring at her. "What do you think you're doing?"

Sheridan frowned. "Excuse me?" She couldn't fathom what he meant.

The hard expression on his face softened. He held his hand open like he expected to help her out. "You can't drive this while pulling a trailer."

"You've got to be kidding me. Of course, I'm driving. This vehicle is the property of the sheriff's department."

"I don't think so. You're pulling a trailer of my horses." He swung the door wider and stepped aside, waiting for her to get out.

They were slipping back to their old ways and fast. How did she earn this man's respect?

"Carver Love!" Sheridan stopped herself from saying more.

She stared through the windshield, measuring her words, then returned her gaze to the hardheaded cowboy, speaking softer this time. "We have a truce, remember? You're going to have to trust me. What you have to decide is if you are up for that. Are you?"

Sheridan held on to what little breath she'd taken, waiting for his reaction.

His chin jutted out, and Sheridan tensed. "You're right, Sheriff. I'm going to trust you to do your job when that time comes. But between the two of us, I'm the experienced one when it comes to pulling horse trailers."

Oh, he had her there. She'd made a mistake. Hated admitting it.

Head cocked to the side, a grin tugged at the corner of his mouth. "What do you say, Sheridan? Let me do my job, and I'll let you do yours."

Sheridan? Had he just called her by her first name? While she should set him right about how to address her, the sound of her name on his lips did startling things to her insides.

Regardless how the man affected her, she couldn't allow anyone to accuse her of letting pride get in the way of good judgment. "I can't argue with you there. You're the better man to drive. This time."

Sheridan slipped from the cab but Carver didn't budge, his broad shoulders making her feel small, vulnerable.

He hesitated a few seconds longer than necessary, staring down at her. "Don't worry. My insurance will cover anything I'm driving."

She stepped aside and jogged around the front of the Yukon while Carver climbed into the driver's side.

Chapter 6

That was close.

The last thing Carver wanted was to start this trip battling with the sheriff, so he'd taken liberties and called her by her first name, hoping to reason with the woman inside. She seemed to dig in her heels when it came to him, wanting to oppose him on every front. They'd made some progress in their relationship—an understanding of sorts, but in his opinion they were standing on a shaky fault line.

The sheriff's vehicle bounced along his driveway, pulling the trailer, and Carver, keeping one hand on the steering wheel, lifted the mug of hot, strong coffee to his lips.

"You make a good cup of coffee." He glanced her way as he steered the SUV onto the main road. Of course, she didn't know he considered that an important skill he looked for in his future wife.

"Thanks. I probably should have made more for the trip. Brought an extra mug." She offered him a quick smile, her eyes illuminated by a passing car.

"Why don't you lean the seat back? It'll take a few hours until we're there. Might as well get some rest."

"I couldn't sleep now if I wanted to. I just drank coffee to keep me awake." She took another sip from her mug then stared out the passenger window.

If it weren't for the circumstances—trying to retrieve stolen cattle—Carver might consider this a dream come true. Hours spent alone with Sheriff Sheridan Hall. Now, if he could just figure out what to say.

"Have you heard from Ray?" she asked.

"Yes. The plan stays in place unless he calls us with new information. I'm hoping they'll drive those rustlers right to us."

"Carver." The way she said his name, so soft this time, she didn't sound anything like a sheriff.

He risked a glance her direction, catching a look of pity on her face.

"What?" His tone was a little brusque, but he didn't like that look from her. Not one bit.

"You know the chances. . ." She squeezed his arm, sending his mind reeling. "It's wide-open country out there. The chances that your guys will find those rustlers, much less herd them—"

"Are good." Carver nodded as if reassuring the sheriff, but deep down he wasn't as confident as he let on. "The way I see it, you've got to think like a rustler."

He wished he could call her by her first name on a regular basis. Would he ever get to that place with her?

"I'm listening."

He didn't look at her, but heard the smile in her voice. She had a way about her, warming more than the cab of the Yukon. Carver switched on the vent to allow in the cool night air. "My brother, Justin, took some cattle once on a dare."

Carver looked over at Sheridan and saw the serious look he expected. "He's a bounty hunter now, just so we're clear."

"Is that right?"

"He was just an idiot kid. I don't remember what started the dare, but our daddy had to step in and make things right with a neighboring rancher and sent the rest of us boys after Justin."

"So now you can think like a rustler, is that it?" Her question was teasing, letting him know she had no intention of taking him seriously.

"Make a joke if you like, but yes, I'm telling you there's a good chance we're going to catch these guys." A small one, but all he needed was one.

"You'll get your chance to make a believer out of me."

Man, was that a loaded statement. Carver wanted to make a believer out of her, all right. But he was having trouble believing he was actually with her right now, in the same vehicle, having a civilized conversation.

"Look, if those cows belong to me and those men are the rustlers, they've only got one place to go and it's not over Hart Mountain or to Steens Mountain. My guys are spreading out to cover a broad area, making sure nobody slips through."

When Sheridan didn't say anything, Carver glimpsed her way, seeing the back of her head. She was probably thinking that it was still a long shot.

"My daddy taught me to be an optimist, to persevere. I think God sent me out for my cattle a little early this year, and I made the discovery they were gone in good time because of

Him. I can't let go of hope, of trying."

In the corner of his vision, he saw Sheridan turn her head toward him, felt her gaze on him for a long while. What was she thinking?

"Now that's something I can believe in." Her voice held promise.

He sighed, wishing for so much more with her. Wishing he could take her in his arms and kiss her properly.

Just once. He hadn't had that chance years ago when he'd acted like a heel.

For Carver's sake, she hoped he was right. Catching the rustlers would benefit the county as well.

Sheridan stared out the window at the moonlit landscape passing by, trying to stay awake even with the strong coffee. She thought she knew the man sitting next to her. Thought she knew he was an arrogant, hardheaded, wealthy rancher who liked to get his way and stomped around town like he owned the place.

Sure there were plenty who admired and respected him, but it didn't help that everyone knew he didn't approve of her as sheriff. Every time she had any dealings with him, he gave her a hard time.

But now, sitting here with him as he drove them to the middle of nowhere on a measure of faith that he knew where to look for the rustlers, Sheridan decided she hadn't known anything at all about the real Carver. Maybe he'd been off-putting to

Sheridan those years ago, but there were a hundred reasons men acted that way. Maybe he'd just needed to grow up.

By spending time with him again, she was getting to know the man a little better. And she liked what she saw inside. A lot.

"Sheriff." At a nudge on her shoulder, Sheridan opened her eyes to gray dawn.

"Sheridan. . ." the familiar voice, softer now.

There it was again. Carver said her name. Sheridan sat up. She cleared her throat, embarrassed that she'd dozed. "I'm sorry. I can't believe I fell asleep."

"No harm done." Surprising tenderness skirted his tone. "I would have done the same if I hadn't been driving, believe me. We could have some hard riding ahead of us."

Unease weighed his last words as he turned off the ignition and looked at her. She searched his eyes, understanding passing between them. He was concerned about her ability to handle the next few hours, maybe days, in the saddle for their mounted posse of two.

The vehicle was parked at the side of a gas station situated next to a café. Sheridan turned in her seat, taking in their surroundings. "Where are we?"

"We're halfway on Hogback Road in the northern Warner Valley. We can leave the trailer here, that is, after you make arrangements with the property owner." Carver grinned over at her as he unbuckled.

"What if we spooked them with the plane and they changed their plans and head to Steens? We'd never find them there."

"That's a possibility, but I don't think they'll do that. Too far. We have to go with what we have."

Sheridan glanced at her watch. They were at the designated point at least forty-five minutes sooner than she'd projected with their late start. She slid a suspicious glance at Carver, who proffered an innocent look, telling her he knew exactly what she was thinking—with her asleep, he'd taken the opportunity to speed. He climbed from the cab without an explanation.

She smiled to herself. They were on sheriff's business, so she'd let that pass, but the man was beginning to endear himself to her. Following Carver's lead, she stepped from the vehicle and made her way around to the back of the trailer.

"I'm going to speak to someone, explaining our use of the property, and grab us more coffee."

"I'll get the horses saddled and packed with our food and supplies in case this is a long search." Carver opened up the trailer and began ushering the horses out.

Sheridan left him to it.

"Sheriff?"

She turned around. "Yes?"

"I appreciate you helping me with this." He nodded and tipped the brim of his hat.

She wanted to tell him it was her job, but that would only tear down the progress they'd made. "You're welcome." And the words felt good, sincere.

Her reward? Carver smiled at her—a smile that spoke volumes, turning her insides soft, rather than hard like any good sheriff's ought to be—his attention on her rather than the half ton of horse flesh he encouraged from the trailer.

She refocused on her task as she made her way to the gas station in search of the person in charge, worried that whatever was going on between her and Carver could be a dangerous distraction.

Inside the gas station, she grabbed two cups of coffee from the dispenser. After paying the cashier, she was directed to the café where she'd find the property owner, Mabel Follis. Sheridan explained that she didn't anticipate this taking more than a day, but she'd ask a deputy to retrieve the Yukon and trailer if it took longer. After squaring things with Mabel, Sheridan walked outside and started toward Carver and the horses.

A truck pulling a trailer loaded down with cattle slowed and prepared to pull into the gas station, then suddenly increased speed, the driver apparently changing his mind.

Her gaze followed the trailer, unable to read the license plate covered with mud. As she jerked her head to Carver, a cup of coffee slipped from her hand.

Chapter 7

All Carver's next thoughts and actions collided, happening at once in slow motion, which wasn't fast enough for him.

His eyes locked on the sheriff's startled, wide-eyed gaze—she held his, her suspicious expression mirroring his questions.

Were those his cows? Why had the driver changed his mind after putting on his blinker and preparing to turn into the gas station? If he spotted the sheriff, her vehicle, and the horse trailer—an obvious mounted patrol—*and* if he was guilty, that could very well be the reason.

"Unhitch the trailer, Carver!" Sheriff Hall ran toward him, the one coffee cup in her hand, sloshing liquid everywhere.

"You hold the horses." He handed off the reins. Her reaction time was faster than his, and if he had time to think on it, he was sure he'd be impressed.

Carver did as she asked and unhitched the trailer. He hated leaving her with the horses, but they didn't have time to reload them and tow the trailer if they were going to catch that truck possibly hauling his cattle. When he'd finished with the hitch, he jogged over to the driver's side of the Yukon but before he made it, the tires spun out, pulling the vehicle away from the trailer.

What the. . . He saw now that she'd tied the horses to the back of the trailer and now drove the vehicle. What was she thinking? He was supposed to drive. Go after the rustlers.

He ran after her, waving his arms. On the radio, she stopped where the parking lot met the highway and rolled down her window.

Pulse racing, he had seconds to make his point. "What are you doing? Those could be my cattle. I'm going after them."

"You don't have any authority to stop that truck or arrest those men. Remember your place." She turned her attention back to her radio and the road, looking both directions as she gave instructions to her deputies.

"Sheriff!"

She peeled from the parking lot, turned on the flashing lights, and roared away down the highway after the cattle-trailer truck.

Carver whipped off his hat and slapped his thigh, spewing a few unsavory words. He tugged his cell from his shirt pocket, thankful he'd learned to keep it close, or it would have been in the Yukon and out of reach, and dialed the sheriff's number.

She answered on the first ring. "I don't have time for this. Now, let me concentrate on driving, on doing my job."

Though her tone left no room for argument, Carver wasn't giving in so fast. "If those are my cattle I want to be there. Come back and get me."

"Do you really want me to risk losing them?"

"How are you going to lose them? There's only one road and they're pulling a trailer? You can drive faster. Sheridan . . .please."

"I'm sorry I didn't wait for you, but you can't leave the horses alone anyway. Now, you're just going to have to trust me, Carver. And, please, address me as sheriff."

Then you can just call me Mr. Love. He thought it, but he didn't mean it, and wouldn't say it. That would put too much distance between them. He'd overstepped one too many times, calling her by her first name, but he thought they'd crossed that threshold.

Maybe it was too much to hope for.

Unable to think of anything else he could say to bring her back, Carver hung up and trudged back to the trailer where his horses waited patiently. He felt like one of them, left tied to the trailer with nothing to do but wait. That had never been one of Carver's strong points. He pressed his hands against their muzzles, feeling the softness, reassuring them as he considered his next step.

Pacing on the unpaved side of the parking lot, he kicked up dirt and rocks. Should he unsaddle the horses and trailer them because the sheriff would have the rustlers in custody? Were they even the right men? And if not, he and the sheriff were wasting valuable time.

Carver made a call to Ray and got no answer, but within seconds, the man returned his call.

"We've been in the saddle for more than an hour now. Haven't seen a thing." Ray sounded weary. A lack of hope often did that to a man.

"Before we got on the horses a truck pulling cattle passed us. The sheriff went after them and left me here."

"You think that was the rustlers? Maybe they made better time than we thought, pushed the cows long and hard to the highway?"

"I don't know. I want to get a look at those cattle myself."

"Well, if it's like you said, the sheriff likely caught up with them by now. She'll call, Carver, don't worry. Then you can let me know if we should call off this search."

"Will do." Carver hung up. Now he had no choice but to face the uncertainty and his impatience alone.

He hated being stripped of any control over his life, control over the situation. And as the minutes ticked by, Carver started to worry about Sheridan, the woman sheriff, as Ray liked to call her. She was a sturdy one, and she was beginning to earn his respect and confidence that she could do the job Carver thought was meant for a man. But that didn't ease his anxiety. Not one bit.

There was only one thing he needed to get a grip on the current unfavorable circumstances. He grinned when he saw the hardy truck with a sturdy trailer hitch turn into the gas station. An ordinary sight on any given day in open range cattle country, but especially this morning, it was a sight for weary eyes. Now, to convince the woman driving it that he had an emergency.

ꟹ

Sheridan accelerated, driving as fast as she felt necessary but at safe speeds. Ronny was on his way, but weaving through the

Warner Mountains would take time. Her other deputies were spread over the county, handling other problems. She'd also apprised the Oregon State Police of the situation. Ronny was only one of twelve deputies under her direction covering the entire county, and right now, she didn't think that was nearly enough if they were going to see more days like today or like the day she faced off with that mobster.

Normally, her county didn't see this much action. But she was trained and ready to meet the call of duty. Her cell rang again.

Carver.

Let him stew, she didn't have time for him. Where was that truck? She passed a slow-moving tractor trailer and swerved back into the lane as an oncoming car drew near.

Didn't these people know they were supposed to move over when they saw flashing lights? She ground her teeth, her heart pumping adrenaline through her veins, preparing her to face whatever was ahead of her. It couldn't come soon enough.

At this speed, she should have caught up with that truck by now.

Sheridan looked in the rearview mirror and spotted dust flying up in the distance. There wasn't another main road intersecting the highway, but there were a few private roads and driveways. She screeched to a halt on the shoulder, allowing a truck to pass, then made a U-turn, and called Ronny, letting him know she was still in pursuit, giving him her approximate location.

After all this, those boys could turn out to be innocent.

But the way the driver had changed his mind about getting gas once he'd spotted Sheridan erased almost all doubt. If the cattle belonged to Carver, all the better—it would save them time spent in the saddle roaming the endless backcountry without any clear direction.

Sheridan drove to the property entrance, opting for her siren in addition to the lights for good measure. Turning onto the unpaved drive, the bumpy path did its best to jostle her insides, but she kept a good pace over the dirt road. About a mile up, the dust began to settle, allowing Sheridan to see a house, and the cattle trailer she was after.

What were they up to?

Keeping her senses alert, she continued the drive, but flipped off the lights and siren. By now, they knew she was there. She pulled to the side of the drive behind the trailer loaded with cattle, but not too close. The hair on the back of her neck and arms rose.

At that moment, she realized part of her had hoped this was all a mistake, but. . .something wasn't right.

She stepped from the vehicle, her eyes scanning the surrounding area, the house, the trailer. Nobody was around. She tugged out her notepad and wrote down the plate number. If the driver didn't show his face soon, she'd knock on the door.

If these men were the rustlers, she didn't like facing off with them out in the middle of nowhere, but in her county, waiting for backup was often a luxury. Ronny would take too long.

Her cell rang inside the Yukon. Probably Carver again, and

she fought the urge to answer. The screen door creaked and a man stepped onto a porch needing a coat of paint.

"Something I can do for you?"

"Yes. Would you please step out of the house? Bring your driver's license, insurance, and your papers for transporting these cattle." Although branding wasn't mandatory in Oregon, every truck transporting them for transfer of ownership out of state or for slaughter needed branding inspection papers.

The man laughed. "You followed me all the way out here for that?"

"Sir, please do as you're told."

He slipped back inside and when he returned, another man—younger, maybe his son—followed him out. He proffered his license. "What's this about? I wasn't speeding."

Sheridan took the license and read the name, Frank Driggs, and wrote down his license number so she could call it in. "And the papers for the cattle."

"They're all mine. I don't need papers. But you need a warrant to search my property."

Slipping her hand onto her firearm, she tensed. "Sir, I have probable cause to believe stolen cattle are being trucked out of state. We're searching every truck. If those cattle belong to you then you have nothing to worry about. But I need to see them."

She would call out the brand inspector, too, if there was any doubt. Lee Holder worked part-time these days, and he wasn't going to be happy.

The man's expression grew dark. Sheridan's training kicked in.

"All right." He glanced back at the younger man then

marched to the back of the trailer.

Sheridan kept her distance as he opened the trailer door wide. The cows began to shuffle, expecting to be released from captivity, but he didn't roll out the ramp.

Mr. Driggs turned his attention to Sheridan. "We trucked them back from where they were grazing and stopped off at the house, that's all. Have another thirty miles or so to take them. You'll understand if I don't want to unload the lot of them. You can see what you need to."

What he said didn't sound right. Sheridan had a bad feeling about these men, but she'd manage the situation with all caution. "Step away from the trailer, please."

The stink of manure was strong as Sheridan approached the open trailer and studied the cows, looking for brands, specifically Carver's, and calves without brands. Chances were she'd need the cattle unloaded to see what she was looking for, but one step at a time.

A shadow gave her a millisecond warning before the trailer door slammed into her, knocking her to the ground.

Pain sliced through her head. Her vision ebbed, darkening at the edges. The ramp slid down with a deafening jar, and the cows stampeded to freedom in a panic, some leaping out, avoiding the ramp and nearly trampling her. Sheridan pulled her weapon out and rolled under the truck in one fluid motion.

Chapter 8

"This should be it." Carver pointed to the side road on the left, just off the main highway.

He leaned forward, practically on the edge of the passenger seat in Janice Holston's truck. Itching to get out, he hadn't even buckled his seat belt.

"Whatever you say, cowboy." The pretty blond smiled his way and turned the dually, pulling his horses into the rutted, dirt road.

From a distance, he'd seen the sheriff's flashing lights head this way, but he couldn't be certain if she had taken this detour or another from the main road. He wished Janice would drive faster. She hadn't been willing to let him behind the wheel, but at least she'd agreed to help.

The truck and trailer crept along the path, Janice slowing to an almost complete stop at every pothole.

Carver's patience ran out. The sheriff might have run into trouble. Finding his cattle was one thing, but if something happened to her, he'd never forgive himself. Why had he called her?

"Tell you what. Let me unload one of my horses, and I'll

ride ahead of you."

"I'll pull over."

"Don't bother. Just stop here. Nobody's coming, so you're fine at the moment." Carver opened the door, but before he could slip out, Janice reached toward him.

"Remember, you promised to meet me for coffee." Her contact-enhanced lavender eyes were warm and inviting. But. . .she wasn't Sheridan.

"I'll remember." Carver nodded, slipping out of the cab, then slammed the door. Surely, she didn't believe she wouldn't see him again. He had to get his trailer and horse.

He jogged back to the trailer, grateful he hadn't unsaddled the horses yet. As quickly as he could, he unloaded the first one, and prevented the second from escape. "Sorry, girl, you're going to have to stay in here for a while."

"You talking to me or the horse?" Janice leaned against the trailer, poised to show off her curves.

"The mare. She's staying in the trailer. You're driving the truck and meeting me up the road a bit." He couldn't help his sharp tone.

Without another look at the woman, Carver climbed onto Kodiak and pressed him into a gallop.

Hold on, Sheriff, I'm coming.

What was he doing? Sheridan was the law and didn't need his help. She'd left him behind to prove her point. But she also needed her deputies to back her up, and as far as Carver could tell, help hadn't arrived.

He didn't bother glancing back at Janice, trusting that she

would follow. As long as she didn't run off with his trailer and horse, he didn't care. If only the sheriff would look at him like Janice, who didn't even know him.

But Sheridan had once, a long time ago. He'd blown his chance back then.

A couple of miles farther on, the road curved around a bluff, preventing him from seeing what was up ahead. He urged Kodiak off the main path and up the rise to save time and get a better look. At the top, he could see for miles. The drive ended at a small farmhouse. He pulled his binoculars from his pack and peered through them. The sheriff's vehicle was parked a little ways behind the cattle trailer. Cows poured haphazardly from the trailer into the yard around the house instead of a holding pen.

No one was there to guide them or handle the mass exit. What was going on? Where was the sheriff? The coffee in his stomach curdled.

Oh Lord, am I too late? Staying alert to his surroundings, Carver maneuvered Kodiak down an access in the bluff, then charged toward the house.

He meant to save the woman he loved.

Weapon at the ready, Sheridan peered out from under the cattle trailer, searching for the suspects, waiting for the press of hooves to clear from her line of sight. The dust to settle.

Coughing, she covered her mouth to filter the dirt stirred by the cows, growing more aggravated with Ronny, her backup, by the millisecond. If only she'd brought Carver with her, this wouldn't have happened. But then, he wasn't her deputy, nor would she want him to get hurt.

The cattle began to settle. Sheridan crawled toward the clearing air, hoping for a way out. Were the suspects waiting for her, planning to shoot when they saw her? She could make out the house. Crawling out near the front of the trailer would make her vulnerable. The sound of pebbles and dirt, scraping from somewhere behind, pinged her alarm—someone was making their way under the trailer with her. She jerked her weapon around, ready to fire.

Carver! Sheridan lowered her gun, hands trembling. "I could have shot you."

He pressed a finger against his lips and motioned for her to follow him out. She scooted across the dirt, then climbed to her knees, crouching beneath the trailer near the back. Carver's strong arms reached underneath and pulled her out, propping her steadily on her feet. Concern creased the skin around his eyes. The Carver she knew, brusque and arrogant, was gone.

He wrapped his arms around her, hugging her to him. Surprise engulfed her. Sheridan allowed herself to rest in the comfort and shelter he offered. And. . .just for a minute, she was a woman, and not a sheriff in pursuit. The last few hazardous minutes of her life suddenly swooped down on her, and her knees shook.

What was she doing? She couldn't afford to be weak. She pushed away from Carver's embrace.

"I was worried about you." He rubbed his thumb across her

cheek, scrubbing at something. Probably dirt. "Are you okay?"

"Of course I'm all right. What do you think?" She swatted his hand away. She'd worked hard to become tough as steel, and here he treated her like she might break. Weapon in position, she crept around the side of the trailer. It was then she realized Carver had his horse, leading him.

"What are you doing here?" She peered around the trailer. "You could get hurt."

Carver sighed. "Your boys took off on their horses and into the wilds of Oregon."

Figures. They'd released the cattle as a distraction so they could escape. "Why didn't you tell me?"

"I'm telling you now."

"We need to go after them."

"I don't know if there's anyone in the house that we need to worry about," he said.

"I don't even know if the house belonged to them."

"Well, I can tell you the cows belong to me. They've got my brand except for the calves, which haven't been branded yet. Obviously, though, this isn't all of them. But this could just be their first load. Ray is still searching."

"Why don't you go help Ray, then? I've got my hands full with these men. Ronny should be here soon. We'll take it from here."

"There's no time to get more horses for you and Ronny, Sheriff. But definitely, you should wait for him." Carver climbed onto his mount and rode off, herding his cattle into a nearby corral.

Tired and frustrated, Sheridan shook her head. She hiked back to her vehicle, wary that someone in the house could cause them harm. She reached inside the Yukon and radioed dispatch, who informed her Ronny had been detained by a traffic accident that shut down the left lane of the main highway through the mountains. Great. The state police would be there, but Ronny wouldn't be free for a while. Two other deputies couldn't meet her for another hour, if that.

When she looked up again, she spotted Carver closing up the corral filled with cattle. He was fast. He looked her way, tipped his hat, then he pressed his horse into a gallop, heading in the direction he'd indicated the men went.

"Carver!"

Sheridan scrambled into her Yukon, turned on the ignition, and shoved the gear into DRIVE. She swerved around the truck and off the road, bouncing across the yard and unfenced pasture behind the house.

Honking her horn, she wanted Carver to know she was in pursuit, not him. But she couldn't stay in the SUV, following the suspects through Oregon Outback scored with geological scars, bluffs, and mountains. That's why they'd brought the horses to begin with.

Carver stopped at the top of a slope and waited in the saddle. She pressed the accelerator, steering and bouncing over the rough terrain. Near the top of the rise, she yanked the steering wheel around in a hard stop. Hopefully, Carver had control over his horse, because he certainly didn't have control over himself. The man was a wild mustang. Someone needed to tame him.

Sheridan leaped from the vehicle. "What do you think you're doing? I've about had it with you. You cannot take off after those men. You are not the law."

He didn't even look at her but lifted his hand from where it rested on the pommel and pointed. Sheridan's gaze followed where he indicated.

Two men on horses were riding hard and fast. The rustlers. . .

"I needed to see where they were headed."

"Well, you can't go after them alone, and I can't follow them without a horse." Sheridan looked back at the house. Another truck sat in the drive now. A dually with a horse trailer. Carver's trailer. She'd not had a chance to wonder how he'd caught up with her on his horse.

He guided his mount to where she stood. "Looks like Janice finally arrived with the other horse."

"Janice?" She stared at him.

He grinned and winked. "Let's get you in the saddle."

Oh boy. Sheridan held her shoulders high, despite the weight pressing down. She'd had the rustlers. Why had she allowed them to get the best of her?

Suddenly, she realized Carver was watching her. To her surprise he dismounted and stepped over to lean against the Yukon, his face inches from hers. "Don't blame yourself they got away. You're alive. That's all I care about. But if you still insist on going after these men, I still insist on going with you."

I know. The way he stared at her, the way he'd said the words, Sheridan could swear something about this whole chase had changed them—changed their relationship.

She had to shake herself from the way the man affected her. “We’re wasting time.”

Opening the door, she nearly knocked him over. She climbed in and closed the door, then leaned out the window. “I’ll race you down the hill.”

Chapter 9

By midmorning, the sun had begun its climb into the sky, and Sheridan, finally in the saddle, raced behind Carver after the rustlers. She'd never ridden at a gallop like this over such rough and rocky terrain, but trusted Carver's horses were well-trained for the challenge. After this experience, she wished the county could afford a full-time, well-trained mounted patrol. A mobile command trailer would be nice, too.

How she wished they had bullet-resistant vests. It was a matter of economics, but since facing off with that mobster, Sheridan had applied pressure to those in control for the purchase of new vests. The current ones were purchased years ago. They'd been taken off the market because they didn't work. She'd tried one—it didn't fit, choked her, and she couldn't even drive.

She was still waiting and prayed today wouldn't be the day they were needed.

They'd unhitched Carver's trailer and sent Janice—who had an eye for Carver—on her way. Sheridan radioed their location and would update Ronny, using her mobile transmitter unit.

Now that the stakes had risen, and they were chasing real

fugitives, a couple of her deputies would acquire more horses and join her and Carver in apprehending the rustlers on horseback.

Legs squeezing the saddle and the powerful beast beneath her, Sheridan focused on the terrain ahead. The rustlers had cut into a crag-lined ravine, hoping to lose their tail. She and Carver had lost time, but not much. At some point Mr. Driggs, if that was his real name, would have to slow down. He must have thought he had nothing to lose by running.

While the ravine offered the men cover and possibly an escape into the mountains if they could evade the law, their strategy could also backfire, cornering them with no way out. On the other hand, the ravine was dangerous for Carver and Sheridan going in after fugitives who were waiting on them.

They could easily be ambushed. Sheridan knew firsthand the rustlers weren't afraid to tackle the law. Carver slowed when they reached the ravine's entry point, and leaned on the pommel.

He removed his hat and wiped his forehead with his sleeve, his gaze sliding to meet hers. She'd bet he was thinking the same thing.

"It's too dangerous."

"You're right. I can't ask you to go in there. These men stole my cattle. I'll handle it." His voice sounded strained. He tore his gaze from her and looked over the expanse. "By the time your deputies get here, the rustlers might be long gone, but I think you should wait on them. At least we know where the rustlers are holing up for now."

She'd heard his mantra too many times. He didn't want her getting hurt. She frowned, uncertainty enveloping her like never before. He was right—if they waited on the other deputies, they could lose the rustlers.

"I don't think they're going to kill us. They wouldn't want murder on their list of crimes. If they'd wanted to kill me, they would have done that back at the house."

"Maybe they tried. Thought you'd be trampled and they could say it was an accident. But you scrambled under the truck, and they made a run for it."

He had a point. And just thinking about it again made her mad.

"Maybe I should at least deputize you, though I don't think anyone's done that in a hundred years," she teased, hoping to add some levity.

He pulled a 30-30 saddle rifle out and placed it across his saddle. "Wouldn't want the sheriff's department held liable for my actions. I'm prepared to make a citizen's arrest if necessary."

The bruise on his face a stark reminder that he was serious, she read in his eyes that she couldn't stop him from pursuing the rustlers. She radioed again, providing the location of the ravine for Ronny and the others.

"We're going in together. I'll make the arrest." She urged her mount ahead of Carver, ignoring his unsmiling, disapproving expression. "I don't need people saying the sheriff can't handle a couple of rustlers."

Sheridan couldn't be positive that she wasn't letting her pride get in the way of good judgment. Regardless, letting these men get away from her twice wouldn't go unnoticed. She was the sheriff; she was trained to face dangerous situations. Carver needed to accept that.

On his horse, he sidled up next to her, though he wouldn't be able to do that for long. The path narrowed considerably. "Sheriff, let me lead you."

"I'm trained to apprehend suspects, I'm carrying the weapon that's going to protect us, if need be, so put away yours. I know what I'm doing."

"And I've got more experience riding a horse on this kind of ground. One wrong step and those rustlers will be the last of your worries."

She slowed up and sighed, peering at Carver. "Looks like we're going to have to work together."

He grinned. "Don't tell me it's come to that."

"After you." She gestured for him to go ahead of her, and as he passed, she whispered, "We should keep conversation to a minimum."

He nodded.

No need to alert the rustlers of their presence, even though they were probably expected. She watched him nudge his mount in front of hers. She'd bet they'd have to dismount at some point. Maybe even leave the horses. She hoped not.

They successfully picked their way down the rocky descent into the ravine, each second packed with worry, while she watched the crags, searching for Driggs.

Was he watching them now?

God in heaven, I hope we don't have to camp here tonight.

At the bottom of the gorge, the river was low, affording them a shallow bank. They watered the horses, and drank from the supply that Carver had stowed in their packs. The sun had risen high in the sky, blazing down into the river-carved canyon. Sheridan couldn't remember when she'd been so thirsty and guzzled the water.

Carver pressed his hand against her canteen, lowering it. He shook his head slightly, making her understand she had to go easy on the water. She was beginning to read his every thought—it was a little scary, understanding this man who'd grated on her for so many years.

But not anymore.

He stared at her long and hard, and she shifted her eyes to the river that ran clear and true. Confused at every turn where Carver was concerned, she wished her thoughts about him would do the same.

Carver touched her arm, gaining her attention, then pointed at something on the ground.

Tracks in the sandy loam—two horses and two men—hedged the river as far as she could see.

☙

Carver hated that his search for cattle had turned into this hunt for rustlers in the worst possible scenario.

On foot, he led Kodiak along the riverbank, following tracks that seemed to lead on forever, his senses alert to the slightest sounds or movement ahead of him. Why had it been too much of a strain for him to think of bringing a good dog? That would have these boys sniffed out in no time.

If they were still in the ravine.

They were here. Carver could feel it. Living on a ranch, managing cattle in this harsh land, he'd trained his senses to be in tune with everything around him—the animals, the trees and plants, the wind, and the sounds. He'd learned to pay attention to his gut. The smallest of things could be important.

But it didn't take a sensitive man to recognize that the sheriff was tiring and quickly. She wasn't accustomed to this pace. To be fair, Carver was feeling the pinch, too. If they didn't remain alert, and at their best, they could get killed.

They'd walked the entire afternoon, and now the sun was setting, though it would grow dark quicker in the gorge. He studied the shadowed crags farther on and was keenly aware when the sheriff stood next to him.

How had he let this happen? One phone call to inform her he'd had cattle stolen, and now the two of them were hiking in a ravine, chasing men who could kill them. Tearing his gaze from what lay ahead to look at her, he studied the shadows beneath her eyes. The sweat and smudges across her face. He'd done this to her.

No. She would have gone after these men, one way or the other. She was a strong woman, wanting to prove herself at every turn.

"We should go back now," he whispered.

Should have headed back an hour ago.

"We won't make it out before dark, Carver. We both know that."

He nodded. "We'll make camp."

"It'll have to be minimal. No fire, nothing to draw attention."

They found a small fissure to hole up in for protection from the weather. Hidden behind a rock, Carver could keep watch—he could see, but couldn't be seen. He hoped the sheriff wouldn't argue with him.

He dug out a few protein bars in different flavors and held them up like cards. What he wouldn't give for this time alone with her under different circumstances. Maybe one day he would get his chance. Another chance, that is.

She took a peanut caramel bar. After tearing into the wrapping, she bit into it and looked up at him, watching her like an idiot, or a love-starved puppy, take your pick. Her emerald eyes had lost their sheen in the heat of the day, and now, the dusk of a forgotten ravine.

Carver wanted to take her in his arms again, like he'd done earlier that morning. To wipe the grime from her face, feel her soft skin beneath his fingers. At first, she'd clung to him, clearly upset by the turn of events. But all too soon she'd shaken free, her steel-plated veneer back in place.

"While you eat, I'm going to keep watch."

Her eyes grew wide and she froze, midchew. He knew exactly what she thought—she was about to object. If he'd been smart, he would have waited for her to make the call.

Before she could swallow and speak her mind he cut her off. "You might be the sheriff, but you can't keep watch all night. We'll take turns. I'll be on the first shift. You finish your dinner, drink, and rest." Carver stood and adjusted his shirt, tugged at his pants. Why couldn't this night be different? Why couldn't they be on a date? A real date.

Would they make it out of this alive? He had a bad feeling in his gut, which he never ignored. Regret seeped into his heart.

So much wasted time.

Looking down at her, he grinned. "Listen, when we get out of this, I'd like to take you out. You and me spending time together under better circumstances. Maybe we could eat at a nice restaurant."

Without waiting for her reply, he shimmied around the rock to keep watch. He hadn't phrased it as a question, just a simple statement, letting her know his intentions. He probably should have waited to see her reaction, but giving the idea time to sink in was best—for both of them.

Now, he had to figure out how to stay awake and keep them safe.

Chapter 10

After she finished her second energy bar for the day, Sheridan was still hungry. Disappointed in the way things had played out so far, disappointed in herself, she snuggled into the thermal blanket Carver had supplied—one like his boys used when they were working the range. She trusted it would keep her warm, but it wouldn't keep her safe if Driggs and his partner found them.

If the matter weren't serious, she'd chuckle. Today's experience riding horseback in the outback, trailing a fugitive, made her feel like she was living in the Wild West, during the 1800s.

She'd expected Ronny and the others to catch up at some point, but they hadn't, and down in this gorge, Sheridan couldn't contact them on the radio—the mobile unit wouldn't transmit. Nor Carver's satellite phone. She yawned, the tug of sleep pulling at her eyelids, and gazed up at the stars, her head positioned on a sham of a makeshift pillow.

If it weren't for moonlight shimmering into the canyon, she probably couldn't see her hand in front of her face. Still, the stars shone like she'd never seen before. The darkness had a way of making them brighter.

That must be what happened with her and Carver. Two people who couldn't get along, but now, the shady dealings of a cattle rustler had brought out the good in Carver, shining light on the man he really was.

Sheridan wasn't sure why she'd refused to see before. Maybe he'd seemed to have a low opinion of her as well, but she'd never given him a chance, preferring to think the worst of him. Now, she saw that because he cared about her, he was just plain overprotective. It wasn't that he thought she couldn't handle the job as sheriff.

Sheridan had read him all wrong. The last thing he'd said to her about having dinner today. . .well, warmth spread all through her again at the thought.

I'd like that, Carver. I'd like that very much. . .

Now if they could catch Driggs and his cohort, and take them to the county jail, Sheridan would be one happy sheriff.

Sheridan woke to a crick in her neck. No. That wasn't it. She'd heard a noise. Her head propped on a flat rock, she sat up as realization dawned—she was in a ravine out in the middle of the wilds of Oregon. With more effort than she was accustomed to, she scrambled to her feet and worked the kinks out of her back.

She glanced at her watch, but couldn't read it. If she turned on the flashlight, she might give herself away. She had a feeling she'd slept too long. Carver should have woken her by now. Making sure her firearm was secured in her belt, she took measured steps around the rock in search of him. On the far side, more light reflected from the moonlight hitting the crags across the river.

Her back to the rock, she edged her way around, expecting to find Carver. He'd probably tell her to go back to sleep, and she'd give him a look that, even in the dim light, he was sure to understand. After all, it was her turn to stand guard.

But Carver wasn't there, and he'd left his pack.

Where was he? He was supposed to keep watch. Sheridan didn't believe he would leave without a good reason. If only she could shine the flashlight into the gully, or call his name. She crept farther away from their hidden camp, straining her eyes to see. Watching for signs of danger—the first one being that Carver was gone.

Missing, was more like it. Her thrumming pulse climbed a few notches. She forced her breathing to slow, tugged her weapon free, and prepared herself for the worst.

Lord, please, let him be safe.

Here she was, the sheriff, and this whole time she felt like Carver had been the one taking care of her, protecting her. She never should have allowed him to bulldoze his way into coming.

As the gray light of dawn began illuminating the gorge, Sheridan made her way to where they'd left the horses near a patch of grass. She spotted her mare grazing, but Carver's horse was gone.

What was going on?

☙

On his stomach, Carver crawled toward the ledge that gave him a good view of Driggs and another man saddling their horses.

There were four horses, and a third man slipped behind a rock out of view. Where was the other man? Or was that horse for packing?

In the early hours of the morning, Carver had heard voices up farther from where he and Sheridan had settled in for the night. Finding her dead to the world, he thought better of waking her until he'd investigated—she was safer there.

He could be quick and stealthy, and back before she knew he'd left.

The men's easy banter told him they believed they were alone in the ravine. They thought they'd left Sheridan cowering under the cattle trailer, and nobody had seen them leave on the horses.

He was glad he and Sheridan had kept quiet in their hunt. They worked well as a team, but they hadn't counted on more men. He surmised the other men had come from ahead to meet the rustlers. For what reason, Carver didn't know. But he needed to inform the sheriff. There could be someone else waiting up ahead as well, for all he knew.

He slid back out of sight. The sheriff would be relieved to apprehend them, and cattle country would be avenged a wrongdoing. This time.

But before the two men disappeared from his view, they slowly lifted their hands. Carver froze. A few feet away, the sheriff aimed her weapon.

He'd made a mistake leaving her.

She was the law, after all, as she constantly reminded him. Why couldn't he get that through his thick skull? Even though she had a gun, Carver didn't believe they would relinquish their freedom so easily. Did she realize there was a third man, possibly a fourth? She had to see the extra horses.

He couldn't hear what she said, but she fired her weapon into the ground. The two men stiffened at first, then dropped to their knees. Sheridan was about to cuff them. Somehow, Carver had to warn her they were not alone—but calling out would only distract her and make her vulnerable.

Scrambling down from the ledge he found his horse, hoping he'd be more intimidating on his mount.

ଓ

Her knee in the rustler's back as his face pressed into the dirt, she finished cuffing the third rustler, her senses on alert for the fourth man.

And Carver. She forced them to sit back-to-back in a circle, believing her deputies would be along this morning to assist in bringing the men to jail. By now, they had to be.

But she fought the trembling in her knees. Where was Carver? There was no way she'd believe he'd left her behind and fled the ravine—the cattle rancher was trustworthy. Her answer came when the man himself stepped from behind a boulder, the fourth man holding a gun at his temple.

"Drop the weapon," the rustler said.

Oh Carver. . .

Sheridan aimed her firearm at the criminal. She was an expert marksman. Could she take him out without injuring Carver? Was it worth the risk?

He pressed the gun into Carver's temple. "Now."

Carver gave a slight shake of his head, his eyes bearing none of the fear she'd expect to see there. If she released her weapon, he was dead anyway. They both were.

In the millisecond it took to finger the trigger, someone rammed into her, slamming her to the ground. Her firearm discharged. She'd taken aim at the assailant, Carver mere inches from him.

Had she hit Carver instead? *Oh Lord, please no.*

The breath knocked from her, she gasped for air while scrambling for her weapon, but one of the handcuffed men kicked it away and pressed her to the ground with his knee. He sneered at her.

From her peripheral vision, she could see Carver wrestling with the fourth man. More gunfire echoed through the ravine. While the idiot on top of her searched for the keys to the cuffs, Sheridan searched in the dirt for a rock. When she found it, she wasted no time cracking it into the man's head. He fell off, and she rolled to her knees.

A horse galloped toward her, and she dodged out of the way.

Carver!

He reached down and grabbed her arm. Before she comprehended what was happening, she was in the saddle behind him. He carried them both away on horseback.

She pounded his back. "What are you doing? Rescuing me? We have to go back? We can't leave those men. Let me do my job!"

At last, he slowed, guiding his horse behind a boulder.

Sheridan hopped from the saddle, and Carver climbed off as well.

"Great. That's just great. You should have waited on me, then this whole thing would have turned out differently."

"Yeah, we would have been ambushed by the two extra men. Your deputies should be here soon. I hear horses down the other way. Either that or more rustlers."

Carver stepped to the side and glanced behind Sheridan, she turned to see where he was looking. In the distance, several horses carrying her deputies galloped their way.

Relief swept through her.

She turned back to Carver. A man approached from behind him, aiming a gun.

Carver reacted to the look in her eyes and whirled around to face the gunman.

"No!" Carver stretched himself in front of Sheridan.

The gun went off, and Carver slumped.

Sheridan caught him and lowered him to the ground. Through blurred vision, she saw the man climb back on his horse, his eyes studying the landscape beyond—he'd seen the rush of deputies in pursuit. He fled, leaving Sheridan to hold Carver.

Blood poured from a wound in his side. Sheridan pressed her hand against it, to staunch the flow. He peered at her through half-closed eyes.

"Why'd you take that bullet for me? You shouldn't have done that." She tried to keep her voice strong and matter-of-fact, the way any sheriff should sound, but it was no use.

"Because I love you, Sheriff. . .always have. Can I call you Sheridan now?"

Tears exploded in her eyes, and she chuckled a sob. He loved her? "Yes, you can call me Sheridan, but save your strength for now."

He offered a weak smile. "Can we skip the dinner and get married instead?"

☙

Carver opened his eyes to a beam of bright light streaking through a crack in the miniblinds. He felt groggy and stiff. He needed a drink of water. Taking in his surroundings—he was in a hospital room, no doubt—his gaze landed on the beautiful brunette slumped in the chair, sleeping.

The last thing he remembered, he'd taken a bullet for her. His memory fuzzy on the details, his gut told him that things would have gone much better if he'd let her do her job without his interference.

She stirred in the chair and opened her emerald eyes. As soon as she realized he was awake, she moved to his side. "How do you feel?"

"Like I was trampled in a stampede, but other than that, I'm good." His voice was a croak. "Can I get some water?"

She poured some into a cup from a pitcher and handed it to him.

He drank then laid his head on the pillow. "What happened? Did they get the rustlers? Has Ray found all my cattle?"

"Slow down, cowboy. One question at a time. Yes, we got the rustlers. Yes, Ray found most of your cattle. They were kept in different places."

"And what about dinner? You never answered me. Can we skip dinner?"

Sheridan's eyes grew wide. "I didn't think you'd remember saying that. I thought you'd said it because you figured you were dying."

"I did. But those words came from my heart. Every one of them."

Grabbing his hand, she wove her fingers with his. They were long, slender, and strong. "Carver, you don't really know me."

"Sure I do. I've known you for years. Learning all the little things about each other is what spending a lifetime together is about. But if you don't feel the same way, just say it."

The sheriff blinked back tears. She wasn't that tough after all. But she was a woman, too—the woman he loved. Still, Carver prepared himself to be wounded yet again—regardless how she felt, he'd take a bullet for her again.

"I've never witnessed a braver soul than you, Carver Love. I'm pretty sure I'm smitten with you."

Though her words caressed his heart, something in her eyes made him look away. "But?"

"I can't marry you unless you'll agree to let me do the job I was trained to do."

His smile felt like it split his face, despite her somber words. "I won't lie to you. That's asking a lot. It would be hard to let my wife stand in the line of fire every day. But the way I see it, I love you, and I'll be concerned whether you marry me or not."

He pushed himself up. Sheridan assisted with the pillows. He took the opportunity to pull her to him, wrap his arms around her. "This is where I need you to be when you're not sheriffin' and maybe sometimes when you are."

She nestled against him, filling his heart with pure joy. After a while, she eased from his embrace but kept her face near his. "And this is where I want to be when I'm not sheriffin' and maybe when I am."

"So, is that a yes? Will you be my wife?"

"What do you think?" She pressed her soft lips against his.

Until that moment, Carver hadn't realized he was parched and cracked like a forsaken desert. Sheridan's sweet lips poured her love into him, water spilling into the cracks and hard places of his heart. He'd longed to kiss her properly for far too long, and now, he wrapped his arms around her slender form and kissed her thoroughly. Drenched in her love, the pain from his wound was all but forgotten.

Sheridan was everything he needed.

A LOVE RISKED

Chapter 1

Legs burning, he pedaled hard and fast, willing his single-speed mountain bike up the rugged trail, his riding buddy, Rally Hayes, not far behind. As he veered from the track, junipers and sagebrush lashed out at Lucas Love on the right.

The rocky formations, twists and turns of the Dago Gulch in the Sheepshead Mountains tested the skills and endurance of hard-core mountain bikers. An experience with God's glorious creation, the trails didn't disappoint.

Lucas never got enough. He loved rising to the challenge, defying gravity when possible. He had two days off from his ATV and recreational vehicle business, Oregon Adventures, and intended to enjoy it to the fullest. He was an extreme sports junkie. Mountain biking, backpacking, hang gliding, mountain climbing. The riskier the better. Forget about that giant mess that he called an office—at least for today. Forget that owning your own business didn't return the freedom you thought.

Living in that reality was a necessary evil, but it wasn't living, it was existing.

A glimpse behind him revealed he'd lost Rally around the

lofty crags. He was getting too soft to keep up. Getting married and settling down could do that to a guy. That is, if you married a girl who wasn't an adrenaline junkie, too, like Rally had.

Lucas yanked the handlebars around for a hard stop, the back tire skidding a half circle and throwing pebbles and sand into the air. While he waited for Rally, he took a swig from his water bottle.

Rally appeared around the crag, panting through his mouth. By the look on his face, he was willing himself, willing the bike, up the hill.

"I was beginning to worry." Lucas replaced the bottle on the holder and laughed off Rally's glower.

Lucas jumped on his bike and started on the incline again, working his momentum back up. The sound of heavy breathing, wheels crunching against dirt, pebbles, and rocks, came from behind, drawing near and fast. Though Rally hadn't said as much, Lucas knew it was a race to the top.

He pushed himself harder. The muscles in his legs screamed. His lungs burned. And at the crest, he flew over the rise, releasing a shout.

The bike slammed into the ground, off-trail. His back wheel wedged between two boulders and stuck. Momentum threw Lucas into the air. He flew high, arcing over the trail, his arms and legs flailing, then slammed into the brush, thirty-plus feet from his bike.

After the initial shock fell away, Lucas groaned. He shook out his hands and legs, making sure nothing was broken.

Rally's face filled his vision. "Are you all right?"

Lucas laughed. "Man, that was great."

Reaching down, his buddy frowned and gripped Lucas's arm, assisting him up. "One of these days, you're going to get yourself killed."

Dusting himself off, Lucas made his way to the bike and tugged it from between the rocks where it had jarred. "It wouldn't be the same without the thrill, without the risk, would it?"

Rally helped him free the bike. "You're crazy, you know that? You've got no fear."

The tone in Rally's voice made Lucas look up. His friend wasn't smiling.

"What happened to you?" Lucas asked. "You used to call this fun."

Rally's skin gleamed with sweat. "I can't afford to get hurt and miss work. I have a family to support. You need to grow up."

A thousand retorts battled inside, but Lucas ignored the comment and, like Rally, got on his bike again. The frame remained sturdy and strong despite the collision with the boulders. Though he tried to recapture the spirit of the ride, the high it had given him, Rally's comment had sucked the life out of it.

Rally had wanted to join him today, but it hadn't been the same. Lucas had lost another friend to domesticity. Even two of his brothers were married now. But it had to happen eventually.

That was another reality. An existence Lucas wanted to avoid.

The next day Lucas and Rally hit the trails early but packed up at noon for their six-hour drive home from Oregon's eastern border, the Lake Owyhee State Park area. Refreshed from time spent in nature, he steered his pickup into the parking lot at Oregon Adventures. Several vehicles filled the parking spaces. Business was booming today as always. He'd like to avoid seeing the place for one day, maybe two, but. . .not going to happen.

He lived in the apartment at the back of the building.

He and Rally removed their bikes from the truck.

"Got plans?" Lucas asked, even though he knew the answer. "How about hanging out tonight?"

"I've got a wife and a kid now. You might try it sometime."

After seeing what that's done to you? I don't think so. Lucas chuckled. "I'm not husband material. What girl would want me for that?"

Why did Rally have to be so serious?

"It can't be like old times, Lucas. Why don't you come over to my house? We're grilling tonight."

Lucas helped Rally secure his bike on the back of his minivan. "You'd better ask Katy first. It's no secret she doesn't like me."

"Only because she thinks you're a bad influence. Or that you're going to get me killed by not filing a travel and rescue plan. Plus, I need to help with Jonathan. It's not fair for her to be the only one taking care of the baby. But come over and show her a different side." Rally grinned. "You never know. She might change her mind."

"Yeah, that'll be the day."

Rally climbed in and started the minivan. "I'm serious. Come over and bring a date. You haven't broken every heart in the county yet, have you?"

The words stung, but Lucas hid it with a smile. "Sure, I'll bring a date."

After Rally drove off, Lucas started for the back of the building, where his apartment and a hot shower waited.

"Lucas!" Ricky stepped through the front door of the rental business and waved Lucas over.

Ricky was one of the summer employees Lucas hired so he could take a day off. Two if he was lucky. "What's up?"

"There's a girl here, looking for a job. What do I tell her?"

"Tell her we've hired all we need for the summer. And would you take that HELP WANTED sign down, please?" He turned his back on Ricky, his shoulders knotting. He should get an apartment away from his business.

Ricky ran after him. "She's answering an ad you had in the paper for a bookkeeper. Not for summer help."

Lucas froze. She came by in person instead of calling first? He scratched his head, recalling he'd asked for interested parties to stop by. He'd long given up on anyone in the sparsely populated area answering that ad.

Images of an organized office and someone else doing his books danced in his head. Gripping Ricky's shoulders, he said, "Tell her to wait in the lobby. I'll be right with her." *After I shower off.*

This was the one person to answer his ad for a bookkeeper. He couldn't let her get away.

ଓ

Avery sat in the uncomfortable, hard plastic chair and watched the outdoorsy types come and go while she waited. At the moment, a burly man in his late thirties, two rough-and-tumble boys at his side, pounded on the counter, demanding assistance. Behind him, a woman, maybe forty, held hands with a man definitely ten years her junior.

On the other side of the counter, two college-aged kids scrambled to rent the recreational vehicles and appease customers. She felt sorry for them and impressed at the same time.

At least, if she got this job, she'd be in the back office. She wouldn't have to deal with the chaos and stress. She'd left the pressure and hassle behind in Portland, at least for the summer. At least until she decided what to do. Though she'd been laid off along with fifty others, she counted it a blessing.

Ever since her apartment had been broken into three months ago, she hadn't slept well, fearing another break-in. The next time she might be there.

The thought scared her.

A quiet, simple life in a less populated area was definitely more to her liking. She peered over her glasses—which she wore to look the part and not because she needed them except when working—at the framed photographs on the walls. One was simply a poster that read

REALITY:

THAT WHICH DOESN'T GO AWAY

WHEN YOU STOP BELIEVING IN IT.

Most of the other images portrayed people enjoying a sport. The word FEARLESS was in bold print underneath the image of someone riding an ATV over a sand dune. A scripture caption followed. FOR THE SPIRIT GOD GAVE US DOES NOT MAKE US TIMID, BUT GIVES US POWER, LOVE AND SELF-DISCIPLINE. 2 TIMOTHY 1:7

The verse struck a chord in her. Hadn't she just been thinking about fear? The poster also told her that someone at this business was a Christian.

"Hey." One of the behind-the-counter guys addressed her. "Follow me."

Avery shook away her musings and trailed the guy through a door—looking over her glasses to keep her balance as she walked—and down a short hallway to the last door on the right. A nameplate read LUCAS LOVE, OWNER.

Before he opened it, he smiled. "I'm Ricky, by the way. I hope you get the job. He needs all the help he can get."

"It's nice to meet you." Avery smiled, and adjusted her glasses.

Ricky opened the door and gestured for her to enter. Smiling, she stepped into utter chaos.

Her smile faltered when she saw the stacks of papers and files. Books and magazines hung jagged from a cheap bookshelf. All of this, she took in as she stepped into the office.

A dark-haired, sun-kissed man only a few years older than his help stood from behind the desk and came around, thrusting his hand out. "I'm Lucas Love."

He'd laid on the cologne a little thick for an interview, in her opinion, and his hair was damp, like he'd just taken a shower. A navy polo shirt clung to his muscular frame, and cargo shorts revealed bulging calves. Not exactly professional attire, but what did she expect? This was a business about having fun.

"I'm Avery Summers," she said, feeling entirely overdressed in her sure-to-get-the-job professional attire.

"Have a seat." Mr. Love returned to the chair behind his desk.

She tucked her navy blue skirt under as she sat and adjusted her suit jacket. "Thank you for seeing me, Mr. Love."

"Lucas is fine." He beamed at her, his thickly dimpled smile the kind to stop a young girl's heart. Thankfully, she wasn't that young or naive anymore. "You're here to interview for the part-time bookkeeper position, is that right?"

"Yes." Avery cleared her throat and tugged her résumé from her slim portfolio. "Here's my résumé."

He leaned forward, and when he took it their fingers brushed. Warmth spread through her. A warning rather than a welcome sensation.

Skimming the résumé, he cleared his throat. "Says here that you're a certified public accountant recently employed by Baker and Company in Portland. What's a girl like you doing in a place like this?"

Was he for real? Well, here went nothing. Avery shifted in her seat. "Mr. Love—"

"Lucas."

Taken aback, she stared at him then regrouped. "Lucas, can I be straight with you?"

He cocked a dimple-laden half smile. "I'm counting on it."

"My grandmother died and left me her house out here, and after paying the taxes I have a little money left. I'm tired of fighting traffic on the way to work, tired of the city. I used to visit my grandmother in the country, and I miss it." Her heart ached. Her last year of college, her parents died in a car accident in Portland. Her grandmother was all she had left until she died, too. "I'm looking for. . .quiet. Simple." *Safe.* No reason to tell him about her break-in.

His blue eyes were dark like the color of his shirt as he eased against the chair back and studied her. "And you're looking for a part-time job to keep you busy."

"Yes, that's it."

"Avery. . .can I call you Avery?"

"That's fine."

"Are you an outdoors girl? Ever ridden an ATV? That kind of thing?"

Her smile faltered. She'd lost the job already. "No. I've spent most of my time working, and catching up on work, ordering takeout because I'm too busy and too tired to cook. I haven't had much time for—"

"Fun?"

She glanced at her nervous hands. "Right, fun."

"You've come to the right place then."

"What. . .are you saying I got the job?"

He tossed the résumé on the desk. "You've got the job."

Grinning, he leaned back in the chair with his hands clasped behind his head.

"But, wait. I haven't had a chance to ask you any questions to determine if I want it or not. Like what does the job entail?" Avery glimpsed around his office. "Will I have my own office? Am I just doing the books? What?"

"Don't worry. I'm sure you can handle everything and still find time to relax and have fun. You and I have something in common. I grew up on a cattle ranch and did chores every waking minute of the day. That's why I started this business. So I could have fun while I work." He stood and moved to the door, opening it for her.

She grabbed her portfolio and tucked it under her arm, her compact purse hanging over her shoulder. Standing near him at the door, she gazed up at him. He was a little taller than her, but not much. Probably five-ten. "When do I start?"

"Come back on Monday and wear jeans. You can fill out the paperwork. We'll decide where to put your office. Move furniture around."

Maybe it wasn't what she was accustomed to in Portland, but it was new and different. Fresh and exciting. Lucas pulsated with energy and life.

But Avery couldn't stand there and stare at him forever. Nor, could she walk a straight line wearing her glasses. She slipped them off, then looked at Lucas. "See you Monday. And thanks for the job."

The vibrant smile behind Lucas's indigo eyes faded a little. What was that about?

Chapter 2

Lucas paced the small living room in his bachelor's pad, thumbing through the pages in his little black book and waiting for Clarice to pick up on the other end. He'd never had a chance to transfer the contact information over to his phone.

"Hello?"

His pulse raced. "Clarice, hi. It's Lucas."

She hung up.

Clarice was the third girl he'd called, and the only one to actually answer besides Emily, his sister-in-law Darcy's friend. Emily already had plans.

It was twenty minutes until seven. Lucas had told Rally he'd be there with a date. Even if he found one of the few single girls left in town willing to go out with him, it was still short notice.

Was it his fault he wasn't ready to commit? Lucas couldn't help it that he hadn't found the *one* yet, nor was he looking. Finding someone that would tie him down and hold him back terrified him. That he had this bad boy reputation ate at his insides. He didn't deserve it. Nor did he want to hurt anyone.

He plopped on the sofa and propped his feet on the coffee table. If he showed up at Rally's without a date—someone to talk to Katy and distract her—her attention would fall on Lucas and his inability to commit, on how he'd hurt her friend. Make that, friends.

Pressing his head against the sofa, he growled, frustrated with this part of his life. Nor was he one hundred percent happy with running his own business. It hadn't given him the freedom or the time he'd wanted to do the things he loved, but he couldn't think of anything else he'd rather do.

All he knew was that he worked hard and deserved to play hard.

He skimmed the pages of the address book he'd kept for years. Lucas sighed. Just before Avery Summers had left his office, for a split second, he'd considered inviting her along with him tonight. He could tell her it would be a great way to meet people since she was new in town. But he didn't want to be too forward and lose his bookkeeper before she'd had a chance to clean up his cluttered books.

Today when he'd seen Avery glide into his office, wearing her professional navy suit, hair pulled back, wearing glasses and looking like a schoolmarm, he'd trusted she could do the job. In fact, she was overqualified. But he'd understood her dilemma, her need to escape her life in Portland.

Then when she'd removed her glasses, her immense blue eyes had caught him off guard, and he'd noticed her golden hair—she was definitely a natural beauty hidden beneath her prim professional coating.

He recalled Rally's words that Lucas had no fear. Rally was wrong. Lucas feared losing the life he had. Falling in love and getting married could ruin everything. He'd watched it happen over and over—seen his friends fall, one by one. Witnessed his brothers becoming slaves to matrimony. None of their lives had stayed the same. And that's why he wouldn't give Avery a second look—she could be dangerous for the life he'd built.

An hour later, Lucas stood on the porch at Rally's ranch-style home, wishing he'd canceled, but he was tired of eating alone. They'd had a good time today, and he didn't want that to end. Just a few more laughs—the perfect ending to a good day. That is, if Katy didn't start in on him.

The door swung open. Rally stood there with a big smile. He glanced behind Lucas and frowned. "Don't tell me you came alone."

"I tried—"

"After that razzing I gave you today, I figured you'd bring someone even if you had to tie her up to get her here." Rally pulled him inside.

"It's that bad, huh?" Lucas rubbed his jaw, reconsidering his decision. "I can leave now, if that would be better."

His friend looked behind him then leaned closer. He spoke in low tones. "Katy had gotten a babysitter for us tonight since I was gone last night. I was in trouble for inviting you, but then she invited a new neighbor over. That means I'll live. That means she'll want her new friend to feel welcome. As long as you don't make any moves on the new girl, we're good."

Someone new in town? I wonder. . .

Lucas nodded. "I'm sure I can manage that."

"Honey? You watching the grill?" Katy meandered around the corner from the kitchen, holding dishes and silverware. "Hi, Lucas. Glad you were able to come."

Though her smile was pleasant and warm, she didn't fool Lucas. "Thanks, Katy. I wouldn't miss it."

"Rally said you were bringing a date." She looked at her husband.

If she didn't want him to break any more hearts, why would she want him to bring a date? But he didn't dare voice the question. Probably, she wanted him to show signs of becoming husband material, becoming domestic. "I tried, but it was short notice. I guess you're stuck with me all by my lonesome."

"Not a chance. I've got a friend coming over. She's new in town." Katy paused and pointed her finger at Lucas. "Don't get any ideas."

Lucas held up his palms. "I wouldn't think of it."

Katy headed out the french doors. "Rally, the grill."

Rally punched his arm. "Did I tell you I'm glad you could make it? Now I've got someone to talk to. Let's go outside and grill." He grunted. "Be manly men."

Lucas laughed. He was feeling better already about the life he'd chosen. Rally was totally in prison.

Just as Rally stepped through the french doors ahead of Lucas, someone knocked at the front door. Lucas strolled back through the living room. He was curious to meet the new neighbor.

When he opened the door, he was met by immense blue eyes that widened, recognizing him, and golden hair spilling past the girl's shoulders in soft curls.

ଓ

"Um. . .hi." Avery offered a smile to the man who'd hired her less than three hours ago. He wore the same cargo shorts, but had changed into a T-shirt that said FEARLESS and reminded her of that poster at his shop. "This is a surprise."

"For me, too." He swung the door wide. "Come in."

Avery slid past him into the small foyer. Well, this was awkward. She lifted the plate of chocolate chip cookies she held. "I brought cookies."

"I see that." He grinned. "Let's find out where Katy wants you to put them."

The woman herself stepped through french doors from the backyard. When she spotted Avery, her face beamed. "You made it."

Avery smiled at her new neighbor. Katy rushed to Avery's side and squeezed her shoulders. She'd been just wonderful, and so far, the only person to welcome her since she'd moved into her grandmother's old house last week.

"Where should I put the cookies?" Avery asked.

"Lucas, would you mind grabbing that pitcher of tea?" Katie asked. To Avery she said, "Let's go outside. The weather's nice and Rally is grilling. We'll put the cookies on the table out there."

Avery allowed Katy to usher her into the spacious backyard

and away from Lucas. "I see you've already met Rally's friend."

Avery nodded and sat in the lawn chair Katy offered. Lucas came out of the house with the pitcher. "I met him today. He's my new boss."

Katy's mouth dropped open. "Your new boss? I thought. . .I didn't know you were looking for a job. There are several places that have openings I'm sure you'd love."

Lucas placed the pitcher on the table then stood next to Rally at the grill. "No need for that, Katy. I'm sure Avery and I will get along just fine. I need a bookkeeper, and she's already accepted the job."

"How do you want your steak, Avery?" Rally interjected.

"Medium rare is fine." Avery sensed the tension between Katy and Lucas in the living room, but thought she'd imagined it. "He's right. It's part-time, just what I'm looking for."

Katy didn't appear convinced, her gaze wavering between Avery and Lucas. "It's none of my business, but if you change your mind, let me know."

A glower flickered in Lucas's dark-water eyes. What was going on? Avery felt like the two were somehow fighting over her. The whole thing hit her wrong. A small laugh escaped her, and everyone looked at her.

"It's nothing. Been a long day, that's all. Dinner smells wonderful. I'm hungry."

"I hear you," Rally said. "Let's eat."

Grateful that she was no longer the focus of the conversation, she followed Katy and the two men to the table and sat in a cushioned chair. Lucas set the plate loaded with steaks in the middle.

"There are two rares, one medium, and one well-done. Let me know if you want something else," Rally said.

Avery enjoyed the company of her new neighbors, Rally and Katy, and was glad for their invitation to dinner. Lucas was a great guy, and definitely a man who loved adventure. He and Rally could hardly talk about anything else. Avery sensed Katy wasn't happy about that.

They talked well after they'd finished dinner until it grew dark. Rally flicked on the outdoor lights and lit a few candles on the table.

Avery yawned. "Oh, excuse me." She offered a sheepish grin.

"Is it past your bedtime?" Lucas leaned back in the chair, hands clasped behind his head like he'd done in his office today.

"Lucas." Katy scolded him like he was a child.

"I guess I am a little tired. I should probably head home."

Rally's eyes widened. "No, wait. You'll miss the best part."

Clueless, Avery smiled and shrugged. "The best part? What's that?"

"We go to the ridge and look at the stars. It's amazing," Rally said. He glanced at Katy and shrugged. "What?"

"If she's tired, let the girl go home." Katy stood, gathering plates.

Rally took some of the dishes. "She's new here. She won't know what she's missing until we show her."

Curious, Avery glanced at Lucas, hoping for a better explanation. He grinned and stood, reaching for her plate and stacking it on his. "The stars. Away from the light pollution you can see the Milky Way. Rally even has a telescope for nights like this."

Speaking in hushed but argumentative tones, Katy and Rally headed into the house.

"I don't want to intrude," Avery said. She started to pick up a few glasses and utensils to follow the couple.

Lucas placed his hand over hers, pressing it to the table. "Wait. Give them a minute. And. . .you're not intruding. Rally wants you to see the stars."

She stared at Lucas's hand, still covering hers. "I'm more worried about what Katy wants. Why are they arguing? What did I miss?"

She slipped her hand out from under his, regretting the words. She knew little of the people who lived next to her grandmother and didn't want to say something that would offend them.

"I don't know exactly. But if I had to guess, I'd say that Rally decided on the stars before clearing it with Katy. She might have other plans."

Rally came out of the house, a strained smile on his face. "Katy isn't feeling like stars tonight. How about video games?"

Lucas scratched the back of his head and laughed. "You serious?"

Rally moved to finish cleaning off the table. "She doesn't feel good, so let's just hang out here. Sorry."

"All the more reason for me to head home." Avery loaded her arms with as much as she could grab. "Right after I do the dishes."

She ignored Rally's chiding and went inside, finding Katy at the kitchen sink. Avery set the dishes down and touched

Katy's arm, uncertain if she should press the woman. "I'm sorry you're not feeling well. Let me finish the dishes for you."

Katy laughed and wiped at her wet cheeks. "Oh, I'm fine. Rally does the dishes, so you don't need to worry. I'm sorry you had to see our disagreement. And your first evening at my house. Jonathan keeps me up at night, so I'm cranky lately. I'd like a chance to make it up to you. Maybe lunch sometime?"

Avery smiled. "That sounds good. I told your husband I wouldn't stay for video games. If it's all right with you, I've had a long day and need to get home."

Looking through the kitchen window into the backyard, Katy stiffened. Avery followed her gaze and spotted Lucas walking toward the house. He was rugged, sturdy, warm, and friendly. Owned his own business, so he wasn't a slacker.

"I don't get it. Why don't you like him?" Avery asked.

"He's just one of Rally's friends who rubs me the wrong way. Let's leave it at that. You're going to work for the man. I don't want to color your opinion of him."

Gee, thanks.

Chapter 3

On Monday morning, Avery shoved through the doors of Oregon Adventures, feeling refreshed from the weekend. She'd unpacked a few more boxes and hung new curtains on Saturday, and visited a small church in Carnegie on Sunday. That had given her ample time to shove Katy's vague words about her new boss far from her thoughts.

Customers were just beginning to fill the lobby—some renting and others needing parts or repair.

Ricky looked up from the computer screen and smiled when he saw her. "So, today's your first day."

Avery slid behind the counter to stand next to him. "It's nothing I can't handle." After all, she'd spent three years working full-time for an accounting firm.

A man about Ricky's age, wearing shorts and a dirty T-shirt, scowled. "Can you get me this part or what? I need it fixed today."

Avery left Ricky to make the customer happy, glad she didn't have to stand at the counter and face demanding people all day. Though she'd left the stress and chaos of her job in Portland, wanting to take time for herself, at least for a couple of months, she knew she'd go crazy if she gave up work completely. Part-time was perfect for now. She'd have time to fix up her grandmother's house and ultimately, decide if she wanted to stay or not. She hadn't shared that information with Lucas, but in the end, she might decide to stay.

Even though she wanted peace and quiet, and to simplify her life, the slower-paced community would still take getting used to.

She meandered down the hall to Lucas's office. His door stood open but he wasn't there. Avery dropped her bag in one of the chairs, looking forward to having her own office. She came prepared to set that up, wearing jeans and a T-shirt like he suggested.

A motor revved along with shouts from somewhere in the back. Avery continued down the hallway and opened a door to what appeared to be an ATV repair shop. The air smelled like exhaust. Bright sunlight filtered in from the opened garage door, and it was a minute before her eyes adjusted. Lucas stood with another man—the mechanic?—pointing at something on a four-wheeler. They were shouting over the noise as the mechanic revved the motor again.

Lucas appeared grimy and sweaty. Did he also work on the ATVs? She made her way down the concrete steps, hoping he hadn't forgotten he'd hired her.

She stood right next to him before he noticed her. He did a double take like he actually *had* forgotten. His smile made up for it.

"You forgot about me, didn't you?" she asked, teasing.

Deep furrows grew between his brows. "No, of course not." But something in his exaggerated manner told her otherwise. "As far as I'm concerned, right now, you are the most wanted woman on the planet."

At his words, her heart skipped a half beat, but she knew what he meant and recovered. "You must be hurting for an accountant more than I thought." What had she gotten herself into?

Lucas weaved his arm around her without touching her and gestured toward the mechanic. "Avery Summers, I'd like you to meet Mark Thompson. He repairs the ATVs, our rentals and the out-of-towners who brought their own to ride the dunes."

"Nice to meet you." Mark wiped his hands, black with grease, on a rag without much effect.

She hoped he didn't want to shake her hand. If her friends and associates in Portland could see her now, they'd think she'd lost her mind to take a job like this instead of holding out for something at a distinguished accounting firm. But her time here wasn't about the job.

She smiled. "And you, Mark."

"I'll see you later. I've got to get Avery set up on the computer." Lucas motioned for her to walk ahead of him.

She walked to the steps that led back inside.

"Did you have a good weekend?" he asked.

She turned to answer, but he was already in front of her, opening the door, his ocean blue eyes bright today.

"Yes. Thanks for asking." She walked through the door he held, her skin tingling at his nearness. What was the matter with her?

Something about him—his virility and exuberance, she wasn't sure—excited her. The guy was a flirt and a charmer. Was that what Katy didn't like about him? Avery reminded herself she wasn't sixteen.

Lucas led her into his office. "I've decided you can have my office."

"What? But where will you work?"

His gaze flicked over her so quickly she almost didn't see. "You wore jeans like I asked. You can wear that every day if you want. The only room I could put you in is filled with parts and supplies. I'm sorry I didn't work on that this weekend, but that would take days. Besides, you're only here half the day. My office is fine."

"But. . ." Avery wasn't sure how to react. She wouldn't have her own space to put pictures, to store her things. "You're the boss."

"I hate working in an office anyway. With you doing the work that kept me here, that'll free me up for other things. You don't mind sharing, at least for a while, do you?"

"No, not at all, but. . ." Avery hesitated.

"Say what you're thinking. I promise it won't hurt my feelings." His charm-loaded grin tickled her insides.

She laughed. "Well, would you mind showing me the room where you thought to put me? Maybe I can work on it in my spare time."

"Sure. I'll show you. But I don't want you moving things by yourself. No offense, but you're a little puny." He chuckled. "You could get hurt."

She smiled, wanting to gift him with a friendly smack, but refrained. Lucas strolled out of the office, and Avery followed. He entered a door down the hall to the left. The room was stacked with boxes of motor parts, but he crossed the space to another door.

He cracked it and slipped through. When Avery followed, she shoved the door completely open, disturbing a box crammed on a shelf.

"This is it," he said. "I bought this business from a guy who'd had it for years. You can see he got behind. I haven't had the time either."

"This is where you planned to put me?" Another room filled with boxes and parts. Disheveled couldn't describe it. If it took her a thousand years, she couldn't get it clean. "How does anyone find what they need in here?"

Suddenly, the box above the door shifted and tumbled from the shelf.

"Watch out." At lightning speed, Lucas moved her out of harm's way, pressing her against the wall. Parts tumbled across the floor.

Breathless, Avery stood in his protective hold and looked into his eyes. Though he'd thrust her out of the box's path, he hadn't manhandled her. His hands gripped her arms, but gently.

"See what I mean?" His face near hers, his voice was tender. Lucas's gaze brushed over Avery's face, lingering on her lips.

For a split second, she could swear he was going to kiss her. For a millisecond of that, she wanted him to.

A slight frown morphed over his expression. He stepped

back. "Avery, I love the outdoors. I spend every minute I can living for adventure. For fun."

"I get it. You're addicted to thrills."

Lucas leaned his hand against the wall. "You understand me then. That's good."

"You don't have time for anything else like organizing your business, or. . .dating."

Avery hoped her smile hid the cringe inside. She wasn't flirting, but it sounded that way. Why, oh why had she blurted that?

Six thirty Friday afternoon couldn't have come soon enough for Lucas.

Jerry Seymour stood at the entrance to the garage, holding the keys to his ATV. He grinned, despite his frustration. "Glad I was at least able to rent one while you fixed this, but I don't get why it took you so long. I'm leaving to head home to the coast today. That's cutting it close."

Lucas left Mark to explain and assist Jerry in driving the ATV onto his trailer, and he headed back inside. He thought hiring Avery would free up his time. Instead he'd never been so busy—but maybe he'd taken care of a few things that were long overdue.

In the restroom, he washed his hands and face. He'd left her on her own earlier in the week—her first day to be exact—to face what he considered an accounting nightmare. But with her experience it should be a no-brainer. He'd made good on his decision not to give Avery a second look because once he'd tucked her in his office, he hadn't seen her except a few times when she had a question.

Unfortunately, he'd struggled with not giving her a second thought. She was *all* he'd thought about throughout the week ever since that moment in the back office. A box weighed down with carburetor parts had almost fallen on her. He'd prevented that, but he hadn't prevented her cute smile from driving through the sandbags around his heart. Hopefully he would recover—repair the damage and divert his attention back to important things like having fun. Planning what he'd do on his next day off.

He exited the restroom and walked around the corner to his office to lock things up and there sat Avery, staring at his computer. What was she still doing here?

She worked a half day in the mornings, didn't she? He wasn't sure when she came and left, but he trusted her.

Lucas leaned against the doorframe, crossing his feet at his ankles and studied her, figuring she'd notice him. Her hair was loosely pinned on top of her head, a few thick sections hanging down willy-nilly, mingling with her butterfly earrings. It was an untamed look for her, but contrasted by the dark-rimmed glasses she wore, and the pencil she'd tucked in her ear.

Beautiful. Lucas sighed. *Why are you here when I've avoided you all week?*

"Avery," he said, when she didn't notice him. "Avery. . ." a little louder this time.

Nothing. Wow, she'd become engrossed in her work. Lucas

crept around the desk and leaned in, his head next to hers, and hovered just above her shoulders.

"Avery!"

She screamed and jumped, whirling the chair around to face him.

Lucas burst out laughing. The look on her face told him she didn't find it funny.

"I couldn't help it. I stood there forever watching you. Even called your name. You never budged."

She blew out a breath, ruffling the blond strand that hung over her face. "Really?" She had the sweetest voice.

"Really." Lucas had avoided her this week, he realized, for good reason. He liked her. A lot.

"I'm sorry. I just. . ."

"You're only supposed to work part-time. What are you doing here?"

"Your books are such a mess that I'm stressed. I can't relax until I fix things." She said it all matter-of-factly and stood to stretch.

Lucas noticed her slim figure—what he'd called puny earlier. Her jeans hugged her and her button-down collared shirt, rather than a T-shirt, which everyone around here normally wore, accented her slight form.

He averted his gaze. "Have you got plans tomorrow?"

Dude. What are you doing?

Her big baby blues—innocent and clear—searched his. "I. . .uh. . .probably."

He snorted a laugh. "Probably? Do you want to go hang gliding?"

"Are you crazy?"

"No. You look like you could use some sun. You're pretty pale. Did you know that?" Good way to encourage the new employee.

She pressed her hand to her cheek. "I am?"

"What I mean is that fresh air and sunshine would be good for you. My guess is that you've been inside all week."

"I'd planned to work tomorrow. I can't stand this"—she gestured at the computer screen—"this drives me nuts. And besides. . ."

Lucas realized that he stood too close, cornering her behind his desk. He quickly put space between them, strolling around the desk, and dropped into one of the chairs across the room. Plenty of space. Was it for her, or for him?

Avery appeared to breathe easier. He was such a moron. Katy was probably right about him.

"You were saying?" he asked.

"I like you, Lucas. But you're my boss. Aside from the occasional dinner with mutual friends, I don't want to. . .get involved. I'm not an action-adventure girl. I like to garden and sew and bake bread. That's one of the reasons I wanted to live in my grandmother's house, well, now my house. It reminds me of who I was, who I lost. I want all that back."

"And instead you're stressed because of my terrible accounting practices." Lucas injected a smile, hoping to deflect her serious tone, even though her rejection had stung a little.

"Don't worry. I'll have things repaired in no time. Then I'll have time for fun. Only I have a different definition than you do." She looked down at the desk, pink coloring her fair skin. Finally, she glanced back at him, her gaze soft and tender, making this even harder for him. "Are we good?"

Lucas grinned, willing it to reach his eyes. "We're good."

Though he stood his ground, a few grains of sand slid away from the wall around his heart.

Chapter 4

Avery stood at her kitchen sink, preparing to boil pasta while her olive bread baked in the oven.

Another Saturday. She'd worked for Lucas for three weeks now. What crazy adventure or extreme sport had he done today? After she'd explained she wasn't interested in thrill-seeking and had drawn the line regarding their relationship, he hadn't invited her again. Nor had he said much to her that included his dimple-faced, broad grin.

Avery missed that.

The truth was he'd planted a small seed in her for adventure. Part of her wanted to do something risky for a change. Feel the vibrant passion for life burn inside her that she saw in Lucas. He made her realize she had a certain fear of living. She was tired of that.

But keeping him at a distance was for the best, wasn't it? Besides, focusing on her job was difficult when Lucas was near.

He'd bought accounting software, thinking that would make his life easier, but he still hadn't figured out how to use it. So, she worked to enter all the previous information for the year while processing the current month's business, and correcting errors he'd made along the way.

Fortunately, she'd have his things in order soon and could work part-time like she was supposed to. Then she wouldn't have to worry about avoiding him. The guy was all power and brawn, the exact opposite of the men she knew in Portland. Actually, there were plenty of extreme sports enthusiasts in Portland, athletic types, but none of them ever noticed Avery. Only other accountants had asked her out, and they hadn't been into anything more than miniature golf. Nor had anyone ignited her senses or pervaded her thoughts like Lucas.

Maybe it was ridiculous to believe Lucas had noticed her, but she sensed there was something between them. From his perspective, that was probably because there weren't many women around for Lucas to choose from. Or maybe it was like Katy said. He'd already hurt every woman within a hundred miles, including Katy's closest friends. Maybe he was just like all the other guys she'd known—he ran when he got too close. That made more sense.

Avery frowned at the thought. Through the kitchen window, she watched a coyote traipse across the back of her property. Good thing she didn't have a small pet to worry about, except that having one to keep her company would be nice. Living in such a sparsely populated area—Carnegie boasted only four hundred people—loneliness hounded her.

She'd wanted this—the quiet and simple life, but she'd had difficulty sleeping. Sometimes at night the silence would give way to the coyotes or wolves howling, all manner of creatures and their noises.

Avery pushed aside her dismal thoughts. She focused on making pasta for one and checked on the bread in the oven. She loved the aroma that filled the house, but her newfound hobby making artisan breads wasn't much fun without someone to share it with. She'd attended the small community church where her grandmother had attended, and had met people who knew her grandmother, but relationships were slow going, except for her neighbor Katy, of course.

Finally, Avery poured off the water from the penne just as someone knocked on the door. The thought of a visitor made her happy. Had to be Katy.

"Just a minute," Avery called. She wiped her hands on a towel, left the pasta steaming in a colander in the sink, and rushed to the door to peer through the peephole.

Lucas? Avery swung the door open to find the man who never left her thoughts leaning against the brick wall, his legs crossed at his ankles, and looking like he was born to make girls swoon. He wore his signature cargo shorts, exposing his muscular legs, and a T-shirt tight enough to outline his well-formed chest. And he wore that grin framed with dimples that she hadn't seen in over a week. Her heart surfed a giant wave of emotion.

"What are you doing here?" she asked, trying to hide her smile. But it was no use. She was glad to see him.

Lucas opened his mouth, about to say something, but then paused. "What is that amazing smell?" He shoved from the wall and stood there, waiting for her to invite him in.

"I made olive bread. It's baking, and I need to take it out soon."

His deep-sea eyes grew wide. "You *made* olive bread? That explains all the white stuff on your clothes and face. Are you going to invite me in to share, or leave me standing outside, cold and hungry?"

"I thought we discussed this. I work for you. There is a line drawn between us. Why are you here?" Avery laughed a little, going for teasing banter, instead of a harsh tone.

Lucas straightened his face, growing serious, though his eyes beamed with a smile. "I came by to scold you for bringing work home with you."

"Uh. . .how did you know?"

"I can see it spread across the coffee table from here." He laughed. "Now, can I have some bread?"

His laugh melted her resolve. "I would love to share my bread, but you can't stay because Katy might see your truck, and then I wouldn't hear the end of it."

"Oh." His smile faltered.

"But I have an idea. Why don't you take me to see the stars?"

"The stars?"

"You know, that night at Rally's, he wanted to see the stars. We'll take the bread with us. It's a big loaf, and I'm glad to share it with someone."

He smiled again. "Olive bread under the stars? That's the best idea I've heard in a long time."

She giggled and hurried to the kitchen to pull the bread from the oven, leaving the door open and Lucas to trail after her. Thankfully, she caught the bread before it baked too long. She dumped the loaf out of the cast-iron pot onto a cooling rack. One of several bread-baking methods she'd experimented with.

"That looks wonderful. I don't think I've ever tasted fresh bread, warm from the oven."

"And you won't at my house."

"Huh?"

"It's a myth that you should eat it while it's hot. The bread is still cooking while it cools." She wrapped the round olive loaf in a flour sack towel. "You grab the sodas from the fridge. The bread will cool while we drive."

"What about that pasta in the sink?"

"Leave it. It's nothing special. The bread is enough." Avery wiped her face with a towel and dusted her clothes to knock off the excess flour. Her kitchen floor also showed evidence of her bread-baking, flour everywhere. She loved that.

As Lucas backed from the driveway, Avery looked out the window and smiled to herself. She was taking a risk tonight, but it felt good. Right.

Katy stood in her own yard and waved at Avery. She waved back. Lucas shifted into DRIVE and soon, Katy slipped from view.

"Sorry that we didn't escape Katy," Lucas said. "I'm sure she had to fill your head with stuff about me."

"I've never been big on listening to rumors and conjecture." Though Katy's words were spoken from the experiences of close friends, there were always two sides to every story. Avery hadn't heard Lucas's side. She'd give him that. And she wanted to enjoy this evening.

It was one thing to avoid Lucas at work and try her best to stop thinking about him, but his appearance on her doorstep and her desire to be with him had buried all her well-intentioned resolutions in the sand.

☙

Lucas steered the truck out of town. "You know, I can hardly believe you're with me right now, going to see the stars, holding that loaf of bread. My mouth is watering it smells so good."

"You and me both. How far is this place?"

He glanced her way, admiring the soft golden curls splayed across her shoulder, the curve of her jaw, her unblemished, peachy-cream skin, which had a little more color to it than when he'd first met her.

She peeked at him, caught him staring. "You need to watch the road."

"Oh, sorry." He stared straight ahead. "It's about fifteen or twenty minutes. There's a ledge where we like to park. The stars are clear just about anywhere in this area, but getting a little higher makes it all the better. Tell me about making bread. You do that often?"

Lucas wanted to hear everything about her. For one thing, he enjoyed her sweet voice—like cream and sugar on a bowl of strawberries in the morning.

He listened while he drove. She was meticulous in detailing every aspect of making bread—the types of yeast and flours to use and slow fermentation meant more flavor—that she made the topic interesting to him.

"Who knew there was so much to it," he said. Could there be more to enjoying life than his kind of fun?

He had a feeling that if he spent much time with Avery, she could open up a new world for him. Where was his resolve to stay away from her because she could ruin everything about the life he'd built?

She continued on about the different breads she'd made, and the feel of the dough under her fingers. Lucas drove, listening to her passion-filled voice.

At last, he reached the base of the rise. He steered his truck along the bumpy incline, taking care to watch the road, though it wasn't completely dark yet. He backed up so the bed of the truck was nearest the ledge. After he parked and turned off the ignition, he climbed out.

Avery came around the truck to meet him. "Wow, this is an amazing view."

"We usually sit on the tailgate, or if I'd known, I could have brought chairs. But I do have a blanket in the back in case you get cold."

They settled on the tailgate. Avery tore off a chunk of bread and handed it to Lucas. He took a bite and savored the taste. "You are one amazing cook. The bread tastes like olives."

A long-forgotten memory drifted forward. He was five or six. His mother baked bread and pies, filling the house with good smells. Lucas had forgotten how much he liked that. He could get used to good smells again. He washed the bread down with the soda—what was he thinking? Good smells went hand in hand with being domestic. He thought about Rally and how little fun he had. Lucas never heard Rally mention that Katy made bread.

"You never told me why you stopped by," she said. "I mean, really. Because you didn't know that I'd taken work home with me, so why did you come?"

Avery looked small sitting on the tailgate compared to the expansive, dusky sky. He wanted to curl her into his arms and protect her. From what he didn't know. "I've been thinking about something. Since you work for a recreational business it's important for you to experience at least some of that."

She choked on her soda then slid the back of her hand across her mouth. "You're going to have to do better than that."

What? She didn't believe him? Not only could she bake a mean loaf of bread, she could read people.

"Can I be straight with you?" He grinned, hoping she remembered when she'd asked him that same question during her interview.

"I'm counting on it." Her perfect lips curved into a soft smile.

Good. She remembered. But that meant he would have to open up. He sighed, unsure if he was ready. He waited until he had her full attention—her baby blues focused on him and nothing else.

There. Her amazingly big eyes, shaped sort of like teardrops, watched him. The only thing giving him courage to speak his mind was the fact that she was here with him now. Her idea, in a manner of speaking.

"A couple weekends ago, I went hang gliding. I invited you,

but you didn't want to go and handed me your spiel about our relationship. But. . ."

Her smile didn't falter at the mention of her spiel. "Go on."

"All I kept thinking was that it would have been more fun with you. Avery, come with me. I can show you things you can't imagine." *And experience everything for the first time again through your eyes.* Where had that come from?

Her soft smile spread wide, revealing her perfect white teeth. "You realize this is what Katy warned me about. That you would try to charm me."

"Is that what you think? Because I can tell you that I never led anyone on. All I ever wanted was friendship. Camaraderie. I never meant to hurt anyone. I wouldn't do that intentionally."

"I know. . ." She looked away, her eyes on the valley below.

The night fell, the stars filled his vision, except for Avery. Did she really believe that about him? Would she give him an answer to his invitation?

Their conversation lagged, both of them caught up in their own thoughts. The silence was comfortable as they lay back in the truck bed and looked at the stars and the swirling oval that was the Milky Way galaxy.

"How do you like living in no man's land so far?" Lucas asked.

"If I could get your books in order I might have time to find out." She elbowed him, laughing. "I admit, though I wanted to work part-time, I find it beyond difficult to let it go. Work for me is like a compulsion, kind of like your addiction to adrenaline."

"I don't know if that's a good comparison considering you're afraid of the very things I live for."

"From what I can tell, you're very much afraid of the accounting required to run a business." Avery sat up. "Did you see that? It was a shooting star! I mean, huge."

Lucas hadn't seen it and even now, he couldn't pull his eyes from Avery. He remembered that day in the back room when the box had fallen. He'd been so near her and her sweet lips—he'd wanted to kiss her.

Leaning back on her arms, her hair cascaded behind her head and almost touched the truck bed. Lucas couldn't help himself. He slipped his hand through her thick, blond mane and cradled her head, turning her face toward him.

When she didn't resist, but instead closed her eyes, Lucas brushed his lips against hers, gently at first. He cupped her face in his hands, relishing her response and the electric charge she sent through him—like nothing he'd experienced. Instantly, he sensed when her response reversed on him, and she pulled back, breathless. Hurt and anger swirled in her eyes.

Chapter 5

I shouldn't have done that." Lucas let go and leaned away, his expression taut. "I'm sorry."

She slipped from the tailgate and wiped her slick hands down her jeans. "Not your fault. It was my idea to come here alone with you. And I kissed you back."

"Then what's wrong?" Lucas hopped off the truck and slammed the tailgate. "It's Katy, isn't it? You're afraid what she said about me is true, that I'll hurt you."

Oh, she was afraid all right. Afraid of what this man could do to her heart, but she wasn't about to admit that to him.

"You said it yourself. I'm afraid of the very things you live for. We're too different. We work together. And. . .the truth is. . ."

He'd been open with her, sharing that he'd wanted her to be with him when he went hang gliding or biking or all the other things he loved to do. She studied him for a moment. She could barely see his face but for the stars in the night sky, still she was close enough to see the frown lines in his forehead and around his eyes. That her reaction bothered him this much touched her. His dark blue eyes penetrated hers. She could feel him searching for answers. But she had none.

"What is the truth, Avery?"

"Part of me wants to do something new, something risky. I'd love for you to show me a slice of your life. Maybe—maybe we could help each other. Maybe you can free me from being a workaholic. Maybe I can help you to settle down, enjoy life outside of adrenaline-pumped thrills. But, I don't want to hurt you, Lucas. Let's just be friends."

She'd flipped things a little on him, made him the one at risk. Would it work?

Under the star-flickering night sky, she could make out his big dimpled grin and her heart jumped—she wanted to kiss him again. He took a step toward her, and Avery sensed the attraction between them growing stronger, despite her words.

With his next step, she thought to back away, but she didn't. She let him draw near and slip his hands over her arms, then slowly around her back. Avery stepped into his embrace and lifted her face to receive the kiss they both wanted.

"Tomorrow, Avery." His lips hovered near hers and, when he whispered, his breath warmed her cheeks. "Tomorrow we can be friends. But for this moment, it's too late."

He covered her lips with his. Joy and warmth spread through her heart and mind, all the way down to her toes. Without realizing it, she'd slipped her hands around his neck, and now she pulled him closer. Was this how love was supposed to feel? And if she wasn't in love, if he didn't return it, should they be kissing? The thought battled for her attention and lost. She could stay in his embrace forever.

He eased his lips from hers, slowly and gently, keeping her wrapped in a cocoon of his affection. His forehead pressed against hers, they lingered in the afterglow. Avery didn't want to break the connection.

She smiled, and his lips spread wide in return. "Tomorrow is going to come too fast."

"I know." He drew in a languishing breath and released it slowly. "Are you going to hold me to this friends-only thing?"

"Yes. Remember, I don't want to hurt you. In the end, you could fall in love with me, but I can't fit into your lifestyle."

"I've never met anyone like you before. Can I still come over to your house and eat bread?"

With that, Avery allowed her head to rock back in laughter. "We'll see," she teased.

He gave her a cockeyed frown then brushed his hand down her cheek. "What would you like to try first? Hang gliding? Four-wheeling? Mountain biking? The list goes on."

Avery twisted her hair behind her head, drawing in a strained sigh. "I don't know."

"Don't worry. I'll take it easy on you."

"Surprise me."

"Tomorrow, I'll pick you up after church. I used to go to your grandmother's church. Is that where you attend? It gets out at eleven thirty, right?"

Her grandmother had known Lucas, then. How Avery wished she could hear what her grandmother would say about him. "Why don't you come with me?"

"I go to a cowboy church where my older brother Carver

and his wife go. It makes them happy and keeps him off my back. But I'd rather go somewhere else. Sure, I'll come with you."

"Off your back about what?"

"It's the older brother arrogance, thinking he's the head of the family and has to watch out for everybody. He thinks he needs to ride me all the time about. . ."

Avery snickered. "About growing up, settling down, getting married."

He ran his hand down his face. "Yeah, that. But he waited long enough to get married. He's in his thirties, and he just married the sheriff six months ago."

"Well, you're a good younger brother to at least go to church with him and keep him happy, as you put it." Avery climbed into the truck.

Lucas drove her home. She was taking the biggest risk of her life where he was concerned.

Fearless. . .something told her she'd need to be fearless.

Sitting on his quad, Lucas squinted in the sunlight. Over ten thousand acres of sand dunes waited to be explored. Just one of the dangers lay in all the other explorers that would be out there today as well. Sometimes, people got hurt. Collisions happened.

The dunes had fascinated him since he was a boy and now were the source of his livelihood. He decided that since this was his business, riding an ATV over the dunes should be the first thing for Avery to experience, and probably the easiest compared to all his other activities.

She stood next to her quad and adjusted the helmet that accentuated her big blues while it dwarfed the rest of her. When she slid over the top of the quad her movements were lithe and graceful. Lucas looked away.

Let's just be friends.

He'd been insane to kiss her. Then he'd been insane to go along with her friends-only request. How was he going to stick with her wishes to be nothing more than friends? But hadn't he said that friendship and camaraderie was all he'd wanted from the other women he'd spent time with? He didn't want to get serious and end up in a commitment.

Avery had turned the tables on him. The fact that she was giving him what he'd said he wanted—friendship, someone to enjoy his activities with—said a lot about Avery as a person.

Lucas liked challenges. He could do this.

Let Avery be the girl he didn't hurt.

In the end, despite that Avery was different from all the others, that kissing her had changed something in him, and that he couldn't get her baby blues or the smell of her bread baking out of his head. . .in the end, Lucas still prized his freedom. He wanted the same thing as Avery.

The challenge ahead of him was more than remaining platonic for her sake. The life he'd built and cherished was on the line. He'd have to backpedal on the emotions she'd stirred in him. She'd done it without him realizing what happened. She'd somehow caught him off guard—but that wasn't right either. He'd known he shouldn't give her a second look.

Oh, he'd known.

Sigh. It was no use. He'd lost but a little of the control he'd had, and here he was spending time with her.

Life wasn't the same without the thrill, without the risk. Somehow he knew that life wouldn't be the same without Avery either. That was a new reality for him.

What am I going to do?

"Lucas." Avery's soft voice spilled into his thoughts. "You okay?"

He grinned. "Sure. Now, remember where everything is? The clutch, gears, kill switch, front and rear brakes? We practiced on the pavement but the dunes are different. You'll get the hang of it."

She nodded, but her face was drawn. A lot of beginners were anxious at first, but as long as she took things slowly and built up her skill level, by the end of the day her face would be glowing.

Lucas's heart pounded at the thought of her face flushed from the thrill. Though he didn't want to wish the day away, he couldn't wait for that moment.

Dude, you are in so much trouble.

He started the ignition of his quad, revved the engine, and drowned out the warning sirens blasting in his head. How had he gone from committed to remaining uncommitted, to fearing that Avery wouldn't want to be anything more than friends?

"You ready?" Lucas watched Avery.

She held up her thumb.

And. . .they were off.

Lucas's ATV lurched forward beneath him. He'd installed mirrors for use when instructing a beginner and watched Avery—she drove like a granny. He laughed, thinking of the moment when he'd tease her later.

Yep. Trouble.

Chapter 6

Big Indian Gorge," he said.

Avery admired the view, though fearing what was ahead of her while Lucas shifted into PARK and turned off the ignition.

After a rough and bumpy four-wheel drive over the second half of the loop that was the Steens Mountain National Back Country Byway, in which Avery thought she might get sick, they'd parked and climbed out of his truck, planning to hike a developed trail. At least, Lucas had assured her it was developed.

Wearing her hiking boots, Avery jumped from his truck and looked at the massive cliff face on either side of the grass-filled gorge.

"This is the best way to hike to the Steens Mountain summit," he said. "Unless you want to drive up."

"It's breathtaking." Though the scenic road had shown them much of the mountains, Avery couldn't wait to get out and hike, to stand on the summit. "But I bet this isn't the way you'd normally go, am I right?"

He started off on the Big Indian Gorge trail. "Are

you coming or what?"

She jogged to catch up and walk next to him. "If I weren't with you today, would you go this way to the summit?"

"I don't need to climb the rocky side every time I go somewhere."

"That's what I thought." She sighed. "Tell me about the rocky side."

"Nothing much to tell. You have to know what you're doing. Be able to climb mountains. The eastern face is steep. There aren't any trails. And the ridges are jagged and sharp. It's dangerous even for a skilled rock climber."

Despite the beautiful day, and that Lucas was giving her a taste of his life, shadows grew long over her thoughts.

They walked for a few minutes in silence, enjoying the view. Though it was July, snow still lingered in places along the cliff face. Lucas stopped and drank from his pack.

"You can almost see the summit from here, just to the right." He gestured toward a rocky top where a radio tower stood.

Avery sat on a boulder protruding from the tall grass. "I'm holding you back."

He jerked his gaze around to her and scrunched his face. "What?"

"This isn't an extreme sport, Lucas. You can't share that part of your life with me like you wanted because I'm not able to participate. I'm not in shape for long hikes. I'm not trained to climb mountains or much of anything."

She turned her face from his dark-eyed scrutiny. Why did she have to open her mouth? Why couldn't she simply appreciate that he'd wanted her with him?

Lucas said nothing for the longest time. Avery pulled her gaze from the ridges surrounding them to look at him. The man was gorgeous, especially when he was in his element like today. Why hadn't he responded? Her words must have hit their mark.

She'd not meant to ruin their day, ruin the hike by bringing up what had bothered her for weeks now. They'd even gone white-water rafting last weekend, driving several hours so she could enjoy the beginner's version in the Deschutes River. Lucas had gone out of his way for her.

"I'm grateful for all you've done. But I feel like a burden."

He stalked over to where she sat on the boulder. She couldn't recall seeing him with such a grim face.

Hovering over her, he glowered, but then his expression softened. He sat next to her, forcing her over a little. "All my friends are married and have kids. It gets complicated planning a trip. Having fun. You're far from a burden. So I have to go a little slower, that's better than going it alone. Eventually, maybe you'll get to the place where you're ready for more challenging levels."

Lucas brushed a hair from her face. It was the first time she'd felt his touch in weeks. She closed her eyes and forced her emotions into submission. So far, they'd managed to keep their distance. He'd honored her wishes that their friendship remain platonic. Now that she thought about it, it seemed a strange request, considering the kiss they'd shared. Avery quickly shoved that memory from her mind. She had her reasons.

"We had a deal to help each other. But it's having the opposite effect. Instead of me helping you, you're making an adrenaline junkie out of me—well, at least making me love the outdoors. But I haven't done anything for you. You're still a junkie."

She remained still as his gaze drifted over her face and lingered on her lips. Her breath caught in her throat.

"You're wrong, you know. You've brought meaning to it all. I didn't even know it needed meaning, so that's a start."

"That isn't enough." She smiled, wanting to climb out of their somber discussion. "I'm supposed to cure you of your addiction and help you enjoy the little things."

The light returned to his eyes, and he rewarded her with his multiple-dimpled grin. "You *have* cured me. I am enjoying the little things in life. Maybe I'll get the chance to prove that to you." His smile wavered and something—was it fear?—flickered in his eyes. "Maybe I'll get the chance to tell you what I've been thinking about us, if you give me that. But right now, we need to finish this hike. It'll be late when we get home as it is."

What I've been thinking about us. . .

Avery's pulse rippled through her.

He stood and offered his hand. She took it, loving the strength in his grip. Wishing she could feel his arms around her once more. But. . .what had he been thinking about them?

He released her hand and they continued hiking.

She'd drawn a line, claiming they shouldn't have a relationship outside of work. Then she'd crossed that line and drawn another, stating they were too different to be more than friends. But now their lives were melding together—they'd spent every weekend together, sometimes evenings during the week after work, too. He claimed he couldn't get enough of her bread. The thought made her smile.

Avery had given herself the summer to decide if she would stay in the house her grandmother had given her, or if she would begin a job search in Portland or some other city.

And then, Thursday, she'd gotten a call. A friend had given her name to someone who wanted to hire a CPA—full-time, benefits, great pay—for a prestigious accounting firm.

And now Lucas was talking about having the chance to prove something to her?

What had he meant, if she gave him the chance? Trudging behind him, she sighed, realizing that she needed to tell him she might be leaving. Although she'd told herself she didn't believe Katy's remarks about Lucas, now it hit her. Because of Katy's warning—that Lucas was nothing more than a playboy, not to fall for him—Avery hadn't considered that Lucas would actually fall for her instead. She hadn't for a moment taken his interest in her seriously.

Which was why she'd guarded her heart.

But had she toyed with his? Had she—the practical, no-nonsense one—made sport of their friendship? No. That wasn't it. She cared deeply for him, and she feared admitting just how much. But he needed to know she might leave in a few weeks. Sooner if she was offered a job.

He would need someone to do the books in her place. She was almost finished getting everything organized, and whomever he hired next should have no problems.

Hiking a few feet in front of her, Lucas suddenly turned and walked backward. Slamming more water and then squinting, he scrutinized her. "What's wrong?"

Avery stopped. "What makes you ask that?"

Lucas came toward her and placed his palm against her cheek.

Avery leaned into it. What was he doing?

"Because, Avery Summers, I know you. What's wrong?"

Avery had shoved aside his questions, claiming she was fine.

But Lucas knew better. They'd finished up their hike, and now, he steered his truck through Frenchglen, the gateway to Steens Mountain, and parked at the Frenchglen's historic hotel where he planned to treat her to dinner before they headed home. Lucas had hoped the place would create the right ambiance.

After one of their adventures, she always appeared relaxed, happy, and open. He wanted to take advantage of that. Over the course of the last few weeks, they'd grown close. Though she doubted herself, believing she'd held him back, she'd given him everything he'd wanted in a companion, making his life that much fuller.

In fact, before she came into his life—he hadn't been living at all, he realized.

He'd adhered to her wishes to remain friends, at least on the surface. But he'd not held to his own commitment to remain emotionally and romantically unattached. He clung to the ridge by his fingers, slipping fast and, if he lost his grip, it would be a hard fall.

Before he spent any more time with her, he had things to say. He wanted to tell her how he felt, hoping tonight was the night. But earlier that afternoon something in her demeanor had changed. He'd heard her troubled sighs, and her eyes, usually full of life, held shadows instead.

Through dinner they discussed the hike and where they might want to go next, but Lucas could never bring himself to bare his heart and soul. Avery held back something as well, whatever had gotten her down during their hike. No way would he tell her how much he cared for her until he found out what was bothering her.

At last he pulled the truck to the curb of her house. She looked over at him, her hand on the door handle. "Thanks, Lucas. It's been a great time. As always."

Her words sounded hollow. Insincere.

The way she pursed her lips, he could tell her smile bordered on a frown. She hopped out and headed to her door.

What was going on?

He'd long stopped escorting her to the door because then the moment became a little awkward. He wanted to kiss her. She was thinking the same thing, he knew. They both ignored it. He'd wondered how long their friendship would last. But he never thought he'd be the one to give in first.

Now. . .*now,* he understood how the women who claimed he'd hurt them felt. His pulse took flight at the top of a dune and soared, then plummeted.

This was déjà vu in reverse. He was the one about to lose everything that meant anything to him. Lucas pounded the steering wheel. He couldn't take it anymore. He had to face this fear—was she about to dump him?

"Avery!" He jumped out of the truck, jogged around, and caught her at the door. "Avery. . .we have to talk." He pleaded with his eyes, feeling desperate, hating that he *was* desperate.

She sighed. "Lucas, it's almost midnight. I have church tomorrow. Can't it wait?"

He swatted at the bugs swarming the porch light and his face. "I need to know something."

Frowning, she opened the door. "Come in."

He trailed her into the house and closed the door behind him. He was overreacting. Had to be.

"Can I get you something to drink?" she asked and filled a glass of water for herself from the tap.

"No. Listen, I'm sorry for keeping you, it's just that you never told me what's bothering you." He should tell her everything. That he might even. . .

What? Love her?

If he was going to get hurt—and it would be a first—he didn't want another soul to know about it. Not even Avery. Especially not Avery. He wasn't fearless, after all.

Coward.

Avery plopped on her sofa and rested her head. "I'm sorry I was so distracted. All you had to do was ask."

"I did."

Her laugh was nervous. "Yeah, during the hike. I just wanted to forget about it so I could enjoy things."

He sat across from her on the longer sofa. "So, what is it?"

"I wasn't sure how to tell you, but I got a call on Thursday. Someone asked me to interview for a position in Portland. They seem really interested. When I got laid off, I thought it was a great chance for me to spend some time living in this house. See if I wanted to stay here. Change things. Simplify my life. You already know all that."

Lucas leaned forward, his elbows on his knees, bracing himself against the onslaught of confusion. He hadn't expected this, and in a way, it was worse than her dumping him. Deep down, he believed she returned his affection, and couldn't imagine she'd actually end their friendship or the affection they both denied. But if she left, they wouldn't have their chance to see things through.

Her usually clear and honest baby blues masked something. What else was she hiding?

Lucas hung his head. "I see. . ."—then he glanced back up and stared, tempering the scowl—"When were you going to tell me? I need time to replace you."

Make this about her job. He might survive that way.

"I'm telling you now. And a phone call doesn't mean I'll even get the job. I still have to interview."

"But you're considering it. If they offered you'd take the job."

Avery bolted from the sofa. "Oh, I don't know, Lucas. That's why I didn't want to tell you. I have to think things through."

"This is just great."

Avery paced the living room but didn't say anything.

"We're supposed to be friends. Why couldn't you share this with me? We could have figured it out together."

"There's no point in having an argument about why I didn't inform you the exact moment I got the phone call. And if you're worried about me finishing things up for you, I'll work harder over the next few days and make sure even you could do your books, if you can't find anyone else."

Lucas stood, stepped around the coffee table, and caught her arm as she passed. He drew her up to face him, look him in the eye. Could he do it? Could he tell her how he felt?

"Is that all?" he asked.

She huffed. So unlike her. "What do you mean?"

"Don't you have a reason to stay?" If she could just give a little, show him she cared.

The edge in her expression softened. "Don't worry. I'm sure I could still meet you for a weekend adventure. There's plenty to do around Portland, too."

Lucas nodded. He had his answer.

Chapter 7

Lucas sat at his desk, his legs extended, resting his feet—hiking boots and all—on the desk.

He chewed on a pen and stared at nothing. His deep scowl and dark mood had sent Mark running. Ricky and his other summer employees had taken one look and left him alone. The organized and well-ordered office—books and files in their proper place—reminded him of Avery. If he was serious about ejecting her from his mind, he'd do something besides sit in his office—now the bane of his existence.

But what could he do that wouldn't remind him of her? He'd made a place for her in his world, hiking, biking, kayaking, four-wheeling, though they hadn't made it to hang gliding. Whatever he'd done for the last six weeks, he'd done it with Avery. He'd made a place for her in his heart as well.

Katy would love to gloat over that fact, if she knew.

How could Avery even *think* about leaving?

Because she doesn't feel the same way about you, dude. "Get that through your head," he mumbled to himself.

But he couldn't know her true feelings because he hadn't put his on the line. He hadn't told her about his fall for her.

She'd gone to Portland Tuesday, yesterday evening, for her interview this morning, promising to return later in the afternoon, claiming she had a few things to finish. Should they offer her the job and she decide to take it, she wanted her work completed. Lucas had never asked her to do all she'd done. He'd wanted someone to fix the mess he'd made, and do it while working part-time. Obviously, that had been asking too much. Then again, Avery claimed she was a workaholic. From what Lucas could tell, he hadn't done a single thing to change that.

"Wow. I haven't seen that look on your face since, oh, I don't know, you were ten years old and your dog died." His brother Jonas leaned in the doorjamb, arms crossed. He'd relocated from the FBI's Chicago office to Portland since getting married a year and a half ago.

All he could offer was a beleaguered half smile. "Look what the cat dragged in."

Jonas grinned. "Mind if I sit down?"

"Does it matter?" The hint of a chuckle stirred at the easy banter he shared with Jonas. His brother's unexpected appearance might do Lucas some good.

"Not really." Jonas shoved from the doorjamb and dropped in the chair across from the desk. "Mind telling me what's bothering you?"

Lucas yanked his booted feet from the desk to sit back in the chair. "As a matter of fact, I'm good. Everything's good. What are you doing here?"

Jonas studied him. He didn't believe him. But Lucas didn't care. It wasn't his business. "What? Can't a brother stop by to check on you?"

"Like that's ever going to happen." This time, Lucas did laugh. "Things not working out on the newlywed front? Need a place to crash?"

"Hardly. I'm here on business. Headed down to Carver's to speak with his wife."

"The sheriff?" Lucas sat a little straighter. "What's up?"

"Just pay attention to anything unusual. There's a fugitive we think could make his way through the high desert. Sometimes they go for more populated areas. Other times, they think they can get lost in the wilderness. So I'm just checking out a tip."

"Sounds serious." Lucas should ask his brother to have lunch or something. They didn't see each other often. But he was far from good company, and then Jonas might discover the truth.

"That's my story. That and I really did stop by to see you. I'm glad I did. Now you can tell me your story." Jonas's smile was tinted with concern. Still, he looked relaxed and happy.

Lucas blamed the guy's marriage. *Good for you, Jonas.* He'd gotten a rough start in life, but things had turned out all right in the end.

"Like I said. I've got nothing to tell. Business is good. Life is good." Lucas stood and stretched, feigning a peaceful existence.

Existing was now his reality.

"Right, well"—Jonas leaned forward and stared at Lucas like he was a target, and Jonas the sharpshooter—"a not-so-wise man once shared some rare wisdom with me. I think the words went something like, 'She's the *one,* bro, don't let her get away.' Unless there's something standing in your way, you might take your own advice, Lucas."

The words slammed him, knocking the air from his thoughts, which might as well have been his lungs. He plopped back into his chair. "How did you know?"

"You're the happiest guy I know. You're living your dream. Nothing in the world is going to put that look on your face except a woman. And not just any woman."

"The *one*. . ."

They said it together in an exaggerated tone. Lucas laughed along with Jonas.

"I remembered saying that to you," Lucas scratched his head. "I don't know what I was thinking."

"You were thinking that you knew Darcy was the one for me. You could tell. I haven't met this girl that's turned you inside out, but I've never seen you this intense over a girl. So. . .is there something standing in your way?"

"Yeah. *She* is."

"Hmm. Well. I've got no advice for that."

"Maybe it requires some sort of sacrificial offering on my part."

Jonas laughed. "Oh, for certain, it will require a sacrifice."

Lucas smiled. Jonas had seen right through him, and somehow, sharing his burden had eased the pain. "If you've got time. Let's eat somewhere."

He clapped Jonas on the back and closed the door behind him, leaving it unlocked for Avery, though she had a key. It would be good to be out of here when she got back. If she even came back.

He'd told Jonas that Avery was the one standing in the way

of their relationship, but Lucas wasn't sure if that was the truth. Maybe he was the roadblock.

☙

Avery strolled down the hall toward Lucas's office, thankful she'd decided to come in after hours. Facing him right now would be too hard. Sure, his apartment was at the back of the business, but he rarely spent time in the shop after hours, preferring to play after work.

After her interview in Portland this morning, she'd had lunch with a friend and driven back. She'd changed and did some laundry while she waited until six thirty, when she knew Lucas was certain to be gone. And gone he was—his truck wasn't even parked at the back. She would have seen it.

She'd been so cold to him on Saturday, all day really, and then when he'd followed her into her house, wanting to hear what was bothering her, she'd only shared a half truth. Part of the whole truth.

Avery opened the door to Lucas's office, recalling the first time she'd seen the chaos. Things were in order now, but only in his office and accounting system. Avery's heart was a mess, and she didn't have any idea how to put things right.

She slung her bag into the extra chair, then sat behind the desk and booted up his computer, preparing to finish the work like she promised.

A familiar scent wafted over her—Lucas's cologne. He'd been in the office today. He usually stayed away while she worked at the computer.

Oh Lucas. She'd tried to deny the way he made her feel, and her growing affection for him, hiding behind their friendship. He couldn't hurt her if there was nothing to hurt, but she was terrified of just that. How she'd allowed things to get out of control, she wasn't sure. She'd thought that given time, things would pan out one way or another and so she'd avoided any commitment. She'd done exactly what Katy claimed was Lucas's MO.

Now she was at a crossroads. Could she afford to turn down a job that would be, in essence, a promotion from her last position while she waited to see if her heart was safe with Lucas?

As she stared at numbers on the screen, her chin trembled. Avery swiped at the tears with the back of her hand. *Oh Lord, what am I going to do?*

She thought of the print on the wall out front: REALITY: THAT WHICH DOESN'T GO AWAY WHEN YOU STOP BELIEVING IN IT.

What about that which doesn't go away just because you ignore it?

How could she have known how much Lucas would mean to her? He'd done so much for her, showing her things, giving her experiences she'd only heard about. She'd recovered from her fear of the more impractical and risky side to having fun.

He'd helped her become fearless. Helped her live the scripture, *"For the Spirit God gave us does not make us timid, but gives us power, love and self-discipline."*

But she'd not gotten over her fear of being hurt. And that...

That was keeping her from love.

But it was all too late. If they called and offered her the

job—and she should hear by the end of this week—something would have to happen and fast. She'd need one extreme sign to turn this down and stay in the middle of nowhere with only Lucas and her fear of loving him.

Avery shut down the computer. She couldn't do this tonight.

A man, late thirties, stocky and antsy, appeared in the doorway.

"I'm sorry, we're closed," she said.

"I need an ATV."

Frowning, Avery stood. "You'll have to wait until the morning."

He took another step toward her. "Now."

"I. . .can call the owner. Maybe he'd be willing to rent you something." Avery reached for her phone.

The man pulled a gun from his pocket. "Put the phone down."

Avery's knees trembled. This was for real. Why didn't he just hot-wire the thing, if he wanted it so badly? "Okay—okay. Just calm down. I'll get you what you want."

She slid the desk drawer open, grabbed a key ring, and held it out. "The master key to the key box is on this ring. And the box is in the front."

Sweat beaded on his forehead. "You're coming with me."

Avery swallowed, panic and terror strangling her defenses. For lack of something better to say or do, she walked through the door ahead of him. *Lord, please send someone to help.*

All her thoughts of being fearless bled out her feet. Part of her reason for leaving Portland was because of the break-in.

Why couldn't Lucas be here?

The man shoved her forward. She hurried to the front of the business.

"Now, open that box. Get me a key."

Hands trembling, Avery fumbled with the keys. Finally, the lockbox opened, revealing four keys to unrented ATVs. The man reached forward, his arm gruff against her shoulder, and swiped them all.

Now what would he do? Would he leave her to call the police? As if he was considering her question, too, he looked at her and frowned. He grabbed a couple of helmets off the shelf.

"Let's go."

Too stunned for words, Avery allowed the man to shove her out the door cautiously. She went with him, to the side of the building where the rentals waited.

"I don't get it. Why would you steal one of these from a rental shop?"

He climbed onto the largest one and started it. Avery glanced around to see if she could run, duck and hide, get herself free, but he looked up at her, still gripping the gun. "This will ride two, and the tank is full. Get on."

"Why take me? It's not like you can run away from the police on an ATV."

"Who said I'm running from the police? Now get on."

Avery glanced to the side of the building. Lucas's truck was still gone. How could this happen? This was crazy. "Then why do you need me? Just take the thing and go."

Tears spilled over her cheeks as she stumbled forward.

"I'm not going to hurt you. But I don't want you calling

anyone until I'm long gone, so you're going with me."

"Then why did you involve me? Why not hot-wire the thing?"

His frown deepened. "Someone might notice the wires hanging out. Think it's stolen. This way, we're just two people out for a joyride."

He forced her to sit in front of him, his arms stretching around her as he controlled the machine. At his nearness, her skin crawled. How was she going to get out of this?

Avery held on to the hope that he would eventually leave her somewhere in the dunes. Somewhere alone in the seventeen square miles of desert sand.

Her hopes and dreams for the future, her conflicting thoughts about Lucas, were nothing now.

Survive.

Escape.

Avery's mind scrambled for some way out.

Lord, please, help me. As she slid on her helmet, she discreetly tugged one of her butterfly earrings out and dropped it.

The ATV rumbled beneath her as her abductor accelerated along the unpaved road that led deeper into the dunes. The ride was uncomfortable. Avery couldn't imagine why he bothered with her. But eventually, he steered toward the Sand Dunes Wilderness Study Area—an area remote and completely secluded from other recreational riders because it was closed to the public.

No one would find them out there.

Chapter 8

Lucas steered through the parking lot and spotted Avery's car still there at seven thirty. He frowned. She was serious about working late to complete the cleanup on his accounting system.

Which meant—she was taking the job in Portland. Lucas exhaled long and slow. While he'd enjoyed his lunch with Jonas and they talked well into the afternoon, catching up, his thoughts had never been far from Avery.

His pride stood in the way. But Jonas had convinced him that getting hurt was, in fact, worth the risk. If she rejected him after he spread his heart out for her to see, then so be it.

He parked the truck in the back and jogged around to the side door, letting himself into the business side of the building. The lights were on in his office, and the door was wide open. Avery wasn't there, but her bag was in the chair, and the desk drawer was open. She was around here somewhere.

This wasn't the time or place he'd wanted to share his feelings, but he'd let that chance slip over the weekend. It was now or never. Before she got too caught up in the idea of moving back to Portland. If he knew anything about women, she'd probably want some sort of commitment if she was going to give up a great job opportunity and stay in town. He didn't blame her for that.

Lucas sat in the chair and clasped his hands behind his head, waiting for her to return. Was he ready for more than a confession of love? Was he ready to commit?

If she was the *one*, like he believed she was, then. . .he swallowed. . .he needed to practice saying the words out loud or at least in his head. He leaned forward in the chair. Where was Avery?

He shoved from the desk and headed out of the office, calling her name.

She wasn't in the front room or the restroom. He searched in the back room, fearing she'd decided to move boxes to create her own office. Although why would she do that if she was taking the other job? That might mean she'd decided to stay. Lucas's heart jumped at the thought.

Could it be?

"Avery?" He looked through the chaotic room. She wasn't there, nor was she on the floor somewhere hurt because a box had fallen on her. Though relieved she wasn't hurt, he was getting worried. He stepped through the back to the repair shop. It was dark and empty, other than four-wheelers in mid-repair.

His pulse ramping, he jogged to the front of the building where customers entered and rented their ATVs. The key box hung open. He ran his finger over the key slots. They were all gone.

What was going on? In only a few strides, he shoved through the front door, which wasn't even locked like it should have been. Around the side, he spotted three ATVs that were left for rental. This was his busy season, so most of the rentals were being used. There were four sitting there when he left earlier in the day, but someone could have rented that, or had Avery taken one for a ride?

Avery's car was here, her purse was in his office, and she'd left that in disarray. All were unlike her. No, she'd never take a four-wheeler out alone.

Something sparkled on the ground. He bent over and picked up one of Avery's butterfly earrings.

"Okay, something is weird here." He ran back into the office. Only two helmets were left. If she left on one of the ATVs, did she take two helmets?

Lucas called Jonas. The call went to voice mail. He hung up and tried again. "Come on, come on, come on. . ."

"Lucas. What's up?"

"I don't know. It could be nothing. But it's kind of strange."

"Go ahead."

"Avery's car is here and the office is open. She left her purse, and the desk drawer open, and all the ATV keys have been taken. There are still three sitting there, but two helmets are gone, and I found something that belongs to her on the ground next to where the one four-wheeler was parked. Is there something wrong here? Or do you think I'm overreacting?"

Jonas was silent. Then he sighed. "Don't do anything. Wait for me. I'll be right there."

Lucas stared at his phone after Jonas had hung up. Was

Jonas crazy? After filling Lucas's head about the guy who'd bombed someplace and might be looking to hide out in the Oregon wilderness, Lucas wasn't about to wait on Jonas. He grabbed a helmet and straddled one of the faster model four-wheelers. He yanked the wires attached to the ignition switch and using his pocketknife, cut the red one, then connected the ignition wire, starting the engine.

It wouldn't be the first one he'd hot-wired. He raced off on the four-wheeler, heading toward the dunes, but he didn't have a clue where he was going. He'd either find Avery out for a joyride on her own, or with a friend, or she was in trouble.

Either way, Lucas aimed to find her, even if he had to ride every square mile of the sand dunes and more, looking. Unfortunately, the four-wheeler that he suspected was missing had two gas tanks, and could go a hundred and forty miles before needing gas. The dunes would cut that number drastically, but if Jonas's fugitive had taken Avery and the ATV, where was he headed?

At that moment, Lucas no longer feared loving Avery, or telling her of his love. He'd willingly let go of everything he'd held dear up to the moment he met Avery, for a chance to love her for the rest of his life.

I'm coming, Avery!

Avery feared he would enter the wilderness area, but instead it appeared he headed for a remote campsite. That brought only a measure of relief. Was he meeting someone?

When she'd moved from the city to the quiet seclusion

of central Oregon, she never dreamed she'd face the biggest challenges of her life. Lucas's extreme sports were one thing, but now she'd been abducted, and all because she'd been at the wrong place at the wrong time. But being with Lucas, learning to do things she'd never think of, had doused most of her fear of risk—and *that* was the key to breaking free.

Clenching her teeth, Avery waited for her chance. She prayed she'd recognize it when it came and would know what to do. Somewhere behind her, she heard more quads and leaned around the man to glance behind him. He shoved her forward, but in that instant, she'd spotted a group of riders on four-wheelers. Were they following? Was it Lucas?

Whoever was behind them made her abductor nervous because he steered straight up a steep dune. Avery braced herself, hoping he wouldn't soar over the crest.

They topped the dune. The other side was steep and the man traversed it straight down.

Then. . .she knew what to do. She only had one shot at this—and it was a risk.

She drew in several breaths like she was preparing to dive underwater, then yanked the handlebars to the right. The man cursed and fought to correct his course. But it was too late. All she'd needed was a slight angle.

The quad tipped and Avery jumped. Her abductor wasn't fast enough, and rolled under the ATV. Avery didn't wait to see if he would recover. Going back for the key wasn't an option, with him lying so close to the quad. She stepped into the compressed sand of the four-wheeler's tracks and ran up the dune.

A glance back told her he was stirring, his gun halfway down the dune on the sand. Avery pushed over the top, legs burning, and down the other side, hoping to see the group of riders that had followed.

They were nowhere in sight, though she heard the rumble of vehicles nearby.

"Help, someone help!" she called and continued to run, but the sand slowed her pace, and burned her energy away.

Breathless, she leaned on her thighs. Would he come back for her? Or let her go?

She heard the whir of a quad. Glancing behind, Avery spotted it crest the dune she'd just come from. *He's coming after me. . .*

She ran, willing her legs to carry her through the sand.

But it was no use. The revving whirr of the ATV overwhelmed her. He planned to run her down.

Avery turned to face him. She had no intentions of going down alone. She'd take him with her.

Suddenly, a four-wheeler soared high over the dune to her right, heading straight for her.

Lucas? Her heart thrummed. "Lucas! He has a gun." She knew he couldn't hear her.

On the four-wheeler, her abductor bore down on her, too focused on Avery to see Lucas.

Lucas jerked his quad, slamming against the other vehicle. He threw his body into the man, shoving them both off the vehicles. Avery screamed and dodged. Soon enough, the quads slowed in the sand.

Lucas and the abductor wrestled, but the man had gotten

the better of Lucas, straddling him and throwing punches in Lucas's face. Avery spotted his gun, lying on the ground. The guy couldn't hold on to it. She ran to the gun and picked it up, but she didn't know how to use it. Pointing it could endanger Lucas as well.

Avery rushed over and slammed the weapon into the man's temple. He fell off Lucas, unconscious. Or. . . "Is he dead?" she asked.

Lucas sat up and wiped at his bloodied face. He reached over and felt the man's neck. "No. You didn't kill him."

"Oh Lucas. How did you find me?"

He climbed to his feet and took the gun from her. "Let me hold on to this in case he comes to."

Avery melted into his embrace, and he kissed the top of her head. "Hold on, I'm calling Jonas. He's with the FBI, and this could be the fugitive they're after."

She waited while Lucas told Jonas about her abductor, and gave him the coordinates of their location.

Then he cupped one palm against her cheek. Concern, fear, along with other emotions sprang from his dark blue gaze. "Are you okay? Did he hurt you?"

She shook her head. "I don't know what he was planning." Avery explained how she'd tugged the handlebars and flipped the quad on a steep dune and escaped.

Lucas grinned, rubbing his thumb against her cheek.

Their uncertain relationship suddenly didn't matter. All she wanted was to bask in his attention, enjoy the fact that she had survived.

Chapter 9

Lucas continued to cup her sweet face, unwilling to release her. "As soon as help arrives, I'll get you home. But right now, we need to wait. Jonas was already on his way before I found you, so he should be here soon."

"I couldn't believe it when I saw you. You came just in time, but how did you find me?" Her eyes bright, he could tell adrenaline held her up, but it wouldn't last. She would fade fast and hard.

She'd called him an adrenaline junkie. Looking at her, he knew now that he'd give up his addiction for her. "With all the activity in the dunes this time of year, it wasn't easy, but that quad is heavy and has nineteen-inch tires, so the tracks were deep and wide. I followed a few false trails before I found you."

Lucas relished the feel of her smooth skin against his palm, the softness against his thumb. He didn't ever want to let her go. She could have been killed today at the hands of her abductor or when the quad had rolled over.

An unfamiliar sensation burned the back of his eyes. Tears? Still holding the weapon and alert to any movement from Avery's kidnapper, Lucas rubbed his upper arm over his face, wiping away the emotions. His friends had thought him fearless, and until today, his only fear had been falling in love and the resulting commitment as though it was something to dread. He'd been an idiot.

Now. . .*now*, he knew a different, more fierce, and terrible kind of fear. The fear of losing the woman he loved, losing her so that he could never get her back. Losing her so that he wouldn't have the chance to prove his love. An ache knifed his chest. But she wasn't his to get back. He hadn't told her how he felt, and even if he did, he had no assurance that she would return his love.

"Oh, I have something for you." He dug in his pocket, pulling out her butterfly earring.

Her eyes glistened. "You found it."

"It went a long way in helping me know you were in trouble. Smart girl."

She lifted and dangled it. Then she removed the other from her earlobe. "I don't want to wear these anymore. They're a reminder of what happened."

Avery stumbled back. Lucas caught her elbow. "You should sit down." He hoped she'd let him make her something to eat, let him spend time with her and make sure she was okay.

The deep rumble of a helicopter filled his ears, and soon, it swooped over them. He hoped it wouldn't land in the sand.

ଓ

After Jonas arrived along with his FBI entourage, Avery had told him what happened, and thankfully he'd dismissed her and

Lucas. Lucas insisted on driving Avery home.

He walked her to the door, hating the drained look of her skin and her sagging expression. The adrenaline rush of an extreme situation had finally crashed.

Avery unlocked her door. "Thanks again, Lucas. You were there for me today." Her voice trembled.

Hearing the shattered sound of it tore at his insides. "After I shower, I'm coming back to cook dinner for you."

She frowned. "That's not necessary. Besides, all I want is a hot bath and a nap."

He didn't want to leave her alone. She needed to be with someone.

Lucas sighed. "Look, I know you're tired. Take your bath and your nap. Let me do this for you, please. . ."

When she looked at him, he pleaded with his gaze. Was he being selfish? "Please, let me do this for you."

"Okay, Lucas," she said, too tired to argue, he knew. She dropped the keys to her house in his hand. "Let yourself in."

An hour later, Lucas had showered and dressed in his Sunday best, which amounted to jeans and a button-down collared shirt, and stood in Avery's kitchen, cooking spaghetti with meat sauce, the only decent meal he could make. Store-bought french garlic bread warmed in the oven—she didn't have any of her fresh-baked bread lying around—and he chopped tomatoes for a salad.

He assumed Avery had taken her bath and was napping. He wouldn't disturb her, but hoped the good smells would wake her. She needed some sustenance. Anyone who enjoyed baking bread like she did would stir at the aroma. The table was set and included a bouquet of fresh flowers he'd purchased as well.

He wasn't any good at this romance thing—his track record attested to that—but Jonas had given him a few tips earlier in the afternoon, before either of them knew the danger she was in.

In his head, he rehearsed the words he would say when the right moment came.

I love you. I was too scared to admit I loved you before. But I've loved you from the moment I saw you.

What if the right moment never came?

Funny that life turned things around on a person. His fear of loving, of commitment, had been turned upside down, and now he was afraid of not being loved in return. Avery could reject him.

Especially if he didn't manage to say things right. That was another thing he knew about women, the right word said in the wrong way could be a deal-breaker.

"Lucas?" The familiar sweet voice sent his heart tumbling.

Moisture slid over his palms as he glanced up from tossing the salad.

Avery leaned against a chair at the dining table, her gaze flitting over his handiwork. Her cheeks had a good color now, and her eyes were definitely brighter than when he'd left her. She'd cleaned up, too, and wore white shorts and a pale shirt. When she looked at him in the kitchen, the soft lavender polo shirt she wore accented her big blues.

Beautiful. . .

"Lucas," she said. "You did all this for me?"

He took a glass of iced tea with a wedge of lemon over to her. "Who else?"

Her bright smile shined through his dark places, and she took the glass from him. "I'm impressed."

"I'm sorry about today." Idiot. He was hoping to make her forget.

She watched him over the rim of the glass as she drank. When she finished, Lucas took the glass from her and set it on the table.

He lifted his hand but dropped it. For some reason, he thought if he touched her she would break. A rock lodged in his throat. He ran his hand down her arm until he reached her hand and squeezed it.

Today wasn't a good day to lay everything on the line. Deep in his marrow he knew that waiting any longer wasn't an option. He was terrified.

☙

Avery slid her hands around Lucas's waist and held on. She rested her head against his chest, the sturdy thump of his heart all the security she needed.

She sighed into his shirt. *If he hadn't been there today. Hadn't come when he had. . .*

Lucas rubbed her back like he sensed she needed his comfort, though the day had to be harrowing for him, too. Easing herself from his protective embrace, she stepped back.

He wore a light blue, long-sleeved, collared shirt and

new-looking jeans. "Well, look at you. Cooking dinner, a beautiful table display, and now"—she reached up and pushed a few strands of dark hair from his forehead—"you're dressed to the nines."

He laughed. "Hardly."

"You took a few bruises on your face. I hope it doesn't hurt too much."

"Not too much."

"Dressed like that, you're quite the catch. How did all those women you dated let you get away?" She smiled up at him.

He was an absolutely gorgeous man. His masculine cologne enveloped her and she relished it. Avery had tried to guard her heart. She'd gone from a treasured friendship, to being wary of imminent heartbreak these last few days, and now she was flirting with the man. She had no plans to stop.

He'd worked hard on her behalf tonight. She would do her best to forget today, except for his heroism. Still, niggling at the edges of her thoughts was the fact that any day now someone would call to offer her a job she really wanted. Or did she?

With a flourish, Lucas pulled out a chair for her to sit. She enjoyed this side of him, she had to admit.

"A girl could get used to this," she said, smiling. But shouldn't she be discouraging him? This couldn't end well.

Insane. She was certifiably insane. Avery was crazy about Lucas.

But why was he doing this? He was only prolonging their inevitable parting. She'd fooled herself into thinking that if anyone's heart got broken, it would be his, but that was a bald-faced lie.

Lucas brought her a plate of spaghetti and meat sauce, then returned again with sliced garlic bread. Finally, he sat down to join her and said grace.

Today, when Avery didn't know if she would live or die, all she wanted was to survive. To see Lucas again. Look into his eyes that pooled with the depth of the ocean. She'd made it and she was here. Her uncertainty of their future together didn't matter. For this moment in time, she would enjoy their relationship.

He was a good cook, too. Over dinner, he told stories of his childhood—the four brothers on the ranch and their escapades. Love, laughter, and plenty of smiles. It seemed that like her, Lucas cherished this moment they had together, shoving aside concern for the future.

With the meal finished, Lucas scooped up the dishes and rinsed them all in the sink. Avery protested, but he insisted on cleaning up the kitchen.

Good man.

There weren't many like him around. At last, Lucas joined her on the sofa. He had to be tired, too, after today's events, but he beamed at her, his energy boundless.

Avery exhaled slowly.

Lucas's smile fell. "Avery. . ." He reached up and touched her hair like it was fine china.

"I was afraid today. But being with you over the summer, you taught me how to face all my fears." All except one. She appreciated his attentiveness, but. . .

Hating the thought swirling in her head, she almost wished

he would leave. If he wasn't going to say something about them, then he should just go.

"How was your interview?" he asked.

So now they were down to the talk that would make or break them. Avery stared at him. The furrows between his brows belied his smile.

"It went well, actually. Someone should call me by the end of this week." She toyed with the pillow. Telling a man that she loved him, a man who was reputed to leave a trail of broken hearts behind him, wasn't in her DNA.

"Are you going to take the job?" he asked.

Something in the tenor of his voice—maybe the way it almost cracked—told her that he wanted her to stay. She needed more from him than that, and she needed him to say it. She wouldn't beg. It killed her not to tell him how she felt, and it was more than just pride. It was self-respect. If Lucas placed any value on her, on their relationship, he would man up and say it.

"If the offer is good, yes, I think I will."

"I see." He stood and paced the room, scratching his jaw, weaving his hands through his hair.

Lucas drew up his chin and with a forced smile, said, "I should let you get some rest. You shouldn't worry about coming back to work tomorrow, considering today. Take as much time as you need. Let me know when you're sure about leaving."

Avery didn't answer, but continued toying with the tassel on the pillow. Lucas walked out the door.

Tears slid down her cheeks. How she hated them, and she

swiped at them in a fury. Dark disappointment flooded her soul. She pressed her face into the pillow and sobbed.

Lucas didn't love her back.

Avery drifted to sleep on the sofa, stirring when an hour or more later, someone knocked on the door. She roused herself, wondering if Katy wanted a rundown of her day. Probably heard about it on the news.

But when she opened the door, Lucas filled her doorway. A tenuous grin replaced his usual double-dimpled smile.

The man had the power to stop her heart, but she managed to speak. "Did you forget something?"

"No. I didn't forget. I just hadn't worked up my nerve yet."

Avery's pulse thrummed in her neck.

"I always thought my life wouldn't be the same without the thrill, without the risk involved. Now I see it wouldn't be the same without you. You are my thrill now, and you are so worth the risk. You know how to make good smells." His grin was adorable. "I love you, Avery. I've loved you since the moment we met. I'm sorry that the one thing I was afraid of has kept us apart. I'm sorry that I didn't—"

Avery threw herself into his arms and planted a kiss on his welcoming lips. "I love you, too."

When their kiss subsided, Lucas lowered her to the ground, and put his forehead against hers. "This means we're getting married, doesn't it? I mean, you love someone, you marry them, right?"

"Only when asked. Are you asking?"

"I am."

"I want to hear you say it."

"Avery Summers, will you give up your job prospect in Portland and marry me?"

She couldn't help the joyous laugh that escaped. "Lucas Love, there's no place I'd rather be than with you, my fearless hero."

A LOVE RECOVERED

Chapter 1

He'd found the Judas...

The person betrayed now turned traitor. The person willing to tell him where to find the skip. And that was the first step to locating the fugitive. Usually, the information came from a scorned girlfriend, or rather, ex-girlfriend. A drug dealer. Sometimes close relatives, even parents.

This time it came from the wife.

According to her, he'd headed to Oregon—a state where Justin Love wouldn't be welcome. Standing in line with a dozen others on the blustery tarmac, he scraped his hand over his face and squinted in the midday Nevada sun. The high-decibel whine of the waiting prop plane accosted his ears. Though it sat only a few yards away, it was taking an eternity for him to board.

Justin slid his sunglasses over his eyes. By the look of things, he'd be here for a while. He hated the feeling he got when he wasn't making any headway. But this time, whether he stood here waiting, or sat on the puddle jumper to Nowhere, Oregon, the feeling would be the same.

He was still trying to figure out why he'd taken this job when he finally stepped into the tight fuselage and made his way behind a few sluggish commuters to row ten. A pretty young brunette sat in the aisle seat. His seat. He knew that because he always requested the aisle. She smiled up at him like she hadn't a clue.

"Excuse me, but you're in my seat." He tried to sound pleasant but he was out of practice.

Her bright smile slipped. "Oh? I'm so sorry. . ."

She stood and searched through pockets in her bag.

Justin preferred she simply slide over. He grappled for the ticket stub in his pocket to save them both some time.

"I've got it." She beamed at him and looked at the stub. "Oh good. I thought I'd made a mistake. I'm in the aisle, after all." She showed him her proof.

Justin looked at the row number and seat letter glaring back at him in defiance and frowned. Aware that everyone on the small flight was seated and watching him, he nodded at the woman. "My mistake."

It wasn't the first of his mistakes. This trip had been a mistake. He'd known it in his gut and yet here he was. He folded his body into the window seat and stared out, letting his row mate know he didn't feel like talking. She had that posture about her that told him she was bubbly and energetic, and would jabber all the way to Oregon. She'd want to know about his life. What he did for a living. Where he grew up. Things Justin would rather forget.

He'd decided a long time ago that his job as a bounty

hunter, though Justin preferred the term recovery agent, suited him well. Considering he'd been called a restless spirit more times than he cared to admit, traveling the country to locate and apprehend individuals who'd skipped bail kept him on the move.

If he stayed in one place too long, he might have too much time on his hands. Time to think about his past. Better to run from it.

And that was the real problem with this skip he was after. Hunting the man brought Justin far too close to home.

ଓ

An hour and a half later, Justin landed at Paisley State Airport, rented a vehicle, and now stood at the top of Winter Ridge, the western-most border of the Oregon Outback. The high desert was remote and secluded in places, arid and barren as well. But the region had its redeeming qualities.

Justin hoped for as much himself. That's what this trip was all about.

But returning to the region made him itch for a long hike in the secluded mountains. He missed that.

Winter Ridge hung over Summer Lake and, to the north, the town by the same name. Behind him, the Freemont National Forest—2.3 million acres of wilderness for Benson Reed to get lost. But not before Reed stopped off to see his sister, and Justin would be there waiting. If he arrested the man, he'd get charged with kidnapping himself. This time, Justin had something else in mind. He climbed back into the

Tahoe and made the drive down the winding narrow road into the valley below.

He parked at the Ridgecrest Lodge near the lake where he'd wait for Reed. Sooner or later, the fugitive would turn up here. Lifting his duffel bag from the Tahoe, Justin felt the hint of winter in the gusty late-autumn wind blasting his face.

Shrugging off the chill that swept over him, he trudged into the main lodge to register for a room. A fire blazed beneath the large rock-hewn hearth. Considering there didn't appear to be anyone around to enjoy it, Justin thought it a waste. Most likely, he'd walked in during a lull in the afternoon.

This was big game hunting season. Deer, elk, and black bear. Cougars were hunted year-round.

And hunting fugitives? Well, that was against the law in Oregon.

A twenty-something woman, her hair the color of spun gold and secured at the nape of her neck, stood alone at the counter. She didn't notice as he approached, her attention completely focused on the magazine in front of her.

She wore a pale-yellow flowered blouse, a stark contradiction to the outdoorsy fixtures of the lodge. Looking at the top of her head, he could see her long lashes blinking and he followed her gaze to the image in the magazine. An ornate, lavish wedding dress emphasized the slender curves of an airbrushed, perfect model.

The chill that had swept over him outside burrowed deep into his bones now. Too bad the flames licking the hearth behind him would make no difference.

A LOVE RECOVERED

Darrow Kincaid stared at the gorgeous wedding dress in the bridal catalog and released a dreamy, but heavy sigh.

She might run her own business, but that didn't mean she could afford a wedding dress with a $4,000 price tag. What was she doing looking at this anyway?

Just because Smit had called her on Monday and asked if she was busy on Friday, adding he wanted to take her somewhere special, didn't mean he was going to propose.

Yes, it did. Darrow just knew it.

But she'd die if anyone saw her looking at the wedding catalog she'd picked up a month ago to add to her stack of others. It was presumptuous on her part. She'd given Trace the afternoon off, which put her standing at the front desk during a pause in activity, or she'd not have the chance to browse the pages filled with exquisite gowns. Darrow sighed again.

Someone cleared his throat and rang the desk bell. She froze, her fingers pressed against the slick pages of the catalog. Heat swam up her neck. She flipped the magazine shut and yanked her face up in one fluid motion. Smoky gray eyes bore into her, intense and unforgiving. The dark-haired man worked his stubbled, strong jaw a full ten seconds before his lips formed the hint of a smile.

Had he seen the dress she was looking at? Unfortunately, she cared.

Darrow realized she was staring. She was accustomed to the gruff hunters who frequented the lodge, especially this time of year, but this one was different. "Can I help you?"

"I need a room." His eyes flicked from her to the catalog.

Darrow slid it from the counter and thrust it on the shelf beneath. "Do you have a reservation?" The way he'd said he needed a room, she knew he didn't.

"Do I need one?"

She frowned. "We're usually booked solid this time of year. Without a reservation, I can't make any promises."

The man glanced behind him at the empty lobby. He tugged his cell from his pocket and glanced around the counter. "What's the number here?"

"Huh? Oh." She pointed at a pad of paper with the number then scanned the computer screen. She had a couple of vacant rooms, but they were reserved for a group arriving in two days. Her lodge plus a few cabins didn't accommodate a lot of people, but it was enough to keep her busy. Truthfully, it probably didn't require software to manage, but it made her feel official.

The phone rang, and Darrow answered. "Ridgecrest."

"I'd like a reservation." Darrow slowly looked up from the computer screen at the lone man before her. He held his cell to his ear. "Hello? Can I get a room, a cabin, anything?"

What was with this guy? Darrow allowed a mischievous grin. She'd bite, and she'd play his little game better than he. "Please hold."

She put him on hold and began typing away on the computer screen. He was a potential guest at her lodge and she shouldn't treat him rudely, but somehow she knew he wouldn't mind. He'd started it, after all. When she thought he'd grown impatient enough, she picked up the phone. "What is the date of your arrival?"

An incredulous laugh escaped through the phone and from the man across the counter. He hung up. "All right. I admit, I was being a little ornery. I'm sorry. By the way, you give as good as you get, but you should be glad I don't tell your manager. Do you have a room for me or not?"

Darrow smiled. He wasn't as standoffish as she thought. "First, I *am* the manager, and the owner."

"You?"

She stifled a grin at his stunned reaction. That would be just plain wrong. "I have a room available for two nights, but then it's booked. How long do you need to stay, Mr. . . . ?"

"Justin. . .Love."

Darrow arched a brow. "Really?" *A tough guy like you?*

He pursed his lips, glanced behind him, and ran a hand over his face.

"How long do you intend to stay, Mr. Love?"

"As long as it takes." His eyes grew intense again.

Whatever that meant. "Well, then, if you don't mind moving around as lodge guests with reservations come and go, then you could probably stay here forever." She smiled, hoping to warm the suddenly cold atmosphere.

After taking his pertinent information and payment for the room, Darrow slid the key across the counter. "Your room is on the second floor, up the stairs." She indicated the staircase across the lobby.

Too eager for the key, he grabbed her hand, too. A jolt

of. . .something. . .rushed up her arm. Darrow lifted her gaze to the mysterious man, but he was staring at her hand. Finally he withdrew the key and slid it across the counter.

"The bridal catalog you were looking at earlier. You're getting married?"

Taken aback at his words, Darrow searched for the right answer as her heart raced. "I. . .uh. . ."

"I didn't see an engagement ring. But it's none of my business."

Mysterious Justin Love turned away, lifted his duffel bag over his shoulder, and stalked across the lobby.

Darrow turned her back on the sight and swallowed the thick lump in her throat.

He might be as handsome and sturdy a specimen as she'd seen, and have a sense of humor, but his heart was stone cold. Either that or he'd erected a wall of ice around it. At any rate, he was a stranger and all her thoughts were conjecture. It bothered her that she cared.

White picket fence, a dog and cat, two point three children. That was all she ever wanted. Maybe Smit Cooper wasn't the most handsome of men, and maybe he didn't make her laugh very often, but Darrow had dated Smit for eight months now. He was as solid as they came. At least, solid enough for her.

Like her, Smit ran his own business. Tire sales. Everyone needed to buy a new set of tires or have their old tires balanced and rotated, or have their flat fixed now and then.

That might not be exciting enough for some, but Darrow wasn't interested in excitement.

Chapter 2

Later that evening, after Justin had settled into the rustic room he'd have for the next two days and made a few phone calls, he made his way to the lobby in search of food. Dinner was served at five o'clock, and he didn't want to miss it.

Plenty of guests milled about in the lodge now—a lot of them hunters coming in for a hot meal, or preparing to head out. He followed three men down a wide hallway decorated with photographs of bird-watchers, fishermen holding up their colossal catches, and men standing next to an eight-point stag.

Justin had enough practice at blending in without being noticed. Once he entered the dining room, he selected a small booth in a dark corner without waiting to be seated. A wood-burning stove sat at the far wall, and dimly lit sconces accented wildlife images, both photographs and oil paintings. A glance around the room told him Reed wasn't there. But then, it could be days before he arrived.

A short pudgy waitress took his order of rib eye steak. She returned with a hot cup of coffee and a carafe. Pouring the coffee she smiled at him, and the next thing he knew, hot liquid was spilling over the table and into his lap.

Justin ground his teeth and slid from the booth, wiping at the steaming brew on his jeans. He'd caught it before it seeped through completely and left him with second-degree burns across his legs.

"I'm so sorry, sir." Her eyes filled with tears. "This is my first day."

"It's okay. No harm done." The quiet in the room was palpable. A glimpse told him he had an audience. So much for blending in. He waited for her to wipe out the booth and he took his seat again, not wanting to draw further attention. He should probably go up to his room and change, but his steak was on the way and he was hungry.

Justin blew out a breath. He shouldn't even be in Oregon, but now that he'd made the decision to come, he would see the deed through. After meeting Darrow Kincaid, he'd considered holing up in his room, taking his meals there, but that would hardly put him in a position to see Reed when he showed his face. Reed didn't share the same last name with his sister because he'd changed it in an effort to change his life, escape his past, according to his wife.

Meeting the sister had thrown Justin off balance. He hadn't expected that she would catch his eye, or that her smile would knock on a door he'd bolted shut long ago.

For someone who ran a lodge hedging a wilderness area, Darrow appeared delicate and refined, naive even. The shock that coursed through him when he'd accidentally grabbed her hand while retrieving the key still unsettled him. The way she'd played along when he'd called to make a reservation told him she had a good sense of humor. Gazing into the black coffee, he was torn between a smile and a frown.

He'd caught her looking at wedding dresses, which gave him some relief. She was already otherwise engaged, and Justin could more easily ignore her. Standing there engrossed in the happily-ever-after catalog, looking as lovely as any woman he'd seen, she represented everything Justin ran from. Loving someone was dangerous, especially in his line of work. He'd seen it a thousand times.

The heartache. . .the betrayal.

It ended in disaster, one way or the other. He was already paying the price for his part in a tragedy, the cost more than he could ever repay.

His stomach growled. Where was that steak?

A plate flaunting a steak, baked potato, and green beans, and a side of buttery rolls slid across the table, jarring him from his thoughts. "It's on the house."

He knew that voice. Justin looked up at Darrow. He saw now that her dainty yellow flowered shirt was actually a dress. She was a little skinny for his taste, that is, if he were looking. He offered his best leave-me-alone expression. "That's not necessary." Justin turned his attention to his plate. He bowed his head and thanked God for the meal, said a silent prayer asking God to make Darrow go away, then began slicing into the juicy, tender rib eye. But Darrow still hovered at the table. He could only ignore her for so long.

Finally, he gazed up at her, steeling himself against her

sweet face and golden hair. Though warm and kind, her light blue-green eyes, the color of Summer Lake, searched his. He noticed faint lines around her eyes that told him she was nearing thirty, if he had to guess.

"Do you mind if I join you?" She gestured at the booth opposite him.

He didn't get it. He acted cold and unfriendly. Why would any woman, especially a woman like her, take an interest in him? But maybe he had it wrong. Maybe his credit card didn't go through. Maybe he shouldn't have played with her, using his cell to book a room while standing right there.

"There a problem with my reservation?" He pressed the mug against his lips to hide his wry grin as he recalled their conversation earlier in the day.

She apparently took his question to mean she could sit down. "Your reservation is fine." She'd emphasized the word *reservation* like it was their little joke. If Justin didn't want to be something other than a jerk, it *would* be their little joke.

He buttered his potato and seasoned it just right, and continued eating as though she weren't there. But all he wanted to do was look across the table at her. Did she know that? Was that why his ignoring her didn't seem to bother her?

"Mr. Love. . .I wanted to say I was sorry about the mishap. That's all." Her warm, soft voice swept over him.

If he wasn't careful, she could thaw the cold heart he'd worked so hard to maintain. Justin leaned against the seat and sighed. "As I already said, it was no trouble."

"I'm happy to launder your clothes for you, once you've

removed them." Crimson rushed to her cheeks.

Her comment had been innocent in itself, but the resulting blush made Justin shift in his seat. Why wouldn't she just go away? He'd never had a problem like this, and wasn't sure how to get rid of her. "I can manage."

"You're not here to hunt, are you?" Darrow examined her short nails.

He couldn't exactly tell her the truth.

Oh, I'm hunting. . .

Using her lodge like a deer blind—a place to hide while he waited for his prey. "Why do you want to know?" He eyed her over the rim of his cup.

Justin didn't want to be too unobliging because she could easily deny him a room after his two days was up. But how did he discourage her? Her interest or curiosity, whatever it was that kept her sitting across from him, was unwanted.

"Part of what the lodge offers is resources and information. Usually, people have a reason to stay here. They are here to hunt, hike, explore the petroglyphs, bird-watch, you name it. You caught me off guard earlier today. I should have told you when you checked in, and I'm sorry. If you're not here to hunt, then what can I help you with?"

He'd only caught her off guard because her eyes were on a wedding gown. "Nothing. Really."

"On Saturdays, I usually take a group hiking, depending on the interest."

Hiking, huh? "Honestly, I'm just passing through."

Her fishing for information disturbed him. Had Reed

contacted her, told her to be on the lookout for anyone suspicious?

ଓ

Darrow slipped her shaky hands from the table. "I'm sorry to take up your time. I see a lot of the same faces every year. Since you're new to Ridgecrest Lodge, I wanted to make sure you know about things to do in the area."

She slid from the seat before she made a bigger fool of herself. Could he see right through her?

When he looked up, his shimmering gray eyes held a glint of amusement. "I appreciate the personal touch, and if I have questions, you'll be the first to know."

His answer made her smile, and to her delight, he cracked a grin in return, revealing a flicker of warmth in his rugged, but unapproachable, hard exterior. His reaction infused her with hope, but for what, she didn't know.

She nodded and left the room with as much poise as she could muster. Once she exited the dining hall, Darrow stepped to the side and pressed her back against the wall, taking several deep breaths.

What was the matter with her?

She reasoned that she just wanted to make sure Justin Love, a new guest at the lodge, had everything he needed. Sitting across from him, her pounding heart uncovered the lie she'd told herself.

What she really wanted was to experience again the spark he'd ignited. The current she'd felt earlier today that left crazy thoughts swirling in her head. Pestering him while he ate his dinner attested to that. But this was wrong. All wrong. He was a stranger. And she was in a relationship.

A relationship between a man and a woman shouldn't be just about the spark.

Darrow wasn't the kind of girl to throw herself at a man like that. In fact, that was the gutsiest thing she'd ever done—talk to a stranger while he ate his dinner—and on the surface it appeared innocent enough.

What was it about then?

The answer hovered in her thoughts just out of reach. . .but then. . .she snatched it. Was what she had with Smit enough? She'd better be sure before she took the next step, if it was ever offered.

Lord, help me to know. . .

Trace stood in front of her. Darrow hadn't even noticed her approach.

"You okay?" Trace asked.

"It's nothing. What are you doing back? I gave you the afternoon off."

Trace Mulligan had worked at the lodge with her for the last decade, and continued to work after Darrow bought the lodge with the money her grandfather left her when he died.

"Jeremy's watching Lauren now. He's back from Bend. I can't afford to lose the hours, so I'm here again. Was on my way to grab a plate in the kitchen when I saw you."

That was just the excuse she needed. "I'm feeling a little queasy, that's all. Heading home now."

Darrow lived in a cabin near the lodge and hurried down the wooded path, tugging her sweater around her. This time of year, she needed to shed the light and airy dresses and wear jeans and boots. She hated giving up the spring and summer, but she couldn't deny that fall was about to fade to winter. Darrow was in denial about a lot of things. Wrapped in a blanket, she sat on her porch and listened to the stream trickle only a few yards away.

An hour later, the porch creaked, and she looked up to see Trace, her hand gripping the post. "Stopped by to see if you're feeling better."

Darrow shook her head and stared into the woods, which would soon be completely dark except for the security light if she chose to turn it on.

Trace's boots creaked across the porch until she stood next to Darrow. "We've known each other a long time. I can tell when something's bothering you."

Darrow took a breath. "How did you know that Jeremy was the man for you?"

Her friend eased into the other rocking chair. "That's a hard one to answer. I think it's different for everyone. But for me, it was a lot of little things, and in the end love is a choice. Why? Something happen between you and Smit?" Trace's eyes grew wide. "Did he ask you to marry him?"

Despite her confusion, Darrow laughed. "No, nothing like that. Not yet. But I'm scared he's going to."

"Scared? I thought you wanted him to ask." Trace leaned forward in the rocking chair. "All right. What am I missing?"

"Have you ever wondered if you made a mistake marrying Jeremy?"

"Wow, you're getting pretty serious and personal here. I'll answer you on one condition; you tell me what's going on. I mean what's *really* going on."

"Okay." Though Darrow wasn't exactly sure how much she was willing to share.

"In moments of anger, fits of rage, frustration, sure I wonder if I made a mistake. But that passes very quickly when I realize how wrong it is to think that way. Most of the time emotions stemming from anger shouldn't be trusted."

"You're a wise woman for your age. How did you get so smart when you're only thirty-one?"

"Is that what this is about? You're afraid that you're getting too old and Smit is never going to ask? Your biological clock is ticking?" Trace's soft, pleasant laugh eased some of the tension in Darrow's neck. That was what she loved about her.

"You are the sister I wished I had." Instead, Darrow had a brother she hadn't seen in five years. He'd gotten into a lot of trouble when they were growing up. Darrow didn't know where he was or what he was doing. She hated that.

"Okay. Now tell me what's on your mind. What else are sisters for?" Trace asked.

Darrow frowned. Sharing the dark thoughts in her heart would probably make Trace see her in a different way. "I think Smit might propose on Friday night."

"And?"

"He's a good stable man. He can offer me the only thing

I've been missing in my life—a family of my own." Darrow had imagined what her life would be like if Smit ever proposed. "I've counted on it for so long, I've even selected the color schemes in each room of the home we'll have together. I still can't decide between the yellow-flowered wallpaper with the blue drapes or vice versa." She infused her last statement with humor and they both laughed.

"You're just getting wedding jitters before the engagement."

Darrow stood from the chair and moved to stand at the porch railing, tugging the blanket tighter against the evening chill. She could just make out a doe quietly picking her way through the thicket.

"Smit is a good stable man. But it's better to find a man who really makes you feel alive before it's too late," Trace said, her voice soft.

"How did you know?" That a stranger had ignited a flame in Darrow that Smit never had.

"I didn't. It was just a guess. I've never seen much chemistry between the two of you, frankly."

"But it's not just about chemistry, is it?"

"No. There's so much more, and it's a decision that requires prayerful consideration. You shouldn't go into a marriage without knowing if he's the one God has for you."

"You're right, I know. But, maybe it's like you said, I've just got pre-engagement jitters."

Darrow couldn't stop the doubts. If she married Smit, would she be settling?

Smit was here and told her he loved her. Justin could be

married for all she knew. And he said he was just passing through. He could be a serial killer, a drug addict, or he might not know the Lord—although he'd prayed before his meal. Why had Darrow allowed this man to become a rockslide, blocking her straight and narrow path?

Chapter 3

Sitting behind the ancient pine desk that had come with the lodge when she bought it, Darrow finished tweaking details for the upcoming Thanksgiving weekend, which was a big holiday for the lodge. Hunters didn't start pouring in until late Thursday and early Friday morning, after they'd enjoyed Thanksgiving with their families. All the same, the lodge would offer the traditional meal: turkey, dressing, and cranberry sauce—the works. Though that was several weeks away, she knew it would sneak up on her if she didn't pay attention.

She managed to keep her thoughts off Justin and focused back on Smit, like a good and faithful girlfriend. She wasn't his wife or fiancée yet, but that didn't matter. Thinking of Justin made her feel like she had a cheating heart. Smit was a good man, and Darrow would do her best to focus on his qualities.

Things were going to work out, she told herself.

Repeatedly.

Thankfully, she hadn't seen Justin yesterday and that helped to ease the wild murmurings of her heart. Today, Justin would need to move to a cabin if he planned to stay. A couple, the

Whiteheads, who frequented the lodge, was due to check in, and Elise didn't like the cabins. She enjoyed hiking while her husband hunted. That was all she'd allow the man. Darrow didn't know whether to feel sorry for him or not, but considering how he appeared to adore his wife, she thought not. That was the kind of marriage she wanted. A man who adored and cherished her.

I should feel the same way. She sighed, determined to push her doubts aside.

"How's my girl?"

At the familiar voice, Darrow jerked her head up. Smit leaned in the doorframe. Working long and hard running the business and doing the manual labor required to install tires gave Smit a sturdy form. His hair was thinning a little at the top, and his chin wasn't strong and defined, but that didn't matter to Darrow. He had a good heart.

Darrow smiled. "What brings you by?"

"Wanted to see you for a second. Say a quick hello." His dusky brown eyes held much of the adoration she often saw there, but something was missing. What was it? "Walk me out?"

Heaviness pressed on her heart as she stood. "Okay."

He grinned. "I'm sorry I haven't been by in a few days."

"I know you're busy. You don't have to stop by just to see me." Darrow edged around the desk and went into his arms. She rested her head against his chest, searching, straining for reassurance. "But I'm glad you did."

Smit kissed the top of her head then released her. He led her down the short hallway to the lobby. Trace and another employee, Renee, were busy at the counter, and glanced over at Darrow as she passed. Trace gave her an encouraging smile. Darrow winked, letting her know everything would be okay. She would make it through any misgivings.

Smit grabbed Darrow's hand, holding it as they meandered across the large area rug, passing the fire blazing in the hearth and a cluster of guests in animated conversation. When he squeezed her hand, Darrow kept her gaze on her surroundings.

"What's bothering you today?" Smit asked, stopping next to a photograph of bird-watchers. He took her chin and lifted her face, forcing her to look at him.

Darrow's heart jumped, but not for the right reason. "I'm tired, that's all." How could she share her deepest thoughts when they were so dark and hurtful, even to her?

"Come here." Smit tugged her around the wall into a corner. He leaned in to kiss her, but she pressed her hands against his chest.

"You know I don't like to do this in public, especially at work in front of the guests." She wanted to keep her personal life just that.

Smit pressed his lips against hers anyway, lightly and gently. Darrow got the strange feeling he was searching for answers with his kiss. When he eased back he brushed his hand down her face, a slight frown on his lips.

"I'll call you tomorrow to confirm our plans for Friday night."

He was always so thoughtful. Darrow smiled. "I'm looking forward to Friday." In truth, she was terrified. Smit dropping by today had only made it worse.

"Me, too. I have something special planned, remember." Holding her hand, he took a step away and studied her. Darrow had the odd sense that his behavior had nothing at all to do with the doubts she wrangled with. He couldn't know anything about them. No. The change was in him, not Darrow.

Smit nodded good-bye then stepped through the lodge exit, brushing by Justin, who paid him no attention. The light bounced off the brilliant gray of Justin's eyes as he entered, and seeing her, he paused.

Please, just keep going. But it was no use. He just stood there staring, contemplating. Darrow pushed away from the wall to go back to her office. Justin walked next to her, matching her pace, which was probably considerably slower than his. He was at least a head taller than she and had long legs compared to Darrow.

"So he's the one you're going to marry." Justin's statement startled her.

She forced her palpitating heart to calm down and kept her face straight ahead. "Keep your voice down, please."

As they walked by the front desk, Trace glanced her way and knit her brows. Darrow headed to her office with Justin in tow, something she wouldn't have done had Justin not mentioned her marriage to Smit. He followed her into the office as if he'd intended to do that from the beginning, as if she'd invited him. Without asking, he closed the door behind him then sat down.

Leaning back in the chair with all the confidence in the world, he crossed one leg over his knee. His deep gaze had her cornered. His presence seemed to fill her office.

Darrow struggled to breathe. "I'll thank you not to mention again that I'm getting married. I'm not engaged. I haven't received a proposal. You could ruin everything."

He didn't answer but ran his hand down one side of his face and then the other as though judging the quality of a new razor.

"It doesn't concern you," she said.

He dropped his chin and looked at her. "Are you sure about that?"

What are you doing? He'd gotten to her with that, and now he regretted his words.

To a degree, she was right. That she was planning to marry a man she didn't love wasn't his business. But it was a great misfortune all the same, and he was all about preventing tragedy these days, if it was within his power.

Justin had seen it in Darrow's eyes. She didn't love the man. Probably her intended fiancé knew it as well. But Justin needed to tread carefully where she was concerned. His usual modus operandi was to act aloof, keep his distance. Push people away. But with Darrow, there was something about her. . .

Her chest heaved. "Look, Mr. Love. Is there something I can do for you?"

"First, call me Justin. Second, you said I need to move to another room today."

"The front desk can help you with that."

"I was at the front desk earlier. I was told I didn't have a reservation." With a grin, he paused to let that sink in, hoping to disperse the tension in the room. "I explained the situation, and the girl told me that I should speak to you."

Darrow appeared to shrink, her frown deepening. Was she reacting to Justin or what he'd said? He hated that he'd wiped away her sweet smile. That hadn't been his intention.

"How did you know?" Her question was barely audible. "You weren't even there. You came inside the lodge as he was leaving. You didn't see us together."

What could he say? That he was trained to be observant? "I saw you together through the glass door as I came in. It doesn't take a rocket scientist." But he'd seen enough. He also saw that Darrow Kincaid wasn't ecstatic, wasn't brimming with excitement, with the hope of engagement. Something was wrong.

She shoved away from her desk. "Your cabin should be ready. I'll get you the key."

"How long do I have to stay in the cabin? I prefer the lodge if something opens up." He didn't want to risk missing Reed.

"How long do you plan to stay?"

According to Reed's wife he was driving all the way from Florida, taking the back roads, everything he could do to escape notice as he made his way to Oregon. From the sounds of it, he was desperate to see his sister. But why? "Could be a week or two. Maybe more."

The gorgeous, soft-tempered blond shook her head slightly, her usually bright Summer Lake eyes dark. He knew the question going through her mind. She wanted to know why he was here. What he was waiting on. But she didn't voice her thoughts. Justin was grateful for that. He was being far too transparent with her.

She could very well know that her brother was headed to see her, could be on the lookout for someone like Justin. But chances were that Reed was counting on Oregon's laws prohibiting bounty hunting to keep him safe. Chances were he wasn't expecting anyone to pursue him here.

Justin followed her to the front desk where she recorded his stay in the cabin and retrieved the key.

Rather than handing it over, though, she held on to the key. "I'd better show you to the cabin. It's a little off the beaten track. People often get lost and need help finding their way."

Justin nodded, pondering her statement. *People often get lost and need help finding their way.* Did she know how profound that was?

He followed her through the lobby and out a side door. The weather had warmed considerably since this morning. Clouds had dispersed, presenting a crystal blue sky. A gust of wind caught them as they stepped off the last stair, the air still carrying a chill to it. The breeze lifted Darrow's hair, which she'd worn down today. It hung past her shoulders, curling near the ends. She grabbed it and held it to one side.

As she continued her stroll down the trail behind the lodge, Justin slowed his step to match hers. He was surprised that she had nothing to say, and though he would normally appreciate the silence, he wanted to hear her voice.

"You mentioned there's plenty to do in the area. What would you recommend?" He cringed, hearing the stilt to his question, but he needed her to think he was here to enjoy the environment, nothing more. So far he'd done a poor job of that. Plus, she mentioned she led a group hiking.

"There are brochures in the lobby to answer all your questions."

"But I asked what *you* would recommend. You offer the personal touch at your lodge, remember?" Why was he asking? Did he really care about what she would find interesting? Yes. . .he did.

"This way." Darrow turned to the right, down a barely noticeable path that wound between aspen and ponderosa pine. "Usually, I make recommendations when I know what a person is looking for, their interests." At the cabin she paused and looked at him. "I confess, Justin Love, I don't know anything about you."

"Do you want to?" Justin sucked in a breath. Had he really just asked that? The woman was already planning to marry someone. "Hiking. I would enjoy hiking. Preferably someplace secluded. Someplace with you."

You're heading into dangerous territory.

The corners of Darrow's mouth lifted. Though tenuous, her smile had returned full-tilt. Justin couldn't help himself. He brushed a strand of hair from her face.

If he spent time with her, could he talk her out of her current path leading to marital unhappiness? Should he? He had a feeling that would lead him to his own tragic heartbreak or worse.

Darrow held the key out to him. "I'm in a relationship, remember?"

Justin took the key, allowing his hand to grab on to hers and hold it, feeling the tension between them once more. "I remember."

Chapter 4

Late Friday afternoon, Darrow rubbed the tense and aching muscles in her neck. She peeked in on the kitchen to make sure all was well for the evening meal. Then she checked on Trace at registration.

Trace was cleaning out the shelves under the counter while it was quiet. The weekend crowd would soon keep her busy. She thrust her arm in deep and pulled out a catalog. Trace looked at it, then flipped it over for Darrow to see.

"You wouldn't know anything about this, would you?" Trace gave her a wry grin.

Darrow pressed her hand to her head. "Give me that." She snatched it, her cheeks warming.

Trace smiled. "No need to be embarrassed. What are you still doing here, anyway? Tonight's the big night, isn't it?"

A couple entered through the front door and gazed around the lodge then spotted the registration desk.

"I don't know. Smit was supposed to call me yesterday to confirm." Darrow was disappointed and yet relieved at the same time.

After a sympathetic look at Darrow, Trace turned her

attention to the couple approaching the desk. Darrow left her to her work and headed to her cabin, unsure if she needed to prepare for a special evening with Smit or not. She should just call him herself but that had never been their way. Smit liked to keep things old-fashioned. He was the one to call or stop by.

Darrow stared at her phone as she absently exited the lodge and decided to call him to make sure they still had plans for the evening. The phone rang before she could call. It was Smit.

"Oh," she said. "I've been waiting to hear from you."

"I know I promised you something special this evening but I'm going to have to cancel our plans. I'm sorry." He sounded disappointed. "I've got the flu."

"Let me take care of you. I can make you some chicken soup." Darrow held on to hope that Smit would let her come over. This sudden turn of events caught her by surprise, and all her doubts about him seemed to flee. He'd acted different this week. Was she losing him?

"No. You can't." Smit coughed. "I don't want you to catch this nasty stuff. Best if I sleep it off. I would have called earlier, but honestly, I hoped to feel better. I'll call you tomorrow."

"Smit?" He'd been her sure thing, and now suddenly, she wasn't sure he was there for her anymore.

"Yes?" His voice was scratchy.

I love you? "Let me know if you need me." And she meant it. But her sudden insecurity was pathetic. She'd bring him the soup, ignoring his protest.

"I will." Smit hung up.

Darrow stuck her phone in her pocket. What was the

matter with her? She strolled along the trail toward her cabin and passed it, needing the cooler evening breeze to slap some sense into her. All week, she'd doubted her feelings for Smit, and that, because of her encounter with a stranger. Now that she sensed distance in Smit, apprehension niggled at the back of her mind.

The very idea of her fickle thoughts made her sick. Her mother had run away with another man when Darrow was only ten, devastating the family. Darrow would not be unfaithful like that. And yet. . .she hadn't committed herself to Smit. Not yet.

That thought, at least, brought her a measure of relief. She needed to know for certain it was the right thing to do. She'd been content, completely content, until Justin Love had disturbed her peace. Once he left, all would be well. In the meantime, she should avoid the man, if possible.

Right now, she feared there were too many wild places in her heart. It was an untamed wilderness.

Lord, I need Your guidance and Your help. Please forgive me if my heart has strayed from the one You intend me to be with. Be my guiding light.

Walking with her head down in prayer, she knew the path well as it curved to the left and rose, edged by large boulders on either side. She paused and pressed her back against the rock wall, longing for a certainty strong and unmoving like the rock she leaned on. In the end, there was only One she could count on like that.

As for her own commitments, once she gave her heart completely to someone, Darrow would never bend from that decision. She closed her eyes and lifted her face to the beam of remaining sun that reached down between the rocks, feeling the warmth against her skin.

Darrow saw things clearly. One touch from a stranger had opened her eyes to something more. Now she was afraid to commit to Smit, but she was also afraid of losing him—he had been her dream for so long.

Oh Lord, can I go back? Can I recover what I lost? Wind burst between the rocks, wrapping her body and mind in cold fingers, and bringing with it an animated and familiar voice.

Darrow crept around the boulder and off the path.

Justin stood with his back to her, looking off in the distance, his cell phone to his ear. Reception was spotty in the area, but he'd apparently found a signal.

"Did you lie to me when you sent me here?" Bitterness and pain strained his voice.

ଓ

"Of course not." A sob broke across the phone. "How could you think that?"

"For one thing, you're his wife. You could have sent me here to—" A noise behind him brought Justin around.

Darrow stood frozen a few yards away. "I. . .uh. . .I'm sorry."

Frowning, she lowered her eyes toward the ground and turned around, hurrying back to the trail. She disappeared behind the boulders.

Great. Justin had tried to reach Reed's wife all day and she had to call now, while he was walking a trail. He had to take the call. Still, it was secluded. He hadn't seen a soul on it since he'd been here, that was, until today.

"You still there?"

"Yeah. You could have sent me on the wrong trail."

"But why would I do that? You know what this is about."

He sighed. Once he'd heard Reed was headed to Oregon, he should have left it at that. "I do. That's the only reason I'm here, because I can't arrest him. That's why I need to know now that you're telling me the truth."

"Yes. I swear."

"Have you heard from him?" Justin paced up and down the grassy knoll along the trail, watching for any other hikers, unwelcome eavesdroppers.

"No." Her voice squeaked, and then she started another round of crying.

"I'm going to trace his phone calls and anything else I can do to make sure he didn't lie to you about where he was headed. Or that you didn't lie to me."

"Okay. And Justin. . ."

"Yes?"

"Thank you."

He ended the call and hiked around boulders and onto the trail, following it in the direction he'd seen Darrow go. The sun was dipping low and darkness would close in on him soon.

He hated stakeouts. They forced him to stay in one place too long. Darrow's presence complicated things, especially since she'd overheard his conversation. Just how much, he didn't know. But he had his reasons, and they went much deeper than hunting a man who'd skipped bail, arresting him, and driving him back to the county where he was arrested.

Redemption. It was all about redemption.

He hurried along the path, looking for Darrow. A couple of kids ran past, nearly running into him. Where were their parents? Ah, he spotted them up the trail, holding hands, laughing and gazing at each other like they wanted to recapture the love they once had.

But what did he know about it? Nothing. They were so engrossed in each other they didn't notice the approaching darkness. That was their business. The romantic couple behind him, he pushed down the trail passing a cabin here and there until the trees thickened.

There. Darrow stood on a porch, dimly lit by a small lamp. She leaned over the railing, gazing out into the woods to Justin's left.

Should he approach her? Find out what she'd overheard? It wasn't like he could continue on the trail without her seeing him. Justin hung his head, staring at the trail below and continued on. A stream trickled somewhere nearby. When he neared her cabin, he looked up, hoping to see her. The door closed.

She'd gone inside.

Her disappearance didn't deter him. He marched up the steps onto the porch and clomped over to the door, so she'd know he was coming. He knocked. With the noise he made, he wouldn't give her the chance to claim she hadn't known he was at the door. Maybe she'd invite him in for a cup of coffee, giving him time to find out what she'd heard.

A log swelled in his throat. Regardless, Justin wanted to be with her. With that thought, he turned to go. He was in dangerous territory.

The door swung open behind him.

"Justin?" Her pleasant voice tugged him around.

"I'm sorry if I disturbed you."

Her smile lit up her face, but there was pain in her eyes he hadn't seen that first day. "You didn't disturb me. I was just getting ready to make chicken soup to take to Smit. You can come in, if you'd like."

Feeling thirteen again and awkward, Justin thrust his hands into his pockets and looked away. "I don't know."

She had the boyfriend she was anxious to marry. He should be glad about that. But he wasn't. It wasn't his business. What was he doing here again? Oh yeah—to find out what she'd overheard.

She laughed and grabbed his hand, pulling him inside. "You can tell me if it tastes any good. I should have started it hours ago. It's better when it simmers long and slow. But Smit needs it tonight."

Justin didn't want to hear about Smit. He dropped into the hardwood chair at her kitchen table. "So, you live in one of the guest cabins?"

"Not exactly. This one is bigger, built to my specifications." She poured in chicken stock and noodles and added seasonings.

Some of the earlier stress had eased from her tense shoulders. At least compared to when he'd caught her listening to his call.

She whirled from the pot on the stove. "What can I get you? Coffee, tea, milk, soda?"

"Got anything boring like water?"

Her laugh enthralled him. "Funny."

She poured a glass from the tap then handed it to him.

Darrow slid a chair from the table and sat down across from him. This was nice. Sitting here with her. If only he didn't have ulterior motives. Would he have to bring it up? Or would she?

He downed the water, watching her as he did. There were a lot of reasons he shouldn't be in Oregon, and Darrow was quickly becoming one of them. Justin should stand up and walk out while he could. Leave while he had the chance.

Setting the glass down, he ran his hand over the table, admiring the grain. "I didn't mean to run you off the trail earlier."

Her smile disappeared. "No, it was my fault. I walked around the corner and there you were. I'm sorry if it looked like I was listening in on your call. I wasn't."

Nodding, he looked at the pot on the stove behind her. "So, your boyfriend sick? Is that why you're making him chicken soup?"

She rubbed her finger under her nose. "We were going on a date tonight. It was supposed to be special. But he has the flu."

Jealousy seared him. Surprised him as well. He had no right.

"You have any family that lives nearby who plan to attend your wedding?" He grinned, teasing, knowing she didn't like that he knew her secret. "Or you two going to elope?"

Waiting for her answer, he stood, the chair scraping the wood floor. He made his way around the living room, gazed at her photographs on the wall and the cabinets, all the while glancing back at her, making her feel at ease, he hoped. He wanted to appear natural, not like he was looking for something. How close were she and Reed?

"My mother left when I was young, and my father died when I was a teenager. I lived with my grandfather after that. I haven't seen or heard from my brother in five years. Any family at our wedding will be Smit's. I only have friends." She stood now, as well, moving back to the stove. "I don't know why I said any of that. He hasn't proposed."

"I didn't mean to pry. Just a little friendly conversation."

Five years? Justin's pulse rocketed. Why would Reed come here now? Unless he'd gotten a conscience and intended to make amends.

Reed wasn't so different from Justin. The irony slammed him.

From the small den near the woodstove, Justin watched Darrow stir her soup.

"Here." She ladled soup into a spoon and held it out for him to try. "It probably won't taste very good. It really needs to simmer."

"You could let it cook at his house. He can eat it when he's ready." Justin sipped the soup. He closed his eyes and enjoyed the flavor.

When he opened them Darrow was smiling. *Beautiful.*

"You like?"

He gazed into her gorgeous eyes, her soft expression. "Yes, very much."

Chapter 5

A week later on Saturday, Darrow and her hiking group walked along a well-kept trail through trees shimmering in burnt sienna and golds in the Gearhart Mountain Wilderness. She'd taken Corral Creek Road to the trailhead for Blue Lake. Then it was an easy two-mile hike through old-growth forests. Craggy peaks reached to the sky around them. Ridge tops were crowned with rock formations, leaving her to figure out what the shape represented. Much like she did with clouds.

Darrow sighed. She couldn't get enough of the backwoods beauty and was grateful she lived close enough to hike in the Fremont National Forest on a weekly basis. The day was chilly and overcast. This time of year, the weather could change fast and for the worse. She expected it to snow any day now, especially in the higher elevations.

Only two hikers from the lodge joined her today, so it wasn't exactly a group. Elise Whitehead, who came to the lodge with her husband every year and went hiking with Darrow while he hunted.

And Justin Love.

Smit never went hiking with her because he claimed he couldn't get away from his business, but she knew he didn't enjoy the outdoors as much as she did. To him, traipsing through the woods was a waste of time. That was why his business remained stable and strong—he was a workaholic. She rarely saw him during the workweek unless he stopped by the lodge. This week, she hadn't seen him at all. But that wasn't what bothered her.

Last Friday night, he'd canceled taking her somewhere special because he had the flu. She'd made him chicken soup and taken it to his house, but he wasn't there. He'd warned her not to come, but that was because he didn't want to get her sick, or so he said. Later, he claimed he'd gone out to get some cold medicine. She could have done that for him, if he'd let her.

What was happening to them?

Elise came up next to her as they walked. "Are you sure we shouldn't have gone to Diablo's Rim? I think I smell snow in the air."

"That's my least favorite place to hike." The peak hugged the Summer Lake Valley opposite from Winter's Ridge—a vastly different region, desolate and dry.

"I know, I remember the hike from last time."

"Nothing but sagebrush and bunchgrass. The only nice thing is watching the birds migrating to the lakes in the valley. Or hawks and golden eagles flying high. They're beautiful," Darrow said.

"And I like to look across the entire state of Oregon and see Steens Mountain to the east. Now that's amazing." Elise kept in step with Darrow. "I can see why you like it here, but I don't want to get caught in a winter storm."

"I'm with Darrow." Justin had hung back for most of the hike. Now he walked alongside Darrow, too. "It can't hold a candle to the Gearhart Mountain Wilderness."

What did he know about Diablo's Rim or Gearhart?

He was a guest at the lodge. This was what she did with guests. But Justin's presence made her uncomfortable.

Why had Justin shown up in the lobby when they were leaving for the hike? Why didn't Smit enjoy hiking, too, then he could have joined them? She could have spent time with him, growing closer instead of apart. Instead, Justin was here and she was growing closer to him, despite her best efforts.

These were all things out of her control. Justin showing up in her life when he did, that was out of her control.

A person could tell when someone liked them.

Darrow lifted her face to look at a rocky spire to the north, glancing at Justin while she did. He'd been coldhearted and distant at first, or tried to appear that way. But she'd sensed him warming to her. She sensed, too, that his aloofness derived from something dark and painful.

A secret maybe.

She recalled the words she'd overheard.

Did you lie to me when you sent me here? The words had disturbed her, but they were none of her business. She'd only heard part of the conversation. Still, what could it be about?

That was why it was a big problem that her heart had warmed to him as well. She was attracted to him, yes, but she liked everything about him. The way he smiled, the way he teased, his sense of humor, and to top it off, he appeared to enjoy hiking as much as she did. None of that mattered if he was going to leave. Nothing would come of it except to open her eyes to everything wrong in her relationship with Smit.

"This time of year the leaves are such brilliant colors." Elise was breathing harder now. The older woman wasn't accustomed to walking the distance or in the mountains like Darrow.

"Like God took a paintbrush to them," Justin said, pausing to look at a stream of clear mountain water.

Had he really just said that? She'd seen him pray over his food in the restaurant, right in front of her. She wondered if he was a Christian. His coolness had thrown her on that point.

"In places you can hike for miles without ever seeing another soul," he said. "There are places untouched by human hands."

Yes, that's exactly it. He got it. He felt the same way she did. Justin was a kindred spirit.

"You're starting to sound like a poet." Elise chuckled.

Darrow thought of the wilderness surrounding her, some places untouched. She thought of her untamed heart, of the places also untouched. Somehow, Justin had found his way in. He'd touched one of the wild places in her heart.

But what about Smit?

What about Justin's words, *Did you lie to me when you sent me here?* What did they mean? Why was he here?

"An easy place to get lost, if you wanted." Justin stared at her now, instead of the stream. "Have you ever thought of leaving the world behind and hiding in the wilderness?"

"I love nature, but it's an escape for me, that's all. A brief getaway from the chaos."

☙

Just checking. . .

He wanted to hear her response. Nothing registered behind her eyes that told him she was expecting her brother. But Justin was. Any day. Any minute.

"You sound like you know the area well. Have you been here before? Or did you grow up near here?" Darrow asked.

He'd done it now, opening his mouth. It was more than he'd wanted to reveal. One question would lead to another and would end in questioning his reasons for being at the lodge.

"Let's just say Oregon is a hobby of mine." He grinned, hoping she'd let it go at that.

"A hobby?" Darrow eyed him. "Really?"

Justin glanced at the heavy clouds above, ready to drop their load of snow. When he looked back, Darrow was smiling at the clear water splashing over boulders and rocks.

Behind her the golden and orange leaves framed her spun-gold locks. It wouldn't be difficult for him to forget why he was here, the business he was on. In fact, leaving the world behind sounded like a nice idea at the moment, as long as he could take her with him. She was sweet and innocent—someone to shave off his rough edges—a sharp contrast to the harsh reality of his life.

She'd chipped away at his heart and burrowed in, but once she found out his reason for staying at her lodge, what they had between them, small and fragile, would shatter.

"What's the matter?" A frown fought with a smile on her lips.

He hadn't realized she was staring. "Nothing."

One of the rocky crags rising from the trees around the lake caught his eye. "I'll be right back."

He jogged off, hoping to climb up to the ledge. Some of the most remarkable views could be seen in the Gearhart Mountain Wilderness.

"Where are you going?" she called.

"Just wait here." He laughed. Elise wasn't in shape to climb, and he figured Darrow, if she wanted to go with him, wouldn't leave Elise behind.

He made his way around the lake to the tree line and the base of the crag where stacked boulders made it a simple climb to the ledge. There he'd find a great view.

Despite the chill in the air, sweat slid down his back and forehead by the time he hefted himself onto the shelf. First he looked to Darrow and waved.

She cupped her hands and yelled. "You're crazy, you know that?"

Justin took in the view—forest and mountains and cliffs—beauty as far as the eye could see. The back of his eyes burned. He'd forgotten how much he loved it here. How much he missed Oregon. His brothers.

Justin was a failure compared to them.

He had blood on his hands.

From his perch, he spotted someone traipsing along the same trail they'd taken to the Blue Lake.

Was it Reed? Justin's pulse thundered in his ears. He knew Darrow's brother planned to hide in the wilderness at some point. With no one hunting him, hiding, waiting things out would be easy. Had he come out to find her?

"Darrow!" A man's voice called.

Smit...

Justin's heart sank. He'd allowed himself to forget about Smit for today. Why did Smit continue to pursue Darrow? Couldn't he see she didn't love him?

The man's lithe, tall form exited the tree cover and strode toward Darrow. She glanced up to where Justin stood on the ledge looking like she was disappointed, too.

Chapter 6

Trace slid the key across the counter to Darrow, who put it back in its place. "All taken care of."

Stepping out of Trace's path, Darrow offered a wry grin. "I knew I could count on you."

Darrow had asked Trace to handle any business pertaining to Justin, especially moving him when required. He'd stayed in the cabin for longer than expected, and now the lodge had a cancellation, and he could move back inside, which he preferred.

Trace squeezed her shoulder as she passed. "He asked about you."

"Really?" Darrow tried to stifle her smile. The news shouldn't make her happy. "What did he—you know what, it doesn't matter."

Trace frowned. "I'm not convinced."

A man approached, outfitted for his hunting trip. Darrow ignored Trace's comment and left Trace to do her job. It had been three weeks since she'd first encountered Justin. She didn't trust her heart where Justin was concerned, and there were too many unknowns, so she'd tried to avoid him ever since the hike.

She caught a glimpse of him now and then. If only she knew why he was staying at the lodge.

Did you lie to me when you sent me here?

Who was he? Why was he here? The questions continued to plague her, and the only thing she had in answer was that Oregon was his hobby. Yeah, right.

But it wasn't her business. She wanted him gone because he served as a reminder of her discontent with Smit.

Lord, why can't I be rid of these doubts?

Smit had recovered from the flu and had joined her on the hike the day Justin had been there. Smit had attended church with her Sunday and then yesterday as well. She'd been stunned to see Justin in the back row. When the service was over, she'd caught him staring at her. He nodded and she looked away.

She and Smit had dinner together a couple of times, but nothing more was said about him taking her somewhere special. Something had definitely changed in Smit, but Darrow didn't know what it was.

She stepped into her office.

Arms slipped around her from behind. "How's my girl?" Smit's warm breath caressed her ear.

She turned to see his smile. "You're in a good mood today."

She hadn't seen him smile like this in weeks.

"This Friday, we're going somewhere special." He squeezed her to him then planted a kiss on her lips.

Darrow swallowed. The old Smit was back, along with her pre-engagement jitters. "I can't wait."

Trace found her in the hall with Smit. "Darrow, somebody

needs help on the trail, up by the boulders."

Darrow's heart raced. "What kind of help? Did you call an ambulance?"

"I'm not sure. A woman came into the lobby asking for help. Her grandson was stuck. She sounded desperate."

Smit released Darrow and they rushed from the lobby. Once on the trail, Smit took off ahead of her like he meant to be a hero. She wished she had more information.

God, please let them be all right.

Darrow was out of breath by the time she caught up to Smit. A crowd had gathered at the boulders where Darrow had stumbled upon Justin on his phone. A woman covered her face with her hands and intermittently shouted for someone named Jeffery to be careful. Darrow looked up to see Justin, making his way down the boulders, presumably Jeffery on his back.

Slowly he climbed along the smaller rocks stacked against the large ones. How had Jeffery made that climb? And where had his grandmother been while he was getting into mischief?

She reached out to the woman and wrapped her arm around her shoulders. "He's going to be just fine. Don't worry."

The woman grabbed Darrow's arms and held on.

Justin slipped. The crowd gasped. But he found his footing again.

"I should help," Smit said.

"No. You'll make him lose his concentration." Darrow couldn't stand the thought of Justin or little Jeffery tumbling down the rocks.

Finally Justin's feet touched the base of the boulders and

Jeffery scrambled from his back. The small crowd clapped their approval. The grandmother had already released her grip on Darrow and made her way to squeeze the boy. Darrow figured the woman would scold him much later, but first she thanked Justin.

Darrow approached to thank him as well.

"You're a hero. I want to do something for you," the woman said. "What's your name?"

"That's not necessary." His jaw clenched.

He didn't appear to want all the attention but had been there to aid someone in need.

"Justin Love," Darrow said.

His gray eyes glanced up at her and seemed to drink her in.

Smit cleared his throat and thrust out his hand. "She's right. You're a real hero."

Justin shook it.

"Say, aren't you related to Carver Love, who's got a ranch north of here?" a man in a red flannel jacket asked.

"He's my brother."

Now that was something Darrow hadn't known. An answer to some of her questions and yet the information raised more. She watched him expertly pry himself from the attention and disappear down the trail. Then she glanced at Smit.

He studied her. What was he thinking? Did he wonder if Darrow was the woman of his dreams? Would he finally ask her to marry him? And when he did, what would she say?

ଓ

Justin trudged through the woods not knowing exactly where he was going. He'd driven to Winter Ridge that overlooked

Summer Lake and Darrow's lodge, and hiked in to the Fremont National Park. Maybe he could get some privacy in a remote, secluded place. In the wilderness nobody knew he was a hero. He shouldn't have done it. He shouldn't have gone after that boy, but there was no one else around at the time. Seconds counted when a child was in a precarious situation.

Just like the seconds had counted when he'd failed to do his job as a police officer and someone had died.

With the unwanted attention he'd garnered, he feared that Carver would hear Justin was back in Oregon. He'd left three years ago when his nightmare first started. He hadn't aimed to come back, but the situation with Reed had drawn him here. More like driven him to do the deed he'd promised Reed's wife.

But he knew deep down, the Lord had given him a strong nudge, and Justin, hungry to make things right—hungry for redemption—had allowed himself to bend. It was either that or be broken. But being back in Oregon for a few weeks didn't mean he wanted to face his brothers.

He'd been shocked to hear that Reed hadn't seen his sister in five years. But Justin had stayed away from his brothers, having no contact with them for three. He was no better than Reed on that point.

A breeze blasted over his face. Everything was happening much too fast. Coming back to Oregon, facing the demons of his past and now. . .Darrow. He'd sworn off any entanglements of the romantic kind, seeing too much heartbreak in one form or another, of course he'd have to fall for a woman who had a boyfriend she planned to marry.

Justin's incredulous laugh disturbed the silent forest, bouncing off the trees. Why did he have to be tortured, watching her with Smit at every turn, even at church? Nearby, a brook trickled. He found a smooth rock nestled alongside it and sat, surprised that snow didn't blanket the ground yet.

"God, I know You're there, so listen up. I'm staying here one more week. If Reed doesn't show up then I'm gone." Justin added a silent heartfelt apology for his attitude. But even if he tried to hide his frustration, God could see right through him anyway.

Earlier when he'd rescued Jeffery, he'd almost lost his concentration when out of the corner of his eye, he'd seen Darrow arrive on the scene with her boyfriend. He shoved thoughts of her aside to get the boy to safety. Somehow the child had managed to pick his way up the side, but when it came time to come down he started crying.

Once relieved of his burden, Justin had allowed an errant glance at the beautiful woman who'd remained close to his heart, who'd been a constant companion to his thoughts since the day he'd met her. She'd stared back at him. The admiration in her eyes had almost done him in. But Smit, like a trusted and loyal guard dog, stood by her side.

Justin had tried to shake her from his thoughts, but she wouldn't go away without a lot of effort.

One more week, God. He had a feeling God wasn't about to be given a deadline.

Maybe if he only had one week left, he should confront Darrow about her feelings for Smit. Maybe she didn't feel the same about Justin, but he meant to find out why she was settling for Smit. That Smit was a good man Justin had no doubt. But Smit just might deserve a woman who truly loved him.

Still, Justin hated to put himself as judge and jury over someone else's life.

He shoved up from the rock and began his trek through the woods and back to the Tahoe he'd rented. He'd bartered with the local car rental place to keep the thing for a month. Time was running out.

One more week.

The night already upon him, he hadn't realized he'd stayed in the woods so long. The Tahoe stood fifty yards away when the rain began pelting him. Icy cold rain that would probably turn to snow at this elevation.

By the time he climbed inside he was soaking and cold to the bone. It wouldn't be too soon if Reed showed his face tonight. At least he'd parked in front of the Rimrock Lodge.

His thoughts in a jumble, he rushed up the porch to his cabin before he remembered that he'd moved back to the lodge. He crept off the porch, hoping the new guests hadn't spotted him. A stranger's appearance at their cabin door would probably scare them.

It was still pouring when Justin jogged up the path and, in the fading light from the cabin's porch, he could scarcely see in the dark. Once he was free from the trees, raindrops pounded him and the ground as well. A woman rushed by, covering her head with a newspaper.

Darrow?

Like an idiot, Justin followed her instead of taking the path back to the lodge. She glanced behind her, probably wondering who the stalker was, then kept moving. She ran across the small yard, splashing through the puddles and onto the porch, Justin a few feet behind.

When he clomped up the steps, she faced him, dripping wet despite the newspaper.

Wet from the rain, her face glistened in the soft lamp of the porch. "What are you doing?"

"I don't know." With a grin, he shrugged. "I went to the cabin because I forgot I'd moved to the lodge."

She threw her head back and laughed. "That's great."

He took a step closer. "You think it's funny, do you?"

Her gaze was expectant and wary at the same time. With his next step, he gently gripped her waist and searched her eyes. Would she reject him? Did she want him to leave? No.

He saw what he was looking for. Her eyes sparkled with longing, and she closed them as he drew near. Justin put his lips against hers, savoring their sweetness.

The kiss rocked him to the core.

Something slapped the floor, jarring them apart. A model in an immaculate gown stared back at him from the cover of a bridal magazine. Justin swallowed the acid rising in his throat.

"Are you going to marry him?" he asked.

Regret colored her soft gaze and tore at Justin's insides.

Chapter 7

Darrow stared at the mirror on her dresser as she brushed her hair, teasing it a little on the top to give it lift. She inspected herself, admiring the silky teal dress she'd bought just for this occasion.

"Somewhere special," Smit had said. Later in the week he called to advise her that he'd made reservations at a fancy restaurant. There weren't any near the Summer Lake area, but she wouldn't try to figure out where. After dating the man for eight months, Darrow knew him well enough. He'd always been a complete gentleman, and for their dates, he took her out to eat or cooked for her, or she cooked for him, or they caught a movie together.

But never before had he taken her "somewhere special." A man like Smit didn't play games or waste his time. Darrow had been hoping for this night for weeks. Planning for it for months. Her excitement had led her to ordering the bridal magazine so she'd have plenty of time to decide on the kind of dress she would wear.

She left the dresser and sat on the bed, looking at her hope chest given to her by her grandfather—it had belonged to her mother who hadn't taken it with her when she married. Not every girl had one, but Darrow had been fortunate. She'd filled it with small items for her future home as a married woman, items she'd collected here and there.

What if she'd misread Smit? What if he hadn't planned to propose at all? Even worse, what if he did propose?

Biting her lips, she frowned. For weeks now she'd been excited about a future with Smit. But tonight, all her expectancy was gone.

Her excitement turned to dread.

That, because a month ago she'd met Justin Love. Darrow pressed a finger to her lips. A simple touch from him had planted a forest of doubts in her heart. On Monday night he'd followed her in the pouring rain. And then. . .he'd kissed her. How could she ever forget the feel of his lips on hers or his arms around her?

Closing her eyes, she recalled the moment. He'd poured into her passion, stirred a fire in her belly, and it was then she knew how much he felt for her.

He'd asked if Darrow would marry Smit, but she hadn't known the answer. If he was passing through, why would he care? Why would he ask? He'd made no indications of any intentions toward her. What should she do?

Had anyone ever been this torn? She'd prayed for the Lord to guide her in one of the most important decisions of her life. So far, He'd been silent on the matter. Either that or Darrow wasn't listening.

She weighed her options. Marry Smit, and a home and

children were hers. They would be good together, she and Smit. Or end things with Smit and wait to see if she had a future with Justin Love, a man she barely knew.

Someone knocked on the door, and Darrow bolted from the bed. After a quick glance in the mirror, she left her bedroom, strolled through the small living area to the front door. She opened it.

Smit smiled at her. Dressed in slacks and a nice collared shirt, he looked more handsome than she'd ever seen him. "How's my girl?"

She allowed his familiar greeting to wash over her doubts. "I'm good, Smit. You look handsome tonight." Yes. This was the way she wanted it. She always knew what to expect with Smit. She could count on this man. He wasn't just passing through. He owned a stable and prosperous business.

"And you're too beautiful for words." He took her hand. "Shall we?"

On the drive, Smit talked about his workweek, and she shared a little about hers, though it seemed to go by in a blur. Sitting next to him in his truck, Darrow found that some of the expectancy she'd lost was beginning to return. All she needed was to spend more time with him.

The restaurant in Rimrock was the finest dining Darrow had ever experienced, and she and Smit stuffed themselves with steak and lobster. She couldn't remember when she'd enjoyed herself so much. Yes. They would be great together. He looked across the table at her, his eyes sparkling with love, she felt sure. When he reached across the table and placed his hand over hers, Darrow's breath caught in her throat.

Was this the moment? Would he ask her now?

Once the check was paid, Smit escorted her outside where they walked slowly around a small pond with a lighted water fountain and gazebo. Such a romantic place. Had Smit scouted out the location beforehand? That he'd considered all the details impressed her.

Smit led her inside the gazebo and cupped her cheeks with his hands, his face mere inches from hers. He kissed her softly at first, and then thoroughly. Darrow willed herself to respond. With all her heart she wanted to experience that fire of passion she'd felt with Justin. She loved Smit, didn't she?

He eased away from her, a deep sadness in his eyes. An ache sliced through Darrow's heart. "Smit. . ."

He sighed. "I had hoped that tonight would bring that sparkle back into your eyes."

"You don't see a sparkle in my eyes?" Darrow swallowed the lump in her throat. "Tonight has been the most wonderful time of my life."

At her words, he smiled and ran his fingers through her hair. "I know you have doubts. That something has changed in the last few weeks. And that's okay." Smit dropped to one knee. "Darrow Kincaid, will you marry me? You don't have to say yes now, just think about it."

Darrow smiled down at Smit, looking into his love-filled eyes. "I've dreamed of this moment for a lifetime."

Holding her hand, he stood. "Oh, I forgot something." He tugged a little black box from his pocket. "I hope you like it."

Darrow peered into the box to see a small, but beautiful solitaire diamond ring. Tears streamed down her cheeks. She had no words. It was everything it should be and yet...

Not.

Darrow couldn't bring herself to share all her doubts with him. At least he knew she had them.

Smit tugged her to him, whispering, "I love you. I've been worried you were slipping away from me."

Justin lounged in a high-backed, cushioned chair next to the fire sizzling in the hearth, thinking that his week was almost up.

At eleven thirty at night, everyone except him had left the small lobby. He kept the fire stoked, allowing the flames to mesmerize him, keep him from drowning in his thoughts. Could he leave without finishing? Without finding Reed? Would he leave without seeing his brothers, or facing what he'd run from?

But what kept his heart rate beating an unnatural rhythm was thoughts of Darrow out with her Smit tonight.

He happened to peer out the front door at the very moment Smit assisted her into his truck. The shiny blue-green dress—the color of her eyes—made her look like a beautiful princess. Justin's gut had burned ever since seeing them.

Smit would ask her to marry him tonight.

After Justin had kissed her that rainy night, he'd asked her if she would marry Smit. She answered that she didn't know. But Justin did. Darrow would say yes. End of story.

Why wouldn't she? Justin wasn't husband material. He was much too restless to settle down. Then why had he kissed her?

Feeling the warmth from the fire against his face, he closed his eyes and thought of the dreamy look in her eyes, and the longing. He never thought he needed a woman in his life—too risky, too much heartbreak. People died or were killed in his line of work. He'd seen it all too often.

If only he hadn't played a part in the tragedy that ended a life, and left him walking away from his career, things might be different.

Now, as a fugitive recovery agent, he saw a different kind of tragedy.

Betrayal.

Justin saw the betrayal when husbands or boyfriends skipped bail. The look in their loved one's eyes when they were left behind or left uninformed. When the pressure was on, each person only cared about one thing—his own survival.

In Justin's opinion, the heartache, the pain, wasn't worth the risk.

Darrow had changed all that for him. She'd taken him by surprise, and he'd let down his guard. That was all it took. He couldn't turn her affection away. Couldn't ignore it. Not anymore.

But marrying Smit was the best thing for her because she didn't know the truth about Justin. He didn't have the heart after all to tell her he'd come to the lodge to hunt. He was after her brother.

When she found out, then. . .*then,* he'd see the haunted look of betrayal he never wanted to see directed at him.

But right now, Justin wanted to forget all that. He wanted to remember the desperate longing and the gleam in her eyes as he leaned in to kiss her. He wanted to think about that kiss. About if things were different. If Darrow weren't getting engaged tonight. If she weren't the sister of a fugitive.

That would always stand between them.

A soft sigh to his right drew his attention.

Darrow. . .

She lounged in the chair across from him, firelight flickering across her delicate features and sparkling in her eyes. Deep in his thoughts of her, he hadn't heard her come in.

"You're leaving," she said and glanced at his duffel bag in the corner.

"My business here is almost done." Justin pulled his gaze from the hurt in her eyes and stared at the fire again. He wouldn't wait for Reed much longer.

"I made the right decision." She thrust her hand out and a diamond sparkled on her finger.

The reflection of a thousand lights pierced his thoughts, his heart. Dazzling him, he couldn't pull his gaze away though it ripped at his soul. He squeezed his fist, holding in the pain and anger.

Let her go. . .

"If you call settling for a man you don't love the right decision, then yes, you've done that." Justin leaned forward, elbows on his knees. Why had he said that? This was best for her. Leave her alone.

"He's a good man. And stable. I can count on him. I know where he'll be tomorrow and five or twenty years from now."

Justin rubbed his jaw up one side and down the other. "Stability is overrated."

A sniffle forced him to look over at her again. Exaggerated by the firelight, moisture welled in her eyes. "I've dreamed of this all my life. Why did you have to ruin it for me? Why? And I don't even know you."

"You keep saying that. Don't you know all you need to? Besides, you're engaged now. Would it make any difference?"

Darrow pursed her lips and stared at the flames. She should be happy, ecstatic. Justin had done this to her.

"Smit knew something was wrong. He told me he could tell that something had changed in me."

"But you didn't tell him what changed?"

Darrow stood and meandered to the fire, her lovely dress contradicting her mood. "No. You told me you're just passing through. And now I see that you weren't lying."

Justin rose to join her. He couldn't tell if she was aware of his approach, but her gorgeous eyes—he could live in those eyes—widened when she saw him.

He needed to let her go, do what was best for her, for them both. "I'm no good at this. Never have been. But something has changed in me, too."

Against every good and right judgment in him, Justin did the unthinkable. He lifted her chin and leaned forward to kiss her, fully expecting a slap.

Be true to Smit. End this for us both.

Darrow received his kiss tentatively at first. He slid his arms around her waist and then her back and suddenly, she threw her arms around his neck, turning the kiss forceful and passionate until finally, Justin had to catch his breath.

Still holding her, he whispered, "Why did you say yes?"

"How can I say no to a sure thing? You've given me nothing."

"Haven't I?"

Confusion tempered her soft smile. "You're leaving. I can't count on you."

"Have a little faith." With the words, Justin understood that he'd been waiting on her all along. But now that she'd made the choice, and it wasn't what he wanted, her decision was too much to bear.

"I'll give you the rest of tonight, right here in the lobby, to tell me about yourself. I don't even know what you do for a living, or why you're here." She touched her lips to his, brushing away the shards of ice wall she'd broken down over the last few weeks.

"Darrow?" a male voice called.

Justin released her and they both turned to see a man in the shadows a few yards away.

She took a slow step forward. "Benson?"

Chapter 8

Benson!" Darrow rushed over, leaving Justin standing at the fireplace.

Just short of throwing her arms around her brother, she stopped, hesitating. She missed him and yet, she hadn't heard from him in so long.

What was he doing here? Why had he come? The same questions she had for Justin.

Still. . .he was all the family she had. "It's good to see you."

"You look beautiful." Benson's voice was deeper, richer than she remembered. "Celebrating a special occasion?"

At thirty-five he looked more haggard than she would have expected. Though his dark hair was a little long and shaggy, even for him, he was still a good-looking man.

Not knowing how to answer, Darrow shook her head and smiled. "There's so much to catch up on. Are you staying at the lodge? Did you check in?"

"I planned to, but I wanted to see you first. In case—in case I wasn't welcome. Then I spotted you by the fireplace. . ."

Darrow knew her face flushed. He had to have seen the kiss. His glance traveled down her left arm to her hand, where the diamond engagement ring encircled her finger.

"I guessed you'd be married by now. This must be your husband."

Justin glanced at Darrow, a deep sadness in his eyes. Was he unhappy because she was engaged to Smit? If this situation wasn't so awkward, she'd take the ring off right now.

"We're not married," Darrow said, hoping she wouldn't have to explain further.

"Engaged then. Congratulations." He thrust out his hand to Justin.

Justin shook Benson's hand but didn't correct Benson regarding the misunderstanding. She was engaged, but not to Justin.

"I know it's late." Her brother weaved his hand through his hair, uncertainty in his eyes. "But can we talk?"

Darrow nodded. "Let's sit by the fire."

Justin cleared his throat. "I should leave you two alone to catch up."

"No. . ." Her vehemence surprised even her. "You can stay." To Benson, she said, "You don't mind, do you?"

Reed frowned, hesitating. "No, of course not. Why would I?"

His tone told her that he probably did mind, but if Justin left now, she might not see him again. She might not have the chance to finish their conversation. Besides, she loved her brother, but she didn't trust him completely. Given his past, she had no idea what he was into. He could be dangerous, but she hoped not. She hoped he had changed. But why hadn't he called, written. . .something?

Her brother strolled with her to the couch and chairs positioned around the fire, where she and Justin were only moments before.

"I know you're surprised to see me."

"After five years of nothing, I admit, I'm a little surprised. But I'm glad you're okay."

He sat on the chair kitty-corner to the sofa where she sat. Justin plopped next to her, but not too close, sitting on the edge of the seat. His expression had grown serious.

"So what brings you here after all this time?" Justin asked.

Darrow gave him a sidelong glance. She hadn't invited him to stay to interrogate her brother.

Benson stiffened, clearly not happy with the tone in Justin's voice. Maybe she should ask him to leave after all.

"I wanted to tell you how sorry I am for not staying in touch. For not being a good older brother, a good example. For all the trouble I caused before I left."

Darrow's chin trembled. "You came here to tell me that?"

"Yes. I've changed, Darrow. Changed for the better. I even have a wife now."

A wife? A vise squeezed Darrow's throat. He'd not invited her to his wedding? "Where is she? Did you bring her?"

"No." Benson looked down at his hands. "Something happened."

Oh no. Here it comes. "What?"

Benson squeezed his fists then opened them.

Closed.

Open.

"Nothing for you and your fiancé to worry about. I love you, Darrow. I only thought to protect you when I left. I wasn't any good for you."

"We're not engaged," Justin said. His gaze bore into Benson.

"Then what's going on?" Benson looked at her ring, then at Darrow.

He had no idea.

"Who are you?" he asked Justin.

"I'm a bail bond recovery agent."

☙

"A bounty hunter?" Veins pulsed at the man's temples. He couldn't know that Justin was after him, but he could strongly suspect.

Justin had waited for Reed to tell Darrow what he had to say. His sister needed to hear the words, though they were severely lacking as far as Justin was concerned. All he had to do now was keep everything low-key. Keep Reed from getting defensive, or going on the lam, or worse, turning violent.

Darrow's eyes grew wide as she watched her brother, looking from him to Justin. She didn't have a clue. How Justin wished she weren't caught in the middle. He knew she didn't trust her brother, otherwise she would have asked Justin to give them some time alone. He would have obliged, looking on from a distance. He sensed she wanted him there for protection as much as anything.

Reed slowly stood, his face turning red. "I'll ask you again, who are you? What are you doing here?"

Darrow rose, too. "Benson, you're being rude. My relationship with him is a little complicated, but now isn't the time. He's... wait a minute..." Darrow turned a questioning gaze on Justin.

If Darrow realized her brother was running, if she put the pieces together...

"The phone call," she whispered.

Justin braced himself against the look of betrayal that was sure to come. But it was no use. She'd already shattered any hope he had of protecting himself. He'd let himself fall for her.

"I think you should leave now, Darrow."

"What? I'm not leaving."

Justin recognized the crazed look in Reed's eyes—the man knew Justin was there for him.

"You can't arrest me." Reed clenched his fists. "This is Oregon."

"I could get a warrant, tell the police you're a wanted man, ask them to arrest you."

Darrow gasped, glaring at her brother. "What are you running from? What have you done?"

"You realize this man used you to get to me." Reed pulled a gun from behind him.

Darrow jumped, her hands at her throat. "Benson, no..."

Justin spread his hands out and rose slowly. "Put the gun away. You're not helping your case."

Reed's hand shook as he aimed the gun at Justin. He'd handled this all wrong. Never figured Darrow would be standing between them when Justin faced him.

Darrow stepped in front of the gun.

"Get out of the way, Darrow." Justin's pulse rocketed. "Let me handle this."

"Benson, please. . ."

Reed reached forward and tugged her around, pinning her against him, and pointing the gun at her. "Or, maybe you set me up, little sis. Maybe you were entertaining the bounty hunter, making plans to help him grab me."

Justin shook his head slightly. *You sorry. . .*

"That's crazy. I didn't know who he was." Darrow pleaded with her eyes.

"You think I'm an idiot? You two were really close by the fireplace. You're not the kind of person to kiss someone you don't even know."

"She's telling the truth. I never told her why I was here or what I did for a living. And you can put your gun away. This isn't going down like that. I came here to give you a message. I have no intention of taking you back to Florida."

Still holding Darrow at gunpoint—*his own sister*—Reed began backing toward the exit. "I have no intention of going to jail for something I didn't do."

Justin moved forward, maintaining his distance.

God, please keep her safe. Please forgive me for botching this. Help me make it right.

Reed watched his surroundings, but the lodge was dark and quiet, except for them. Everyone else was asleep. He continued to back his way to the door. No doubt, he hoped to flee to the wilderness a few hundred yards away.

"Your wife sent me here to find you."

"Why that—"

"It's not what you think. She's pregnant. You're going to be a father. She wants you to give yourself up, give up a life of running, and in turn she'll stick with you through the trial to prove your innocence."

Reed's jaw grew slack, and the gun wavered in his hand. "You're lying. Why—why would she send you to tell me that?"

"Because she couldn't get in touch with you, she knew you wouldn't contact her for fear someone would locate you. She bargained with me. Made me give my word that if she told me where you were going, I wouldn't arrest you. As it turns out, I couldn't. But I can give you the message and leave it at that, as much as it pains me."

"Why would you do that?"

"Think about it. The chances of me getting paid for you getting arrested in Oregon are next to nothing."

Reed released Darrow, who ran from him and stood at the far wall, watching. "That doesn't explain why you'd wait for me here. You could have left me a message. She could have left me a message."

"Would that have convinced you?" He took a step toward Reed, ever conscious of Darrow's presence. She had to be terrified. Had to hate him now.

"I'm not sure you've convinced me either. I don't get it. What's in it for you?"

"It's time to stop running. For both of us. Before I became a recovery agent, I was a cop. Years ago I failed to look in on someone for a friend, and my lack of vigilance resulted in a death I could have prevented. It never should have happened. I knew when your wife asked me, I had to do this. See it through. While I can never bring back the life lost, maybe I can help return you to your wife and child."

Reed stood next to Justin and replaced the gun in the holster at his back beneath his shirt. Justin resisted the urge to land a few punches in the guy's face for holding his sister hostage. He also resisted the urge to cuff him. That wasn't why he was here. He didn't know if that was the gun purportedly used in the armed robberies or not. For Reed's wife's sake, he hoped the man was innocent.

"I've never heard a story like that before. It's weird enough, it has to be true."

"I won't lie to you. I was close to leaving tonight, if you didn't show up. Are you going to do it? Are you going back to turn yourself in?"

Scratching his unshaven jaw, Reed seemed not to hear him. "I'm going to be a father."

"Yeah, and Darrow an aunt. I think you need to explain your actions to her."

Realization dawned in his eyes. "Oh man. I didn't mean anything by that. I've been so desperate. What was I thinking, holding her hostage?"

Together they turned to Darrow.

She was gone.

Chapter 9

Justin stood outside the door to Darrow's cabin. Muffled crying left no doubt she was inside. He couldn't blame her for wanting to flee the scene, considering everything had slammed into her at once.

Justin had kept a devastating secret from her. Her brother had held her at gunpoint because of Justin.

He lifted his hand to knock on the door but paused. Should he give her time to catch her breath? The problem was, he'd checked out of his room and now his unofficial business here was done. He should just leave now.

But he and Darrow had left much unsaid between them.

Justin dropped his hand and moved away from the door to stand on the steps of the porch. In the early hours of the morning now, exhaustion weighed on him. After a good night's rest, he might see things with clarity. Know what to do about Darrow. He could sleep in the Tahoe. It wouldn't be the first time he'd spent the night in a vehicle.

The door creaked behind him. Justin turned around slowly, fearing she'd skitter back into the cabin. But he was wrong.

Light spilled from the doorway, illuminating her dark eyes.

She marched onto the porch. "Why are you still here? You did what you came to do. I want you off my property."

Justin couldn't believe it. He didn't think she had that in her. "Fine. I'll go, but not before I explain."

"I think I've heard enough." When she crossed her arms, he noticed the engagement ring was gone. Maybe she took her jewelry off at night. "You used me, Justin. How could you do that?"

"You don't believe that, do you?"

"I don't know what to believe. You should have told me why you were here."

"I think you know why I couldn't."

With a slight shake of her head, Darrow turned her back on him. "Just go."

Justin couldn't give up. Not yet. "This has all been a shock for you. Sometimes we say things we don't mean when we're angry or hurt."

"I don't need psychoanalysis. I just need you to leave."

"I will. But not before I tell you what needs to be said. I knew your brother was headed here to see you so I waited. But I never intended to get involved with you. If you recall, I tried to avoid you. But now I'm in love with you."

When she didn't respond, he continued, desperation burning his words. "I thought Smit would be the best thing for you, but not if you don't love him." He paused, waiting. "Earlier tonight I asked you to have a little faith, and I'll ask again. Have faith in us. If you love me, Darrow, wait for me. There are things I have to take care of, but then I'll be back."

Again, he paused, hoping for something from her. "Wait for me," he said at last.

Darrow crept inside and shut the door, leaving a deep slash across Justin's heart. He left her alone and went back into the lodge, finding his duffel bag waiting where he'd left it before everything exploded. The fire had almost gone out. He glanced around the lobby, committing it to memory. At some point, he might wish he could forget. But he'd hold on to the hope that Darrow loved him. That she'd wait for him. He'd let her make her decision about Smit, about whom she loved.

He climbed inside the Tahoe and started it, then backed from the parking lot. He'd find a place up the road to park and sleep for a couple of hours before the sun rose.

He had more to do in Oregon. He had to face his past and seek forgiveness from an old friend—a man who lost his wife to a crime that Justin could have prevented when he served as a police officer. After telling Reed about what was driving him, he realized he needed to see his one-time friend and tell him how sorry he was.

Instead of apologizing years ago like he should have, he'd allowed anger at himself to fuel him. He'd resigned and left the state. That was when he ended up in a job as a bounty hunter.

He'd come back, wanting to make amends. He thought God had sent him here, but now he was having serious doubts. Recovering Reed for his wife and baby, restoring a family, wasn't enough to ease the pain Justin had lived with. Now, he'd hurt someone else.

Finding a small roadside park, Justin pulled the Tahoe over

and shut it off, then leaned the seat as far back as it would go. He allowed sleep to take him far from his troubled thoughts.

A noise disturbed him.

Justin woke up, but didn't open his eyes. Light told him morning had come too fast. His temples pounded. His back and shoulders ached. A knock came on his window. Justin jerked up, completely awake, now, though groggy.

A man wearing a Stetson stood at his window.

Carver?

Justin wasn't prepared for this. Swiping a hand down his face, he opened the door and stepped out to face off with his older brother, the head of the family, as it were. Justin squinted at Carver, who stood with his back to the rising sun.

"Sorry to knock on your door so early in the morning. You look like a man in need of some coffee," Carver said.

Justin had expected something much different. "At least you didn't tell me I look like a homeless alcoholic."

"I figured you knew that already." Carver grabbed his shoulder and squeezed hard like always.

Justin cringed. "Your grip is as strong as ever."

"Let me take you somewhere for breakfast, and then you can explain to me why you're in Oregon and didn't tell anyone you're here."

Carver hadn't mentioned the last three years, but Justin knew that would come. Eventually. "I could use a plate of steak and eggs and a strong cup of coffee."

"I know just the place." His brother smiled.

Justin climbed into Carver's dually. He hadn't really expected to escape without facing Carver, had he? Fifteen minutes up the road, and Carver drove into the parking lot of a small diner. Justin followed him inside, expecting the questions to come after the coffee had been poured. One thing for certain, he had no intention of answering anything until after at least two big mugs.

Carver nodded at the waitress and made his way through the diner to a booth in the back. Justin came up behind him and froze. Jonas and Lucas sat at the booth, grinning.

"What is this? Some sort of intervention?"

"Not unless you're an addict." Jonas got up and practically shoved Justin into the booth between him and Lucas. "Are you?"

"We just wanted to see you, bro." Lucas punched him a little too hard on the arm. "In case you decided to leave without saying hi."

Guilt and shame tried to strangle Justin for the way he'd treated his brothers. But he'd failed in a big way where every one of them had succeeded. It was hard being the black sheep of the family. He'd never wanted that for himself.

But maybe they didn't look at him the same way he looked at himself.

"Thanks. I'm glad you did," he said, his voice croaking under the weighty emotions.

The waitress brought strong black coffee and menus. Justin allowed himself to drift back in time as he listened to the other three reminisce about their lives on the Love Ranch, growing up. Eventually, they discussed their current livelihoods, and Justin learned that his brother, Jonas, had blamed himself for the death of someone on his team during an FBI raid.

"You aren't alone in the blame game," Carver said. "But if God can forgive us, surely we can forgive ourselves."

Justin smiled, realizing that God had known exactly what He was doing by sending him to Oregon on a mission to restore someone's life. This trip wasn't a mistake.

His own.

Why'd he ever doubt that?

He saw now that his own life could be restored. All he'd lost when he left, the things he missed, recovered. All this time he'd spent hardening his heart against people to protect himself from the hurt or from loving someone. But no more. Now, he was finally ready to love.

Good thing, too, because he was *in* love with Darrow Kincaid.

First, there was something he had to do.

What a bittersweet good-bye.

Benson was innocent. He'd contacted his lawyer to say he was on his way back to Florida and was informed the authorities caught the man who'd committed the armed robbery they had charged Benson with. All charges against her brother were dropped and all that happened within the last few hours.

Darrow was amazed to think that while Justin was facing off with Benson, the real criminal was being cuffed and read his Miranda rights, confessing to a string of robberies.

In the kitchen at her cabin, she smiled at Benson now.

"Bring your wife when you get settled again. I'd love to meet her."

"Or maybe you'd like to see Florida."

He looked like a different man from two nights ago when he'd shown up in the lobby, turning her world upside down. He'd been haggard then, a worn-down excuse of a man, on the run and scared. He hadn't been thinking straight when he'd held her as hostage.

He never meant to scare her. Darrow didn't tell him his action would take her time to get over. But deep down, she knew he wouldn't hurt her. He'd been desperate. Justin wouldn't have let it go that far either. She should never have stepped between them.

Justin...

Benson gave her one last hug then stepped off the porch. "Tell your bounty hunter thanks for me."

Hiding her frown, she offered a soft smile. "Call me when you get home, okay?"

Benson trotted down the path away from her. Could this really be a new beginning for them?

Benson had run, fearing his past had caught up with him and would now put him away forever. But Darrow believed he was a changed man, despite his actions in the lobby.

ଓ

A week later, a chill woke her earlier than usual. She rose and stoked the wood-burning stove to warm the cabin.

Had it really been a whole week? The events of the night

her brother appeared were still too vivid, including Justin's confession of love. On the surface, it appeared he'd used her in order to get to her brother. He'd hidden a terrible truth from her. But what would she do under the same circumstances?

She understood why he didn't tell her.

Then he hadn't arrested Benson. He'd waited at her lodge just so he could catch her brother before he disappeared into the wilderness and off the grid for who knew how long. Justin had pleaded with him on behalf of his wife to return to her and their unborn child.

Justin's deed had washed away any bitterness toward him over the truth he'd hidden. He'd been aloof and standoffish, but in reality, he was a silent hero with a heart of gold. He'd kept his magnanimous plans to himself.

Darrow sighed, wishing she could take back how she'd acted when he'd told her he loved her. Why had she been hard on him? The man had reached into her heart and touched places that no one else had. And Darrow had sent him away.

She didn't deserve Justin.

But where had he gone? How long did he expect her to wait? Or did he even plan to come back? What would she say if he did?

Darrow prepared breakfast and got ready for work. When it was time to leave, she strolled down the path to the lodge—a place she owned and loved. But every time she went inside, memories flooded her mind, leaving her disheartened.

She'd promised to relieve Renee for her break at the registration counter today. Trace was off for the day, thank goodness, because she'd prodded Darrow to share the details of what had happened. Right now, Darrow couldn't explain. There were no words. It was a lot for a person to swallow.

During a slow moment in the afternoon, Darrow cleaned out the counter. She found an old wedding catalog dated several months old. Trace would have found this when she cleaned the shelves, but she'd said nothing to Darrow. Had she been looking at wedding dresses this long? Pathetic. Now it was an out-of-reach dream.

The phone rang and Darrow answered, "Ridgecrest Lodge."

"I need a reservation." The voice sounded familiar and yet. . .not.

Darrow's knees trembled.

"What dates would you like to stay?" she asked. *Please, Lord, is it too much to ask? Let it be him.*

"Is forever available?" With a hint of humor, the voice echoed over the line.

As she stared at the computer screen, it took a few seconds for the words to sink in. Darrow lifted her gaze, searching the lobby.

And then, she spotted him. Grinning, Justin leaned against the wall next to a fake ficus tree. Darrow hung up the phone and rushed around the counter to Justin. She stopped, just short of jumping in his arms. Had he come back for her like he said, or was it something else?

"You're back." It was all she could manage.

Justin's grin faltered. "Yes."

"But where did you go?" Was that so important?

"I'll answer that soon enough. But I have a question of my own."

Darrow could almost guess what it was, but she wanted him to ask.

"Did you wait for me?"

"I'm here. It's not like I was going anywhere."

"Are you going to marry him?" He glanced down the length of her left arm.

She lifted her hand, devoid of the ring. "Smit was everything I thought I wanted. But as it turns out, he deserves better than me. He wanted someone who loved him as much."

Justin's expression grew serious. "Imagine that."

Growing impatient with the conversation, Darrow took a step forward. "Now I'm left with no one."

"I told you to have a little faith."

"I'm trying."

"Come here." Justin tugged her over to him and ran his fingers through her hair, brushing it from her face.

Darrow leaned into his touch. She'd told Smit a hundred times she didn't like to be affectionate in public, wanting to keep her private life just that. But all she wanted now was for Justin to show her he meant business. Tell her his intentions.

"I know I'm not what you thought you wanted," Justin said. "I'm not exactly stable like Smit, the picture of permanence, but I mean to change that. I'm done running. If you'll let me, I plan to stick around and prove to you that I'm all about stability. I know you don't think you know me."

Tears swelled in her eyes. "I know all I need to. . ."

Before she could draw another breath, Justin's lips were on hers. He poured all his passion and longing into her and something much more. Love. Justin's words that night before he left—*I'm in love with you*—danced with his kiss.

When he ended it, Darrow was dazed, unsteady on her feet. Justin lifted her left hand and slipped something on her finger. Darrow looked down.

"A ring?"

"I'm sorry, I did that backward." He pressed his face to hers.

Darrow laughed. What was it with men these days? They didn't know how to propose.

"Marry me," he whispered. "We can spend a lifetime getting to know each other."

"That sounds like a plan. Count me in." She smiled, hating the tears slipping down her face. "I never thought I could be this happy. It's not about the matching curtains or white picket fences after all."

Still pressing his nose to hers, he held her hand and with his other hand at her back, he led her in a small private dance like they were the only ones in the world. "You saved me from a dry and arid, lonely life. You know that?"

Without either of them noticing, an audience had gathered and now clapped softly.

People watched her private moment, but she didn't care. "I love you, Justin Love."

Epilogue

Wrapped in ivory taffeta and satin, and an ornately beaded corset-bodice, she looked over her shoulder at the mirror's image displaying the train of her gown.

Darrow had her wedding dress—the one she'd eyed for the months since Justin had asked her to marry him. He and Trace had conspired behind her back to make it happen. She didn't see any harm in dreaming, but spending that kind of money hadn't seriously been in her thoughts. She'd had to travel to Portland, of all places, to try it on and make the final decision, then to have it altered.

The train was shorter on this one than the one in the magazine, but that was fine. The gorgeous once-in-a-lifetime dress was fancy as it was, for a girl like Darrow. But Justin had insisted. He reminded her that the first time he'd seen her she'd been looking at wedding dresses. That dress was important to her, he'd said.

His brother Carver insisted they marry at the Love family ranch house. Darrow hadn't had any family for years until Benson came back into her life, and now he kept in touch, calling her weekly. When Justin had proposed, he'd given her a whole new family with his three brothers and their wives, children, and babies on the way.

Justin was truly the love of her life. Her dream. She hadn't known love could be like this, and to think, there was much more to experience.

Trace stepped back into the room where she'd assisted Darrow into her wedding dress earlier. "Five more minutes. Let me help you with the veil."

Darrow had asked Trace to be her maid of honor, and she looked gorgeous in her champagne bridesmaid's gown with the floor-length trumpet skirt. Trace stepped behind her and lifted the train as Darrow turned around to face the mirror. Tears welled in Darrow's eyes.

"Oh, now don't do that." Trace tugged two tissues from a box and handed them to Darrow. "You'll mess up your makeup."

"I don't know why I thought I needed to wear it."

"Because today is special. You wanted to look like the bride in the catalog, remember?"

"What was I thinking?" Darrow laughed. "What if Justin doesn't like it?"

Trace lifted the one-tier beaded veil and set it on Darrow's head, gently clipping it to her hair. "Trust me. Justin is never going to forget how beautiful you are today."

Nausea swirled inside. She pressed her hand against her midsection. "All that time thinking that I had pre-engagement jitters. That was nothing compared to this."

Darrow waited while Trace fiddled with the veil.

"You ready?" Now *Trace's* eyes were tearing up.

Darrow nodded. Trace dropped the veil over Darrow's face and smiled. "You're such a beautiful bride."

"You look amazing in your gown, too. I'm sure you'll wow Jeremy." Darrow smiled.

"Oh, and I plan to use that for all its worth." Trace winked then wiped her eyes with a tissue.

Minutes later, Darrow stood behind a partition that was set up outside just for the ceremony, waiting for the moment when she would walk down the aisle to Justin.

"You make a mighty pretty bride, Darrow," Carver said and winked. As Justin's oldest brother, he'd agreed to walk her down the aisle since Benson couldn't make it back to Oregon for the wedding.

Darrow's cheeks grew warm under Carver's pride-filled gaze, but it was Justin's admiration she grew impatient to see.

Holding a bouquet of roses in shades of white and pink, Trace took a step forward, disappearing from Darrow's sight. She held her own larger bouquet, and waited for her turn to make her way to the beautiful white gazebo.

"You ready?" Carver offered his arm. Darrow slid hers into the crook of his elbow and together they stepped from behind the partition. Rows of chairs on either side lined the path. Family and friends from the community, draped by sunlight on a beautiful spring afternoon, filled the chairs.

Suddenly, the pianist started playing the "Bridal Chorus." Darrow's palms grew slick. The crowd, gathered to witness Darrow and Justin's wedding, stood, and many turned to look at her.

A few gasps, mutters of how beautiful she was, rippled through the gathering.

Darrow took her first step, Carver at her side, and then another. She continued walking down the aisle created just for today. Her day. Justin's day.

He stood next to the gazebo waiting.

Justin in a tux. Her pulse soared at the sight of him. She almost swayed on her feet, but Carver held her steady.

One step, then another.

Carver's wife, Sheridan, stood to the right, her appreciative gaze on Carver before moving to Darrow. "Beautiful," she whispered. She smiled and winked at Darrow and her husband, pressing her hand against her large belly. She'd taken a leave of absence from her job as sheriff of Rimrock County while pregnant to keep Carver from having a heart attack.

Now that was love.

One step, then another.

Familiar faces from the community looked on from ahead on both sides. To her left, Jonas stood next to Darcy and held their beautiful little girl, her golden curls framing her face. So precious.

That was love.

Trace stepped into place, opposite Justin's best man—his brother Lucas. Darrow spotted Avery, Lucas's wife, sitting on the front row. Tears streamed from her beautiful blue eyes. Darrow understood. She always cried at weddings, too.

Darrow and Avery had become close, and Darrow knew that the couple had struggled to have a child. Darrow caught

Lucas's glance at his bride, love pouring from his eyes.

Then, Darrow drew her own gaze up to her husband-to-be. She hadn't known him very well when she'd first fallen for him. But now, she felt like there had never been a time when she hadn't loved him.

Justin smiled, his eyes meeting hers, and Carver relinquished her to Justin, who took her hand so they could both step into the gazebo and face the pastor. A warm current rippled up her arm.

Darrow smiled, remembering the first moment they met—that moment when his simple touch had changed her life.

And in the end. . .her life was only beginning.

Elizabeth Goddard is a seventh-generation Texan who recently spent five years in beautiful Southern Oregon, which serves as a setting for some of her novels. She is now back in East Texas, living near her family. When she's not writing, she's busy homeschooling her four children. Beth is the author of several novels and novellas. She's actively involved in several writing organizations including American Christian Fiction Writers (ACFW) and loves to mentor new writers.

Other Romancing America titles available from Barbour Publishing

Seattle Cinderella

978-1-61626-641-7

The Quakers of New Garden

978-1-61626-643-1

Rainbow's End

978-1-61626-686-8

The Midwife's Legacy

978-1-61626-588-5

Available wherever books are sold